Lizzie

Also by Dawn Ius

Anne & Henry

Overdrive

Lizzie

Dawn Ius

Simon Pulse

NEW YORK   LONDON   TORONTO   SYDNEY   NEW DELHI

SIMON PULSE
An imprint of Simon & Schuster Children's Publishing Division
1230 Avenue of the Americas, New York, New York 10020
First Simon Pulse hardcover edition April 2018
Text copyright © 2018 by Dawn Ius
Front jacket and spine photograph copyright © 2018 by Colleen Farrell/ArcAngel
Back jacket photograph copyright © 2018 by Shutterstock
Jacket illustrations of lace copyright © 2018 ajuga/Thinkstock
All rights reserved, including the right of reproduction in whole or in part in any form.
SIMON PULSE and colophon are registered trademarks of Simon & Schuster, Inc.
For information about special discounts for bulk
purchases, please contact Simon & Schuster Special Sales
at 1-866-506-1949 or business@simonandschuster.com.
The Simon & Schuster Speakers Bureau can bring authors to your
live event. For more information or to book an event contact
the Simon & Schuster Speakers Bureau at 1-866-248-3049 or
visit our website at www.simonspeakers.com.
Designed by Sarah Creech
The text of this book was set in Berling.
Manufactured in the United States of America
2 4 6 8 10 9 7 5 3 1
Library of Congress Cataloging-in-Publication Data
Names: Ius, Dawn, author.
Title: Lizzie / by Dawn Ius.
Description: First Simon Pulse hardcover edition. | New York : Simon Pulse, 2018. |
Summary: A modern-day reimagining of the story of Lizzie Borden, casting her as a shy seventeen-year-old whose blackouts become worse after her father and stepmother try to prevent her from studying to be a chef.
Identifiers: LCCN 2017030262 | ISBN 9781481490764 (hardcover)
Subjects: | CYAC: Family problems—Fiction. | Mental illness—Fiction. |
Child abuse—Fiction. | Stepmothers—Fiction. | Bed and breakfast
accommodations—Fiction. | Murder—Fiction. | Massachusetts—Fiction.
Classification: LCC PZ7.1.I97 Liz 2018 |
DDC [Fic]—dc23
LC record available at https://lccn.loc.gov/2017030262
9781481490788 (eBook)

For Karen,
whose love of all things spooky is even greater
than my own—this one's for you, babe

BEFORE

I'm dying.

Sharp pain zigzags across my shoulder blades and trips along my spine. My abdomen is stretched out and bloated. Cramped. I try to lift my head, but it's stuck to the cement, ripe with the scent of rodent feces, stale bread, musky earth. The stench curls under my nostrils and twists into my skin, making me gag.

A steady pulse hammers against my skull.

Where am I?

I lift one eyelid and peer into the heavy darkness. My shallow breaths ripple through air so still my heartbeat echoes like a prayer chant.

In.

Out.

In.

I squeeze my eyes closed and tamp back the bile inching its way up my throat. Try to focus. Process. There's no way it can be night—

I squint into the dark. Fragmented memories slash across my vision like windshield-wiper blades. *Swipe.* My hand on the railing, and me staring down the staircase into the dark abyss. *Swipe.* Shadows dancing across the cellar floor. *Swipe.* My head light, dizzy with confusion. I sway forward—

Swipe. Swipe. Swipe.

My eyes flit shut—

Open.

Swipe.

A black spider scampers in front of me. It pauses, stares—eight beady eyes—tiptoes away. *Rat-a-tat-tat* through the eye sockets of a tiny rat skull, spindly legs dangling against the cream-colored bone.

My breath catches.

Swipeswipeswipe.

This spider is the last thing I remember before everything goes—

Swipe.

It's so dark.

I run my tongue along my teeth, pasty with dried drool, the metallic tint of blood. The left corner of my mouth is pushed into the floor, lips against the cement. I close my eyes and open them quickly, as though speed will bring the light back faster. Instead my vision clouds with tiny dots that swirl like constellations.

I shift my legs and pause.

My thighs are sticky. I force them apart and the strong scent of copper drifts under my nose. I slide one hand along my waist, curling the thin material of my dress in my fingertips. The other weaves over the curve of my hip and between my legs.

Light from the kitchen cuts through the open door at the top of the landing and bathes my skin in a translucent glow.

I am a ghost.

Unable to lift my head, I curl into the fetal position, digging my fingernails into the cement floor as pain snakes through my lower abdomen. My anguish squeaks out in a muted scream. It's barely even my voice.

I wedge my hand between the soft flesh of my thighs and wrench them apart.

The skin is damp.

Tacky.

I pull back and hold a shaky hand up to my face. My chipped fingernails are outlined in deep red.

Blood.

My blood.

CHAPTER

1

FIVE YEARS LATER

There must be a million things cooking can't cure, but I don't know of any. I have whisked away anger, can knead-roll-knead through sadness, despair, even grief. Crank up the heat and negativity simmers and evaporates, just—*poof!*—disappears. I remember every ingredient I've ever used, the textures of the labels I've touched, the tangy scent of each herb.

The kitchen is my fortress, my sanctuary.

Until *she* walks through the door.

A tight flutter of foreboding claws at my throat, *slice, slice, slicing* away at my euphoria. My eyes flit to the polished silver crucifix that hangs over the door, and I mouth a prayer. *Lord, give me strength.*

But even He can't save me from my stepmother.

Abigail.

I work my knuckles through the slab of ground hamburger on the granite countertop, focused on anything but her. The knots in my shoulder blades tense, release, tense. Across the kitchen, the gears on the wall clock click and catch. I glance up just before it strikes ten.

"Lizbeth, that's inappropriate attire for Mass."

Her voice scratches like nails on a chalkboard. I clench my hands into fists, forcing the slimy egg yolk to ooze through my fingertips. "I'm not going."

Abigail steps closer, her thin neck arched and craning downward. A large gold cross dangles from a thick chain, suffocating in the fleshy folds of her cleavage. "Don't be ridiculous," she says. "It's Christmas Eve."

I wipe my forehead with the back of my hand. My nose twitches at the scent of raw beef mixing with the tart evergreen-and-cinnamon wreath that hangs crooked in the window. I gather the meat mixture into a tight ball and slam it into the bowl with enough force that hamburger chunks slap against the backsplash and trail down the tiles like maggots.

Disgust curdles from somewhere deep in Abigail's throat. "Dear God, Lizbeth."

My heartbeat picks up speed. I yank the dish towel off the counter and swing at the mess, smearing rosemary and beef bits into the tile. "I need to take care of the meat loaf," I say, pitch rising.

I draw in a calming breath.

Abigail's arm swoops forward, the gold sequins on her totally inappropriate dress shimmering like reptile scales under the stark overhead fluorescents. She upturns her palm and her tongue flicks out. My eyes lock on the thin gold band encircling her wedding finger. My throat goes raw. It's still so jarring after four years.

"You never miss church," Abigail says. She puts her hands on her wide hips. "It's practically your second home with all that senseless volunteering." She shakes her head, knocking loose a few wayward curls. "This can wait."

My voice drops to a hoarse whisper. "It can't."

She sighs heavily, the weight of her exasperation landing on my shoulders, already burdened with guilt. I shrug it loose and use my forearm to wipe clear the flecks of wet hamburger stuck to my cheeks. Irritation prickles between my shoulder blades, like an intense itch I can't reach, can't scratch. It burns with need.

I drop my hands into the bowl and continue to massage the gooey meat mixture with far more vigor than required. Hamburger spackles the countertop, the wall, and my journal, the place where I have carefully written every revision of this particular recipe, even the subtlest change. I use my wrists to try and wipe it away, but no matter how hard I scrub, the page won't come clean.

Another *tsk* of disgust from Abigail. "Lizbeth, calm down. You're—"

Don't say it.

"—manic."

I breathe out slow and blink to deter my tears.

"Honey, have you seen my car keys?" The echo of my father's voice down the hallway lops off what's left of my oxygen. My throat closes in and I go still as a mouse. Abigail's mouth twists into a cruel smirk. There is a beat of silence and then louder, harsher, "Abigail. My keys."

My father's approaching footsteps pound against my rib cage like a kick drum. *Thump-thump-thump*. My skin feels thin, stretched out like Saran Wrap. I suck in a sharp breath just as his enormous shadow darkens the threshold of my sanctuary. The tension in the room goes so heavy, you couldn't hack through it with a hatchet.

"Abigail?"

A charcoal blazer hangs from my father's shoulders like giant vulture wings, and his polished shoes gleam under the overhead lights. On the surface, he is disguised as perfection, but I know what lives behind that mask. His piercing gaze lands on me with a thud and my pulse skips a beat.

"You're wearing an apron to Mass?" he says, disgust like molasses on his tongue.

I blink.

He gestures at me with his enormous hands, palms stretched out as if in prayer. "I don't expect you to win any beauty pageants, Lizbeth, but at least make a goddamned effort not to embarrass me."

A gaping hole opens inside my chest.

Abigail rolls her eyes. With all the gaudy makeup on her face, they're more bulbous than usual, like they might pop out onto the counter, bounce across the granite, drop onto the floor. "She's not going," she says.

I stuff my trembling hands back into the metal bowl, imagining them wrapped around my stepmother's throat. The meat slithers between my fingers like human entrails.

Dad recoils. "Not going?"

A wave of guilt grips me in a vise, this dark specter of my past, my present, my future. A cruel and vicious voice whispering at the nape of my neck, reminding me that I am unworthy, tainted, undeserving of any freedoms.

The expression on my father's face reaffirms this, and I duck my head to avoid his searing disapproval.

Through hooded eyes, I watch him advance on me, forehead wrinkles exaggerated, lips pressed together in a firm line. I shrink under his oppressive shadow, my throat shriveling, heart racing. He grabs my wrist and squeezes so hard I gasp. "You're hurting me."

"Hurting you?" His tone turns incredulous, wounded even. "For Christ's sake, Lizbeth, don't be such a little girl."

But I am a girl.

Tears spring to my eyes. I *blink, blink, blink* them clear. My father studies my face, as though searching for a map to help navigate the rocky terrain of our increasingly dysfunctional relationship. Things haven't been right between us since Mom died, since Abigail moved in.

"Honestly, Lizbeth, I don't know what's gotten into you," Abigail says. She snaps on a pair of pearl-colored gloves that once belonged to my mother, and glares at the mound of raw meat in the bowl.

I resist the urge to stuff her smug face in it. To rip those gloves—my mother's gloves—from her body.

My father clears his throat. "It's Christmas Eve." The ominous undertone of his voice causes an itchy sweat to spread across my back, and I wait for him to issue his command. Remind me that I have no choice but to do as he says. "What will folks think if you're not with your family, tonight of all nights?"

I bite down hard on my tongue. In this small Massachusetts community of Fall River, my father pantomimes the American dream—success, wealth, the illusion of a wife and two daughters who worship him. Maybe that's true for Abigail and my older sister, Emma, but my adoration snapped the first time the flat of his hand connected with my cheek.

My skin burns now as though I've gone back in time. I hear the crack of bone, the sharp sting of pain. The lump in my chest aches, a phantom reminder of a heart that was once whole. I touch my face to soothe the tingle that never quite fades.

"It is my duty to tend to the inn," I say, calmly wiping my cheek with the edge of an apron soiled with cow's blood. The pungent scent intensifies, filling my nostrils and trickling down my throat. "Besides, Mr. Dent forgot his keys last night. . . ."

"Ever the martyr," Abigail mutters.

Fresh pinpricks of guilt ripple down my spine.

I am expected at church for Mass. Over the years, I've become a staple at Father Buck's side, serving as youth leader, chairwoman of the annual bake sale, and special events coordinator. I've earned the title of Fall River's youngest Sunday school teacher—but my halo is not without tarnish, my service to God not selfless.

Being at the church allows me untethered freedom from the stifling rule of my father's iron fist. It's a place where I'm not forced to pretend that we are a unit, a *family*. To go there, tonight of all nights, with the very forces that trap me under this roof, would strip any solace the church offers, and I'm unwilling—unable—to make that sacrifice. I'd rather play babysitter to the lone guest at the Borden Bed and Breakfast.

My father stuffs his hands in his pockets, drawing my attention to a speck of ground hamburger on his thigh. It will fall off long before he gets to the church, but it gives me a little thrill to know it's there, a flaw in his otherwise perfect facade.

I glance at the giant cross above the kitchen door, my distorted reflection mirrored in its surface, and pray for the Lord's forgiveness.

"It's best she stays behind anyway," Abigail says, her voice thick with disdain. "She doesn't look well."

My spine stiffens.

Dad sighs. "You will lock the door." Not a question, but an order. I nod with rehearsed obedience. "And you're not to set foot outside this house," he adds, as though I don't already understand the consequences of leaving.

Abigail flicks a piece of black lint off her shimmering sleeve. "Oh, Andrew, where would she possibly go?"

The meaning behind her words rings crystal clear. Within these walls, I am no more significant than a pigeon, a nuisance to be caged or eliminated. But beyond them, I am nothing.

No one.

My father stares at me a long beat, expression unreadable. "Fasten all the dead bolts," he says, ever exercising his paranoia and steadfast control. His gaze moves to the meat-loaf mixture. "And turn off the oven when you're done."

My face goes tight with annoyance. "I'm not a child."

Abigail snorts. "Oh, but you most certainly are."

She throws back her head and cackles, and the sound reverberates off my skull and makes my teeth chatter with unease. "Don't you see, Lizbeth? You can never be more than your father's silly little girl."

CHAPTER

2

I press my nose up against the kitchen window, tension draining as my father's Cadillac inches along Second Street. When the headlights round the corner and disappear into the lightly blowing snow, I release the breath I've been holding with a loud *swoosh*.

The tightness in my chest begins to ease off.

Freedom. If only for a few hours.

I rinse my hands under hot water and snag a box of saltines from the cupboard above the sink. A grin spreads across my face. *This* is the secret ingredient in my meat loaf.

A sense of pride overtakes any lingering anxiety. This dish encompasses everything I've learned from watching rerun after rerun of my idol, Chef Emeril Lagasse—he's from Fall

River too. A lot of semifamous people are, I guess.

I crumble three crackers between my palms and sprinkle them over the meat mix like confetti.

BAM! Kick it up a notch.

I stand back and rock on my heels to admire my handiwork. It is a meat-loaf masterpiece, an edible Picasso—

A sudden ache crackles across my lower abdomen. I grab on to the edges of the sink, eyes clenched shut against the sting of soap, and take a deep breath. Exhale. My head starts to spin. A second pain hits me like the blunt edge of a knife burrowing into my gut, and I bite my lip to stop from crying out.

Unease bubbles across my flesh. I turn and lean up against the counter, hand pushed tight against my stomach.

Not now. Please, God. Not now. Is this my penance for missing Mass?

I swallow hard to dislodge the dread, and exhale slowly. *False alarm.* It has to be—it's too early. I flip through my journal, blood and oil and spices smearing the paper like a page from Pollock's sketchbook, and count back the days since my last "incident." Twenty-eight, marked with a bright red dot. I should have at least two days before *it* happens.

My *transformation.*

Yeah, I know how that sounds.

I rip off my apron, gather the material in my fist, and blot my forehead. A meat maggot smears across my skin. I bash my hand at it. Rub, *scratch*, rub until my flesh goes raw. No matter how hard I press, I can *feel* it. Slimy. Wet. A sticky dot of hamburger lingering between my eyes.

Familiar panic rockets up my spine.

It's like this *every* month.

Anxiety. Paranoia. The fear of what happens when everything goes dark.

It's not like I bark at the moon or Hulk out, but each month, at around the thirty-day mark, I . . . change. Our old family doctor says my condition is even rarer than werewolf-ism—lycanthropy, or whatever—if that were a thing.

Most girls my age get their period and their hormones shift out of whack. My older sister Emma turns into a blubbering mess. Abigail goes mad with rage, though her menstrual cycle has little to do with it, as far as I'm concerned.

Me?

I black out.

For minutes. Sometimes hours. And it's not like I'm just lapping up extra beauty sleep—though Lord knows I could use the help. My brain is a honeycomb. Pieces of memory go missing. Erased from existence. Just—

Gone.

I wish I could blame it on amnesia, or one of those diseases that attract massive public fund-raising campaigns in the quest for a cure. Dementia or Alzheimer's, maybe.

Apparently, there's no antidote for my special brand of afflic-
tion. I have postural orthostatic tachycardia syndrome, which
basically means my heartbeat goes into overdrive and I black
out at the exact instant blood starts flowing from my V.

It happened in the middle of Father Buck's Easter sermon once. Talk about a reenactment of the crucifixion. Red
everywhere. Bloodcurdling screams. And then—

Pitch-black.

I always remember the minutes leading up to an episode.
I can account for the blank spaces in between—I mean, it's
not like I blackout-walk. At least, the doctor doesn't think
that's possible. And I've been tracking symptoms, marking
the calendar, anything I can do to predict, if not control, the
blackouts. But lately, strange things have begun to happen.

Strange, inexplicable things—sometimes when my period
isn't due at all. Like that time I supposedly switched out the
salt for sugar in the condiment containers at the B and B like
some prepubescent prankster on April Fool's.

Abigail accused me of trying to poison the customers.

My pulse ratchets up. Enough with her lies! Every word
that slips off her forked tongue is meant to hurt and confuse
me. Fill me with doubt. She's consumed with one purpose—
convincing my father that I belong in a psych ward, that I'm
a danger to others.

A *psychopath*.

The doorbell buzzes, snapping me back to the moment.

I hold my breath and listen. Who could it be? Abigail locks down registration at nine p.m. sharp. We flick on the NO VACANCY sign, dim the lights. It's practically a morgue.

Two more buzzes come in rapid succession.

Now my heartbeat begins to gallop. I close my fingers on the small gold cross dangling around my neck, fear seeping into my chest like a thunderous cloud. I don't deserve His protection tonight, but the cool metal soothes my anxiety.

I lick my lips, contemplating my options. It's probably just Mr. Dent. Last night he rang at midnight, his cheeks flushed, the strong smell of alcohol clinging to his clothes like death, claiming to have left his key at the pub. Another chink in my father's fortress, for which I shouldered the blame.

I consider leaving Mr. Dent out in the cold. To be honest, he kind of gives me the creeps. There's a distinct scent in his guest suite. Musky and sour, like what I imagine it's like after sex. A shiver trickles down my spine.

Thump. Thump. Knock.

I startle.

Outside, dark clouds roll across the face of a half-moon. Clusters of stars twinkle down on a light dusting of snow, making the ground glisten in red and green under the Christmas lights from the neighbor's house.

Fresh guilt slides under my skin—I can't very well leave a paying guest outside on Christmas Eve. Isn't that the precise reason I told Father I would stay behind?

I wipe my hands on a dishrag and tiptoe into the hall. The family photographs that line the wall guide me down the dimly lit corridor, the pictures faded and old, frames peeling at the corners. They're not even hung straight, most of them just strategically placed to mask the cracks in the drywall.

Another knock and my pulse leaps right into my throat.

I flatten my hand against my chest, steadying my heart rate. I'm no chicken, but the amount of security in this place is a clear indication of Dad's paranoia. The B and B doesn't have Internet, cable television, or decent cell reception, but we're sealed up like a high-tech Alcatraz.

To keep the outsiders out, Father says. Like the people of Fall River, who are—allegedly—after his money. Best I can tell, the only "outsider" in this town sleeps beside him and is well on her way to draining his accounts. Unfortunately, my case against her has flatlined, while my unusual menstrual cycle and strange behavior has made me a prime candidate for a straitjacket. Go figure.

And anyway, my gut says Father's obsession with security has everything to do with keeping me here, under his fleshy thumb. Trapped in his prison—for my own protection, obviously. He's an effective warden.

I peer through the peephole.

Blink.

The redheaded female on the other side is tall and thin, with wild green eyes that seem to stare into my soul. A fluttering rises up from my stomach and gathers in my chest, circling my heart.

I jump back and touch my mouth with two fingers. Shifting closer, I peek again. Draw in my breath. The girl runs her hand through the chaos of her hair and adjusts the knitted cap that traps most of her wayward strands in place. A single curl feathers across her cheek, just barely above her top lip. My eyes lock on her mouth. There's a small hole in the right-hand corner, like maybe where a piercing once had been.

A scarf is wrapped around her throat—Earth, Mars, Saturn, the whole galaxy, I'm sure, twists in the wind. I flatten my eyeball to the peephole, so close I can almost feel the glass against my pupil. The girl angles her head to reveal a small crescent shape that curves at the base of her ear.

Her jaw tenses.

She leans closer and I'm sure she can see me, hear me, *feel* me. Her breath fogs up the glass.

I step back and ease the door open, carefully poking my head into the cold. The breeze nips at my nose, my chest, burrows deep in my bones.

The girl's entire face brightens in a mesmerizing smile. "Um . . . hi," she says. Her voice is like a melody.

My eyes grow wide as I take in the layers of her clothing—a fitted plaid shawl draped over an olive print dress that falls to mid-calf. Two sections of flesh, red from the wind and cold, poke out from where her dress stops and purple ankle boots begin. A tattoo winds around the skin there, but I can't read the faded inscription—something Latin, maybe? She adjusts her crocheted backpack on her shoulder. "I'm . . . Bridget."

I draw a blank. It's as though someone has stolen my voice.

Her beautiful smile slips a little. "Bridget Sullivan. The new—"

Maid, I think, just as a wave of nausea sucker punches me in the gut and everything goes dark.

CHAPTER

3

The girl—Bridget—stares down at me from behind the thin curtain of her strawberry hair, her large liquid eyes wide with concern. I'm completely sucked in.

"Welcome back," she says, a hint of Irish accent slipping out.

The back of my head throbs, my mouth is dry and pasty. I wet my lips and squint against the pain pounding against my skull. "Blacked out?"

Yup, she nods.

The first pinpricks of humiliation trickle across my skin. "I'm sorry, I . . ."

Bridget shakes her head. "Don't be! This one time, a snake slithered in front of me and I screamed so long, I passed out. . . ."

Her animated voice turns to white noise as I spot the smear of red on her calf. A knot forms in my chest. She's bleeding. No, that's not quite right. The cramping in my abdomen, the stickiness between my thighs. She's been bled *on*. My cheeks go hot. "Oh, God, I'm so—"

Bridget waves a dismissive hand. "Don't you dare apologize." She uses the inside of her wrist to scrub at the smear of my blood on her leg, and then wipes it on her skirt. The smudge blends in with the whimsical pattern of swirls and flowers. "If anyone should be sorry, it's me. I rolled you off me and left you bleeding for dead."

"So that's why my hip hurts?" Heat crawls up the side of my neck. "How embarrassing."

"Don't be ridiculous—it happened to me just last week."

My traitorous lip curls into a half smile. I push myself up onto my elbows with a grunt. Something inside of me aches. "Sure, and I'm Lady Báthory."

Her head tilts toward the blood smear. "Maybe that's me." She grins, and my stomach flips end over end. "I'm actually an old hag who keeps her youthful appearance by bathing in the blood of beautiful young women."

I feel heat in my throat, my cheeks, and I realize that I'm blushing. I'd turn away, but that would only highlight it more, so I hold still. So very still. Bridget stands taller, glowing, as if her body is absorbing the attention. I'm not surprised. She's probably used to being gawked at.

Her mouth parts a little, and dang if my eyes don't focus in on her lips. They're pink, like cherry blossoms, and it makes me wonder if they'd taste half as sweet. My breath catches. Somewhere deep in my subconscious I've dreamed of this moment before—my first kiss, first love, being with a girl. But on the heels of those thoughts always comes the gut-twist of shame. The knowledge that not only would the church, my father, never approve of such a relationship—or any relationship, really—but also that my feelings could never be reciprocated. What would anyone see in me?

I stare at Bridget with longing, searching her face for some kind of signal that maybe she senses something different between us too, but her expression is playful, unreadable.

A sour chuckle rises at the back of my throat. A girl like Bridget wouldn't have given me a second thought if I hadn't period-bled on her leg. Embarrassed, I drag my eyes from her face, only to spot another streak of blood on the beige tile. Behind it, the Charlie Brown Christmas tree beside the door lies on its side, pieces of broken glass ornaments peppering its base.

"Obviously, you're not a virgin," Bridget says. I gasp aloud. Her smile widens and I'm dumbstruck by her beauty—it's radiant, like the glow from an angel's halo. I touch my cross, silently thanking Him for this gift, if even for a snapshot in time.

"Virgin to the whole passing-out thing," Bridget adds

quickly, shyly. Her sudden awkwardness is utterly adorable, and I find myself grinning like a lovesick schoolgirl.

I blow out a slow breath. "Not even close." Here I could launch into a lengthy monologue about my menstrual condition. Instead I shift to take pressure off my hip. Even the slight movement makes me wince. Behind Bridget, the open doors creak against the lightly blowing wind. A shiver ripples down my spine. "It's only day twenty-eight. . . ." I shake my head. "Never mind. It's not important."

Bridget extends her hand. "Let me help you up." She tilts her head and her hair cascades over one shoulder to fall across her breast. "Unless you're planning to sleep here. In which case, point me to the blankets and I'll build us a fort."

A nervous giggle shoots more pain along my rib cage. Tears gather in my eyes, and I blink them away. Dang it. *Everything* hurts. Even my heart, as though someone is squishing it, trying to mold it into submission.

I won't—can't—give in.

"Okay, no fort." Bridget crouches so we're eye level, her smile crooked and perfect. "You're not okay, are you?" She licks her lips and I'm hypnotized. "You fell pretty hard and I tried to catch you, but I lost my balance and . . ." She shrugs, helpless. "I landed on my ass. You fell on top of me. The rest is history."

I close one eye and squint. "I don't suppose we could forget this ever happened?"

She holds out her hand as if to shake mine. "Hi. I'm Bridget. Bridget Sullivan, the new maid." Her skin is pale and lightly freckled. A giant blue gemstone glints at me from her pinky. My eyes skim across her long fingers, which extend into well-manicured nails painted lavender. She catches me staring and grins. My heart feels like it's free-falling through my chest, making me lighter, freer. "Your turn," she says with a wink.

I blink, as if to reset my racing thoughts. The overwhelming sense of confusion doesn't fade—it gets worse instead, rising up through my esophagus in rolling waves.

"And my name is . . . ," she prods, her grin impish.

"Are you sure I didn't bump my head?" Dang it. What is it about Bridget that makes me off-kilter, a little not quite myself? I limply take her hand. Another shock rockets through my core and I almost pull back. "I'm Lizzie Borden. I own the B and B." I scrunch up my nose. "I mean, I guess my family does."

"Oy," she says. "Talk about making a good impression on the owners' daughter." She leans over and starts plucking pieces of the glass ornaments off the floor, gathering them in the palm of her hand. I'm transfixed by her elegance, her nonchalance. Bridget stands, spots the garbage can beside the reception desk, and dumps the debris inside. As she passes the spot of blood on the tile, she rubs her shoe across it, scuffing it clean. "Got a broom?"

I curl forward, forcing myself to sit. The pain shifts from my hip and flares down my lower back. I'm a dang wreck. "You're not sweeping the floor. You haven't even started work yet." She's actually days early. "Besides, it's Christmas Eve."

We glance at the clock over the desk and in unison say, "Christmas, actually."

"Jinx," we echo, and then share another laugh. I'm stunned by how in sync we are.

Bridget tucks her hands behind her back. "So . . . this is nice." She spins in a slow circle. "The color is pretty." *It's puke green.* "And this desk must have cost a fortune." *Five bucks at the thrift shop.* She spots the service bell and flattens her palm on top of it three times. A warbled *ding, ding, ding* croaks out. "I've always wanted to do that." She cups her hand over her mouth. "Shit! Is there anyone here? Of course there is, it's an inn. Fuck. I hope I didn't wake anyone. . . . Did . . . I . . . wake someone?"

It hurts to laugh, but I do anyway. "I think it's just me and Mr. Dent, and I'm pretty sure he wears headphones so he can't hear himself snore."

Bridget unties her scarf—it's such a beautiful scarf—and drapes it over her slender arm. "Oh man, that's rough. My ex-boyfriend was a real Darth Vader."

A sharp pang of jealousy sucker punches me in the gut, and the small thread of hope coiled around my heart dissolves with a painful hiss. Of course she likes boys. Why would I think otherwise? Because she was nice to me? I'm so naive.

Her voice goes shallow as she breathes. *In. Out. In.* "You know? 'Luke, I am your father . . .'" Her grin flattens. "Never mind. Here, let me help you up."

"Please."

Bridget wraps her cool fingers around my wrist, the low hum of her energy like a sub-bass tingling against my skin. She pulls, I push, and somehow, I stand. A wave of nausea hits and I reach for her shoulders to steady myself. She smells faintly of cotton candy, and I breathe it in.

Standing next to her, I feel strange. Unbalanced.

Her emerald eyes fill with concern. "You're not going to pass out again, are you?"

A small drop of blood trickles down my upper thigh. I press my legs together to stop it from hitting the ground and dribbling at my feet. "I'm ninety-nine-percent sure it's a once-a-month occurrence."

"'Never tell me the odds,'" she says in a deep, sexy voice that makes my knees buckle a little. Her cheeks go pink. "Sorry. Another *Star Wars* reference."

Grasping for some way to keep her talking, joking, to prolong this moment, however awkward, I glance down at her exquisite scarf. "You like things to do with outer space."

"My mom gave me this when I turned ten," she says, scrunching up her nose. "But yeah, I guess I've always been obsessed. I used to take her silver eyeliner and draw stars on my cheeks." She lifts her hair to reveal a small crescent moon tattooed behind her left ear. "I got this when I was fourteen." Her shy grin worms under my skin, filling my entire body with warmth. "I'm kind of a geek."

A gust of wind blows through the open door, bringing with it a fine mist of ice rain. It's enough to shock me back to reality. Christmas Mass will end any second, and Abigail can't see us talking, laughing. "Servants" at the Borden B and B are not meant to be seen or heard.

"We should bring the rest of your things in," I say.

Bridget points to the small rainbow backpack puddled on the floor. "That's everything."

My jaw drops. "Everything?"

Fresh curiosity buzzes through me. I don't own much, but even the few items I care about—trinkets, my rosary and Bible, my journal, pictures of me and Ems—would need a half-decent-size suitcase, at least.

Bridget winks. "It's magic." Her stomach growls, drowning out another of my humiliating giggles. She presses her lips together, but her laughter seeps through.

"Someone's hungry," I say.

Her face goes crimson. "Don't mind him—that's just my guard dog, Seth."

"Sounds ferocious."

"He can be." She bites her lower lip and again my thoughts veer far from innocent. I close my clammy palm around the cool steel of my cross. Oblivious, Bridget grins. "So, you got any food for this guy?"

Fire rushes to my cheeks. "Meat loaf?"

"Sounds delicious."

My voice is too loud, too sure. "Oh yes, it's utterly to die for."

CHAPTER

4

Bridget flops onto the bed, swinging her legs over the edge of the mattress so that the heels of her purple boots *click, click, click* together. Her pale calves are almost white against the pink-and-yellow floral bedspread.

I shuffle my foot across the worn, patterned carpet, my freshly washed toes leaving while ridges in the grime. It's a sin for someone as beautiful as Bridget to be surrounded by so much gloom. "My sister and I painted your room," I say.

She stares at me with eyes that make me think of lush jungles, which is maybe why all common sense gets tangled in my throat. "It's yellow," I add, and my face goes so hot I expect it to burst into flames. "Obviously."

She giggles.

Twirling a strand of wet hair, I focus on the thin strip of wallpaper at the back where the drywall meets the low end of the lofted ceiling. No matter how hard Emma and I scrubbed, we couldn't strip it clean. Like somehow the house itself is clinging to it, refusing to release the memories, no matter how painful or old.

"Where is this sister of yours?" Bridget says, expertly pulling me back into the moment. "I must thank her."

"Oh, she's at college in Boston." I swallow the tightness that threatens to close off my throat every time I think about Emma being gone. It stings that she isn't home for Christmas, that we seem to be drifting further apart. The gaping hole in my chest thrums with a constant emptiness, a hollow ache that until this moment seemed impossible to heal. For the first time since my sister left, the pain isn't debilitating, and that awareness fills me with hope. "Emma picked the color. She said it reminded her of sunshine. . . ."

You are my sunshine.

I *swipe* clear my mother's singsong voice, echoing from the dark recesses of my memory.

Bridget pulls a pair of oversize sunglasses out of her rainbow backpack, puts them on, and falls backward onto the mattress. Her hair splays out like a fan. "I can actually feel the heat. . . ."

My heart is like a hummingbird.

I've grown up in this cold house of darkness and

deprivation, my youth structured around the rigid adherence to church teachings and my father's hypocritical heavy hand. But there's something *bohemian* about Bridget—wild, bright, *free*. Everything I've wished for.

Even things I never knew I wanted.

Bridget lifts her head and smiles. "I'm serious. Check it out." She pats the bed. "Lie down next to me."

It's playful. A teasing invitation. Soft, gentle, and yet it comes to me as a command. Her voice is so persuasive it's almost physical. Something about it makes me queasy and breathless, but I climb onto the mattress and roll onto my back, tingling in quiet anticipation.

She slips the sunglasses over my eyes, fingertips skimming across my skin. "Do you feel it?"

"Yes," I whisper, but I'm sure we're not talking about the same thing. My entire body buzzes with restless energy. I've only just caught my breath when her warm hand closes over mine. I can't move away, not that I've tried.

I push the sunglasses up onto my forehead, and together we stare at the patch of popcorn ceiling Emma and I couldn't scrape clear. It's not a perfect renovation, but the after is so much better than the before.

"This place is charming," Bridget says. "I think I'm going to love it here."

I hope so.

Carefully, I lean in, craving more of her touch. "Still a lot of work to do."

"I could help." She sits up and flexes her arm. "You should see these pipes work a paintbrush." She glances over her shoulder and her eyes are bright, like tiny stars dancing across her pale skin. "Seriously," she says. "That's how I earned my keep at most of the places I've stayed. Manual labor in exchange for room and board. Or bread and cheese, if you're in Italy."

"You've been to Italy?" My voice is low and breathy. I'm sure I sound like an idiot—starstruck, envious. Humiliating, sure, but hardly a shock. Father Buck says I give off that wholesome vibe. I can read between the lines, though: *prude*. I'm seventeen and never been kissed. I'm not even sure I'm allowed to date.

Bridget tugs at the corded drawstrings that hold her backpack together. "My ex-boyfriend and I lived there for three months. Want to see pictures?"

Inexplicable jealousy and disappointment pull my chest tight. As I sit up, Bridget flips the bag over and the contents spill onto the bed. A camera, a handful of loose change, two pairs of black lace underwear, and a sweatshirt rolled into a ball . . . I look away . . . then back. Bridget shoves everything aside except for a manila envelope, the corners weathered and darkened with grit. She dumps it upside down and a thick stack of prints falls into her lap, like the Polaroids in the travel scrapbooks I've borrowed from Father Buck. She grins. "I still print off my pictures like a total geek."

I wind my finger through a strand of hair and twirl it

round and round until it cuts off my circulation, snapping me back to reality. It's so easy to get lost around Bridget, to let my mind and heart wonder: *what if?* My cross grows heavy and hot against my skin, like it might ignite at any moment. I swallow the fire burning at the back of my throat. "No, I—"

"Trust me, I've been called worse."

I perch on the edge of the mattress, careful not to crowd her, wondering for one fleeting second if I imagined her hand on mine after all. She inches closer and passes me a picture. The casual brush of our fingers up against each other sends a spark of electricity through me. My hair stands on end.

"This was my view from the Tuscan villa I stayed—um— worked at," Bridget says.

A sea of golden sunflowers covers every inch of an expansive field, their round faces tilted upward to the setting sun. Billowy clouds swirl in a sky so blue it looks fake.

I've wanted to go to Italy ever since Emeril Lagasse talked about it on one of his shows. "You took this?"

Bridget tucks a strand of hair behind her ear. "It's not one of my better—"

"How did you do it?" My head swims with questions, emotions. "I feel as though I'm standing *in* the field."

The tip of Bridget's nose goes pink, making her freckles almost disappear. I want to reach out and touch her, coax them back somehow. "I was just tinkering with my new camera at that time," she says. "I've had a lot more practice since then."

Bridget flips through the photos until she lands on an image of a cathedral. A giant dome bubbles toward the heavens, disappearing under the glow of early dawn. "This is the Duomo in Florence," she says with a touch of wistfulness that makes my stomach flutter. "It took two centuries to complete and it has, like, a million stairs."

Just over two hundred, according to Father Buck, but I get how they can lend to exaggeration. I study the angle, trying to figure out where Bridget would have had to stand to get such an incredible shot. It's postcard perfect.

"Everyone says, 'If you've seen one church, you've seen them all,' but that's bullshit." She tilts her head, looking up at me with shimmering eyes. "You ever been to Florence?"

I can barely admit the truth without blushing. "I've never left Fall River."

Her face softens—if that's even possible; she's practically porcelain. "How sad." She cups her hand over her mouth. "Shit. That was rude. I never even asked if you want to travel. I just assumed—"

"I absolutely do," I gush. God, *now* who's the geek? "I just can't believe . . ." I exhale. "I mean, your parents *let* you travel alone?"

"They're basically hippies," Bridget says. She digs through the stack again and hands me a photograph of a man and woman—a guitar in his hand, daisy flowers in her strawberry hair. They're obviously a couple, and strangely familiar. "This is Mom and Dad, just before they left Ireland in search of fame and fortune."

I squint for a better look. "Musicians?"

"Mostly I think they just like to travel," Bridget says, quickly tucking the picture to the bottom of the stack, effectively ending further conversation about them.

She moves on to castles and forests, pictures of sea creatures and endless beaches. "My parents gave me the travel bug when I was just a kid," she says, as I'm transported to busy markets, antique shops, circuses, and museums. "Mom says I'm a free spirit. I started traveling on my own when I turned sixteen last year."

Envy coats my esophagus, making it hard to speak. I can't walk to the end of Second Street without a full-blown Inquisition, and until I'm eighteen—probably forever—my curfew has been firmly set for nine o'clock. It occurs to me that it's well past midnight and though I'm trapped in this house, I have never felt more free. "The food must be amazing."

Bridget's eyes brighten and I'm practically blinded by the glow. "Incredible," she says.

She finds a picture of an olive grove. "Can you imagine picking olives right from the tree?" *I can't.* "It's . . ." Her tone goes wistful. "Unparalleled." She searches for another photograph. "Or how about eating a fresh croissant purchased from a street vendor in Paris?" Her voice picks up speed. "Pierogis in Ukraine! Fresh-roasted chestnuts in Italy!"

My mouth starts watering and my voice goes embarrassingly hushed. "How dreamy."

Bridget thrusts her finger upward. "We'll start in Italy, then."

My pulse leaps. "Excuse me?"

Her cheeks are full-on pink now, her excitement creating an electric current between us that buzzes and hisses. "I mean, unless you'd rather travel with your boyfriend or whatever." Bridget shakes her head before I can react. "Wow. That was super presumptuous of me too."

"No, it . . ." My voice trails off, and a strange tingle ripples along my spine. It's such a preposterous idea, the two of us, almost strangers, not yet even friends, traveling, exploring as . . . what? A couple? I can't imagine she's serious. Unless . . . My blood hums. Is it possible she's trying to find out if I'm in a relationship? Whether *I* like girls? Goose bumps of excitement somersault across my flesh.

But then *God's* voice whispers across the back of my neck, and confusion washes over me. A relationship with Bridget is frowned upon by the church, but I know that even if she were a young man, my father would not allow it. Not now. Maybe never.

Abigail's words echo back at me: *You can never be more than your father's silly little girl.*

Sadness pools like quicksand, threatening to pull me
under. I take a deep breath and cling to hope like a lifeline, the ridiculous notion that maybe there's a chance a
relationship with Bridget, for travel, for me to break free
from all this.

"LIZBETH!"

Abigail's shrill voice lops off the tail end of that dream
with the sharpness of an ax. My body stiffens, blood turning to ice. So caught up with Bridget, I'm shocked by the
time. Where did they go after church? There's a loud *thunk*,
a string of curses. Tension spiderwebs across the base of my
neck. "I have to go."

Bridget's face darkens. "Is that your mom?"

"Stepmother," I snap.

She recoils, and I'm immediately filled with shame. My
tone was too abrasive, too harsh. But how can I control the
anxiety, the tension, that takes over whenever Abigail is near?
There is not enough Ativan in the world for that.

"Should I let her know I'm here?" Bridget says.

"I'll tell her in the morning," I say, though if I could hide
Bridget forever, I would. I stand, brushing smooth the wrinkles
in my skirt. It's the same flouncy material as Bridget's dress,
but somehow her faint floral pattern looks stylish, while I'm
more reminiscent of a grandmother. From the 1800s. "She'll
just make you start early."

Bridget tilts her head, and the moon emerges through the

glass window behind her, its round face glowing against her pale skin. "Even on Christmas morning?" she asks.

"Especially."

A much more serious warning lingers on my tongue. I want to tell Bridget to run, to get out while she still can. My father, Abigail, they're like giant clouds of impending doom, trapping you with the fear of what's *out there*. But the words won't—can't—come out. I need Bridget to stay. Need—

Her.

My gut twists like a butter churn. I shouldn't feel like this—not now, not so soon, but it's so easy to talk to Bridget, to share what's been trapped in my heart for so long.

Bridget smiles like there's sunshine in her. I strain forward, lapping up her warmth and calmness before I'm forced to trudge through to the storm raging below.

"Tomorrow, then," she says.

I tuck my hands behind my back and kick at a piece of fluff on the carpet. "Tomorrow."

"LIZBETH!" I stiffen at the echo of my stepmother's screech, leaden with the slur of too much whiskey. Only Abigail would chase God's message with an after-Mass shot. "Get your ass down here. Now."

"She sounds—"

"Drunk," I confirm, my pitch rising as anxiety begins to take hold. "Which is only slightly less humiliating than period-bleeding on your leg."

Bridget's grin practically splits her face in half. "I needed a shower anyway."

A tight knot in my chest begins to slide downward, creating a flutter around my heart, a strange hollowness in my stomach. I realize with alarm that I'm reluctant for my time with Bridget to end, desperate for just a few more seconds in her presence, to capture the sense of freedom she brings, no matter how fleeting or false.

"You should—"

"Go," I say, nodding.

I stagger backward, but Bridget is like a magnet, pulling me forward. She stuffs the pictures into the envelope and sets them on the nightstand next to her bed. My feet swoosh along the carpet until finally I'm at the door. I blow out a deep breath. "Really beautiful, Bridget."

She looks up. Smiles.

My chest expands so fast I worry it might pop.

"The pictures," I add, slowly licking my lips.

Bridget giggles. "You're so adorable." She cocks her head. "I totally knew what you meant."

I'm glad, because for some inexplicable reason, I'm not at all sure myself.

CHAPTER

5

I pause at the top of the staircase, paralyzed like a mouse beneath the claws of a descending hawk. Trapped. My heartbeat stutters.

A door creaks open behind me. I crane my neck and stare into Mr. Dent's wide, white pupils. A shiver tremors down the back of my thin dress. I place my finger to my lips and whisper, "Shhh." He blinks and retreats into his suite. Seconds later, water pipes groan as the shower turns on.

Hushed voices grind up the stairs.

Abigail: "This is exactly the kind of carelessness I've been afraid of. It's dangerous, Andrew. *She's* dangerous."

I grip the banister and clench my teeth.

Father: "Not dangerous, depressed."

My fingers tighten around the railing, and my heart begins to race.

Abigail: "That's the diagnosis, yes, but there must be more to it." Her breath comes out in an angry huff. "The medications don't seem to be working. We should increase the dosage."

Father: "I won't have a zombie for a daughter—she's already a bloody embarrassment."

The hair on the back of my neck rises, like tiny soldiers standing at attention. My father's voice does that, commands a kind of respect born out of fear one minute, squashes you like a bug the next.

More Abigail: "And I won't spend my life babysitting her. Commit her to a hospital and be done with it."

My throat goes raw as I wait for my father's response. I imagine him pacing the lobby, the tips of his ears bright crimson beneath his top hat, trying to decide what will better serve his precious reputation—keep me here and run the risk of exposing his secret, or send me away, not once stopping to think about what is best for me.

The ensuing silence is a noose around my neck, pulling tighter with each passing second. No matter how trapped I feel in this house, the thought of imprisonment by strangers, always watching, judging, is far more terrifying.

Abigail again, clearly exasperated: "For Christ's sake, Andrew."

Her stilettos *click, click, click* across the floor. She bends down and looks up at the stairs where I hover, camouflaged in the shadows. "LIZBETH!" Her screech reverberates like a church organ, off-key. "For the last time . . ."

I step into the dim light and her voice catches. "Honestly, Lizbeth." She presses her hand to her chest. "It's creepy how you just show up like that."

My father joins her at the bottom of the stairs, and they glare at me like they're trying to coax a delinquent puppy out from a cardboard box. Dad points to some vague spot behind him. "Lizbeth, what is the meaning of this blood?"

I blink, and the spot is still there, even though I could swear Bridget cleaned it with her shoe.

Abigail rips off her gloves—my mother's gloves—and slaps them together with a resounding *thwack*. My tongue drags across my teeth in disgust. I know all about the secret things in Abigail's bedside table, her collection of my mother's trinkets, jewels . . . memories.

No, she can never have those.

"On second thought, I don't want to know," Abigail says. "Just get it cleaned up."

"Yes, ma'am."

Her face turns scarlet. She opens her mouth, clenches her jaw. Of all the names I could have called my stepmother, "ma'am" is the one that hurts her the most. A cruel thrill pulses through me.

But in my peripheral, I catch Jesus eyeing me from his framed visage in the hallway. *Swipe.* I try to blink away the hallucination, but He lifts an eyebrow and wags his finger at me in disapproval.

Swipe.

I blush, chastised, and begin my slow descent down the staircase, my fingernails carving grooves into the faded wood. Abigail turns away with a sharp *tsk*, but not Father. His eyes watch, warn. A familiar quiver of unease inches along my back.

My shoulders begin to sag. I let out a shaky breath, earlier bravado sinking beneath the creaky floorboards. My knees buckle.

Keeping my anxiety in check can be exhausting, even with my medications—the cocktail of pills prescribed for my "depression," even though I'm not sure Dr. Driscoll's diagnosis is quite right.

How can it be? He can only assess what Abigail has told him. And maybe it started that way—the blackouts from my menstrual condition becoming more frequent in the wake of grief after my mother's passing and Emma's leaving. But what Dr. Driscoll doesn't know—can never know—is how the anxiety gets more and more trapped under my rib cage with every minute I must live in this house.

My father waits until we're nose to nose—me on the third step, him towering over the lobby like a menacing Goliath—and half sneers. "There is blood—"

Don't look away. Dang it! I always look away.

"—on the floor. The *Christmas* tree is on its side. Would you care to explain what happened here tonight?"

I push away the irrational urge to laugh at the ridiculousness of it all, knowing whatever response I give will still end in discipline. But then his voice softens, so slightly I almost think it's my imagination. "An episode?"

My stomach flips with hope. Glimpses like this, hints of the caring father I knew before Mom died, are what ground me. Make me believe that in time, everything will go back to normal. Him. Me.

Us.

God, I want that so bad.

"Yes," I finally say.

Abigail's breath releases in a loud whoosh. "I told you," she hisses. "She's not fit to be left alone, Andrew."

His eyes harden, and again I shrink under his cruel gaze, suffocating under the weight of his displeasure. It's overwhelming, crushing even, never being enough, knowing that I can never live up to his impossible standards. Can never be . . . normal.

Tears gather in the corners of my eyes. I blink them back and shove past my father, my shoulder knocking up against his solid chest. He is an unmoving wall of hard stone. "You're one to talk," I say to Abigail, under my breath. Not soft enough.

Dad grabs my wrist and wrenches me around. Pain shoots through my arm.

"Do not disrespect your mother," he says, growling.

Step. Mother.

I drop my eyes and stare at the floor, which I know my father will accept as submission. Fresh guilt snakes under my skin. *Honor thy father and thy mother.*

"Sorry," I mutter, without looking either of them in the eye, focusing instead on a blurry scuff mark of black on the tile. It does nothing to tamp back the rising anxiety building in my chest, the "madness" itching to sneak out. That's the word my father uses to describe the scars on my thighs, a patchwork manifestation of my "weakness."

I tuck my hand into the pocket of my dress and thread my fingers through the rosary hidden there, drawing strength. The cool beads soothe my skin, but my thoughts wander to Bridget and in an instant, my entire body feels like it's on fire. I am burning up with fresh shame.

Abigail takes off her coat and lays it across the reception desk, knocking the service bell onto the floor with a reverberating *clang*. I bend to pick up a stray piece of glass from one of the ornaments, carefully tucking it into my pocket while I use my wrist to scrub at the small dot of blood on the tile.

Swipe.

The spot grows larger, brighter, a glowing planet Mars. *Swipe. Swipe. Bridget loves the planets and the stars.* I can't get this spot to go away. *Go, spot, you cannot, must not stay.* My skin turns raw and red and I press down hard enough to leave an angry welt across my flesh, grunting from the effort. Sweat beads between my shoulder blades. The anxiety flutters up along my throat—

"Lizbeth!" my father shouts.

Swipe.

With measured speed, I turn to look up at him, eyes cloudy with tears, and something in the distance catches my gaze. Bridget, crouched at the top of the staircase, peering through the banister as I rub, rub, rub at a speck of blood on the floor like some modern-day Cinderella. Fresh panic trips along my spine. It's one thing for Father to berate me, but the thought of Bridget witnessing his anger—

My throat swells.

Go away, I mouth.

She shakes her head. I say it again, my voice a hoarse whisper.

Too late I remember that my every move is monitored, carefully analyzed. Abigail's hands go to her hips, and her lips pucker with distaste. "Lizbeth, you will look at us when we talk to you."

My eyes flit to Bridget, willing her to go away, to retreat farther into the shadows before she is seen. Abigail's chest heaves, her whole body rigid with and poised for intimidation. "Seriously, Lizbeth, what has gotten into you?"

I cast one last glance at Bridget. My heart *pounds, thumps, thunders* through the tense silence. *Do not look at Bridget. Don't.*

Look.

I steady myself against the edge of the reception desk, my head light.

Abigail runs her tongue over her upper teeth. Her eyes sweep me from head to toe, and a snarl curls her lip. "Sweep the whole lobby until it is spotless." She flicks a manicured fingernail toward the corner, where a broom and dustpan lean up against the wall. "Now."

Anger flashes through me. "But it's Christmas."

"I don't care if it's the last fucking day on earth," my father interjects. "Until the new maid arrives, this is your job. Do it."

I focus hard on not shifting my gaze to the stairwell, praying that Bridget has tiptoed back to the safety of her room. My lips move in a silent prayer. *Lord, please keep her safe and free.*

Tomorrow I will go to church. I will ask forgiveness for missing Mass. For dishonoring my father. For my unholy thoughts about Bridget. I will go to confession. Recite Hail Marys. Repent for these sins and promise to obey my father, Abigail, Him from now on.

Anything to keep Bridget hidden, if only for one more night.

Abigail's icy stare leaves me cold. "Do not talk back to me, Lizbeth."

My gag reflex lurches. I despise the way she says my name. *Lizbeth.* Like her forked tongue's about to have a seizure.

A thump at the top of the stairs pulls my attention, and my skin tingles with nervous energy. I freeze, waiting for Abigail or my father to turn to the noise, but neither of them seems to hear it. I risk a glance.

Bridget's pupils shine white through the shadows, peering at me with confusion and alarm. I give my head a subtle shake. *Go!* The color drains from her face, turning her pale as a phantom.

I quickly look away.

Abigail gathers her dress in her fists and brushes past me, pausing only to address my father with the dramatic flair that always turns moments like these into something out of a B-grade horror movie.

"Come, Andrew. It's late."

I know without looking that he won't follow his wife to the bedroom, that her words are more of a test than a command. My father's face is tight with anger. But there's something else there too: regret for what he is about to do. Every muscle in my body flinches, clinging to the hope that this time will be different.

My hand presses to my cheek, a futile attempt to soothe the forthcoming pain.

"Come with me, Lizbeth," my father says. Dread carves into my bones and burrows deep. "You've been a bad girl, and there must be consequences."

I shrivel into the role of helpless child, cowering in fear of what comes next. Of what always comes next.

My father guides me to the staircase, his hand firm on the small of my back. Traces of sweet sugarcane rum and cigar smoke cling to his clothes. I hover on the first step, hand on the rail to steady myself. Goose bumps whisper along my skin. I move slowly, drawing out the inevitable, my throat swollen, chest pinched with fear.

At the top of the stairs, I glance over my shoulder to where Bridget trembles in the corner, camouflaged by the shadows. Thin lines of concern crease her forehead. Her lips purse, then open. I look away before she can mouth the questions I'm unable to answer.

I've seen all I need to anyway.

After just a few hours in Fall River, the bright light in Bridget's eyes has already begun to dim.

CHAPTER

6

The fuzzy yellow streetlight outside glows through the kitchen window and blankets the checkerboard floor. In the distance, the sun hovers just under the horizon, lingering in the early light of dawn for a few minutes longer. It's my favorite time of day, when the house sleeps and I can pretend I'm the only one home.

Across the street, the neighbor's Christmas tree in the living room twinkles to life. Any second now the Dawson kids will bound down the stairs and tear into their presents like Ems and I did once upon a time, before Mom died and Dad . . .

My throat clogs up.

I close the blinds and flick on the stove light. The

low-humming overhead fan swirls the sweet scent of cranberry muffins throughout the kitchen. I breathe in deep. My stomach tingles with anticipation, and it's almost enough to mask last night's memories.

Almost.

My skin burns like there's a fire in my veins. I peer into the stovetop glass, wincing at my reflection. I touch my cheek. Layer after layer of foundation and still, the bruise glows like an overripe blueberry, plainly visible through the makeup.

It doesn't matter. Not even spray paint could hide what I know Bridget *heard*.

Shame hits me like a cold wave. It's rising, all-encompassing, and the idea of it being exposed outside the house makes my hands tremble. I pause, listening for the creak of the uneven floorboards overhead. A rustle of movement, a sign that Bridget hasn't stuffed all her things—pictures, black underwear, her beautiful constellation scarf—into her rainbow backpack, climbed out the bedroom window, and run straight to the police.

A fresh lump of fear swells under my tongue. Would the authorities investigate? Put my father in prison? I lick my lips. No, he would convince them to send me away, lock *me* up instead.

The stove timer buzzes.

With trembling fingers, I slip on oven mitts and take out the muffins, replacing them with the scrambled-egg casserole layered with smoked Gouda, green onions, and a thick béchamel sauce I whipped up from scratch earlier, whisking the ingredients with an intensity meant to exorcise the demons that feed off the madness lurking inside me.

The kitchen is the only room in this house that doesn't stifle. Doesn't feel as though the walls are closing in, trapping me like a caged pigeon. Cooking, baking, creating—it makes me forget that it's Christmas, and that my sister isn't coming home. It dulls the sharpness of my father's words and even his backhand.

No one should ever underestimate the power of a pear cobbler.

Each monotonous motion of mixing and mincing holds me together by the thin thread of normalcy I cling to, giving me hope for a life beyond this house and the invisible locks that confine me to it.

The warm air from the oven singes my cheeks. I bask in it, allowing myself to get swept up in the mechanics of a new creation, yet another recipe stolen from my idol. Today, under Emeril's tutelage, I have *truly* kicked things up a notch.

A soft hum vibrates from my throat. My feet feel lighter, the weight on my shoulders lifting as I draw in the calming scents of savory and sweet. I twirl once, removing the oven mitts and setting them on the counter. Then twirl again and again, craving the kind of freedom that leaves me light-headed and giddy. *Alive.*

So utterly alive.

A soft gasp raises the hair on the back of my neck and I freeze.

"Is this heaven?"

I spin around at the sound of Bridget's melodic voice, and smile so wide the bruise on my cheek aches. My hand flutters to my face and I watch with horror as Bridget's mouth opens in shock. It's too late to shield her from this, I know, but I silently beg her not to ask questions, not to acknowledge it at all. Without uttering a single word, Bridget has already said so much. I want to melt like butter into the floor.

"I'm sorry," she says, a soft whisper.

I hold up a finger. "Don't say that." Turning, I snag a muffin off the cooling tray and pass it to her with a reverence reserved for far more sacred things. I lower my voice, try to smile. "Merry Christmas, Bridget."

The words sound silly considering all that's happened, but I lack the courage to say all the other things hovering on the tip of my tongue. *Run.*

Leave before you are trapped.

Stuck here. Forever.

Bridget cups the muffin and brings it up to her nose. Inhales. "Cranberry?" Her eyes burn with excitement, and my pulse thrums. It's suddenly so important that she loves it—

Me.

Good Lord, I've never wanted anything so much—the

ability to be untethered, free from guilt and self-doubt. Just . . . free.

Bridget takes another long sniff. "Cinnamon." I nod. "Cloves. A hint of citrus." She lifts her gaze. "What else?"

I wring my hands together and rock back on my heels, my chest swelling with pride. "It's a secret."

Her grin is all mischief. "I'll get it out of you."

She reaches toward me and I dodge her advance, my hip hitting the edge of the stove. It doesn't burn me, but my skin ignites anyway. Her fingers playfully jab into my rib cage, twisting into an older bruise that creeps up my side like a glass of dark wine splayed across white linen. I try to mask my wince with a giggle, and fail. Laughter dies on Bridget's cherry-kissed lips.

Her voice drops to a whisper. "It's my fault, isn't it?"

I shake my head with vigor, fighting the tears. It's not sadness or pain fueling the reaction, but anger and embarrassment. Bridget should never see this. Emotions pool under my tongue, threatening to bubble over, the madness spilling out and onto the floor like vomit. I struggle to contain it, unable to process what this all means.

In Bridget's presence, I am weightless, spiraling toward the unknown, grasping for something to ground me. Some way to keep balanced, stay afloat. I blink, suddenly realizing with surprise that my anchor is *here*—it's Bridget.

"They drank too much," I say softly, my head spinning

with thoughts and feelings and fears. The lie slides easily from my mouth, but it's not enough, not nearly enough, to wipe the concern off Bridget's face. It's etched into her perfect skin with permanent marker, and I hate that I'm the cause of such blasphemous graffiti.

She reaches up and brushes her thumb under my eye, her gaze lingering on my mouth.

My lips quiver. "Ginger."

Bridget blinks, and the moment is lost. "My hair?"

"The secret ingredient. It's . . . ginger."

She smiles like I've unveiled the Cadbury secret, making my insides twist. It's an obvious attempt to change the subject, and I almost gasp with relief when she takes the bait. This place is bad. Abigail is bad. *I'm* bad. But Bridget is the first *good* thing I've come across in so long, I can't stomach the thought of letting her go.

My gut clenches at the realization, and I'm shocked at my selfishness. At the sheer depth of my feelings. It's too soon. *Too fast.*

My throat squeezes shut, making it impossible to breathe.

Bridget slaps her forehead with a flat palm. "Damn it. I should have guessed. Ginger ale is my favorite soda."

My eyes widen. "Mine too. Father B . . . my friend . . . says he ate so much ginger in China, he almost got sick. I can't imagine that." My words string together, almost incoherent with excitement. "Have you ever been there?"

She pops a chunk of cranberry muffin in her mouth, her lips strangely mesmerizing as she chews. A small groan emerges from somewhere deep in her belly, making my skin prickle with pride. The pulse thunders against my eardrums.

"Good Lord, these are delicious," she says, mouth full. "I spent two weeks in Hong Kong." A crumb latches onto the corner of her lip, and I'm desperate to lick it clean. I imagine my tongue sliding across her soft mouth, and heat crawls up the side of my neck.

I drag my gaze to the cross above the kitchen door. *Swipe.* The face of God pinches with more disappointment, more contempt. I am drowning in his judgment.

Grab the anchor.

Swipe.

Bridget bites down on her lip. "Honestly, Lizzie, these muffins are fucking brilliant."

Brilliant.

"You could be a chef—I mean, you're already a great cook, but . . ." Bridget stares at me, and for some inexplicable reason, tears prick my eyes. "A professional chef, Lizzie. Like, you could go to school and everything."

I couldn't. Can't.

My father's words play back at me, a constant reminder that I don't have the skills or resources to make it on my own. In the world outside Fall River, I would get lost. Hurt, or worse.

A fresh blush sets the bruise aflame. I force myself to keep my voice steady while I shift gears. "What was Hong Kong like?"

"Busy." Bridget hops up onto one of the kitchen stools, tiny feet dangling over the edge. She isn't wearing socks, which is ridiculous. My father barely runs the furnace in this place. A silver ring encircles her pinky toe, and purple nail polish shimmers under the harsh overhead lights. I glance down at my mismatched fuzzy slippers, for the first time wishing I could steal something more glamorous from Abigail's armoire, something sleek and elegant. Or maybe just cool.

Bridget manipulates the muffin wrapper into a series of folds. In seconds, the cranberry-stained paper transforms into a blooming rose. She passes it to me, a shy smile playing on her heart-shaped lips. "That's the extent of what I learned in Tokyo."

I grip the stem of the rose so tight the paper sticks to my fingers. A bead of sweat moistens my forehead. Familiar anxiety creeps across my swelled chest, but then I look up at Bridget and my nerves begin to unwind. An unfamiliar lightness begins to spread throughout my body. "I've only seen people make swans," I say. *On TV*.

"That's advanced origami," she says, deadpan. "I barely made it past beginner."

"You took a class?"

I'm totally gushing.

Her laugh stirs up more butterflies in my stomach. I glance down, sure she can hear the flutter of their wings coming to life. But it's the cranberry stain that catches my eye. Red, like . . . *swipe* . . . blood. A low hum buzzes behind my temples.

I pivot away and open the stove with shaky fingers. Cheese bubbles on the surface of the casserole, turning golden under the heat. I release a nervous breath.

"Origami flowers are common icebreakers at bars in Asia," Bridget says, moving closer to the open door. Heat radiates off her skin, bathing me in its warmth. "And I'm a sucker for a good line."

My tongue tangles as I try to find some kind of witty response.

"Boys like my hair," she goes on, like I'm not agonizing over how to keep the conversation from getting even more awkward and confusing. "Girls, too, come to think of it." I hold my breath, daring to hope. "Gingers are easy, they all think." I turn around just as she winks, and the fluttering butterflies begin to inch up my throat. There's this strange tingle between my thighs that keeps throwing me off balance, turns my cheeks crimson. I press my knees together. "Do I give off that vibe?" Bridget continues. "Never mind. Even if I do, it's got nothing to do with hair color."

"Is it real?" My jaw drops. I'm shocked by the question,

my audacity. I've never been so blunt in my life, but being with Bridget is both unnerving and the most natural thing in the world.

Bridget bursts out laughing. "This week, yeah. But I've been every color of the rainbow—even green." She snorts. "An Irish girl with green hair? Shocking, I know."

Ireland.

Another destination on my travel bucket list. The Bible teaches us not to covet, and maybe I'm going to hell, but in this moment, I am coveting *Bridget*. Her freedom, her experiences. If I am a hamburger, she is an exotic lamb roast—we could not be more opposite. But isn't it true that opposites attract? That they can forge some kind of connection that is maybe more than friendship?

Fresh hope forms a ball in my chest, clenched like a fist.

"Why leave Japan?" I say, though what I'm really wondering is why she ended up in Fall River, ended up—

Here.

Bridget sighs. "I make bad life choices." Her shoulders sag. "Or maybe I'm just drawn to bad romances. My ex-girlfriend ended up doing time in juvie. . . ." My breath hitches. *Girlfriend?* Could I have imagined those words? My emotions are on a yo-yo, with Bridget manipulating the cord. *Up. Down. Up* . . . "And the guy I was seeing in Hong Kong cheated. Dick."

The string snaps. "That was his name?"

Bridget smiles. Good Lord, I'm already addicted to the way her lips curve. She is like a mirage, plucked from my fantasies and into my life. A living, breathing manifestation of all the secrets I've kept hidden—my attraction to girls growing even under the church's microscope, her presence here a convenient way for us to be together without arousing suspicion.

"As in, he *was* one. And then there was Miss Italy . . ." She shoves another piece of muffin in her mouth. My tongue slides across my teeth, as if to swipe clear the grit and filth of my sins, my unholy thoughts.

"I don't want to talk about her," Bridget says, pulling me back. She curls her lips in a sexy smile, and I can't help but wonder how many others have been mesmerized by it. The low hum of jealousy thrums through me. "Or anyone else, really." Her voice goes impossibly soft. "I like being here with just you, Lizzie."

My mouth goes dry, and I'm sure I'm imagining it when Bridget slides off the stool and steps toward me. "I like *you*," she says. I blink, blink, blink, but she moves closer. *Swipe.* The tips of my fingers start to tingle. "You're funny, and . . ." She puts her hand on my face, and her thumb brushes across the bruise on my cheek. "Kind."

I pinch my wrist, twisting the skin, willing myself to wake up from this delicious dream.

Bridget isn't gone.

"Do you have any idea how beautiful you are?" she whispers.

I'm not, I think, but the words don't come out. There's no time. Bridget's lips part and she tilts her head. I lose my breath when her mouth closes over mine. Her lips are cool, soft. My limbs stiffen in trepidation and confusion.

This can't be real.

But then her tongue probes between my trembling lips, and she cups the back of my head to pull me close. Her fingers tangle in my hair to deepen the kiss. Tentative at first, and then with more urgency as my mouth yields to hers. My arms move clumsily around her back to settle on her hips.

In all my fantasies, I could never have planned for this.

This utter loss of control.

I am breathless and floaty, trembling under her touch. My heart flutters so fast I'm sure it will—

The oven timer buzzes. We pull apart, startled, and I flatten my hand against my chest.

Bridget presses her fingers to her lips and giggles.

I'm sure I've never heard a more beautiful sound.

"You should get that," she says.

Carefully, I put on my oven mitts and pull the casserole out from the heat to set it on the stove. The aroma is overpowering, breathtaking even. Bridget's warm breath feathers across the back of my neck, a light kiss against my tingling skin. Every cell in my body strains toward her touch, aches to rewind time and experience this "first" again and again.

Bridget leans over the dish, holding her hair back with one hand to reveal her faded moon tattoo. I'm fascinated by the shades of gray that give it a three-dimensional appearance, like it might revolve right off her skin. She fans the steam toward her button nose and moans. A shiver of longing ripples down my spine. "You really should consider a professional career as a chef," she says.

My voice turns to a whisper. "I'd never be accepted in."

Her smile is luminescent, confident. "Of course you would," she says, beaming. "Why wouldn't you?"

A million reasons should come to mind, but in this moment, none of them do.

7

Candlelight casts flickering shadows across the eager faces of the kids kneeling on the strip of carpet stretched out at the base of my lectern. They wait for my teachings, the words that I'll speak from the gospel.

I draw in a deep breath and look up, stalling.

Light from the stained-glass windows dances across the colorful murals of Daniel fighting the lion, of animals boarding the ark, of His savior nailed to the cross. My eyes linger there a little too long.

Four polished columns rise up beside me and form an arch. From it hangs a giant crucifix, Jesus's finely sculptured form nailed to the wood. His gaze weighs heavy on my back, too. I used to believe he watched over me. I wonder now if he simply watches.

Judges.

One of the children shifts, kicking out her legs to point her stocking feet to the side. Her smile slips in apology for the disruption, but it's not her quiet discomfort that has fresh anxiety nipping at my throat.

My sister's latest letter is tucked into the back of my Bible, the edges of the yellow paper poking out to reveal the swirl of her penmanship. The word "love" stands out among the blur of sentences that tell new stories of her life on campus. Her descriptions of Emerson College are so vivid, I can almost smell the rich pastries at DeLuca's Market or taste the dumplings at some hole-in-the-wall in the nearby Chinatown.

I've met someone. His name is Jesse—he's the editor at the paper. I can't wait for you to meet him.

She's happy, and I should be glad, but there's a pit in my stomach that hasn't moved since the morning she packed her bags, the grin on her face shattering my heart into tiny little pieces.

You will visit someday, won't you? I miss you, Izzy.

The hole of grief inside me still throbs, the pain of it nearly taking my breath away. Emma's first letters kept me grounded, but they also carved fresh wounds, and this one is no different. With her newfound freedom, our relationship has begun to erode like sandstone in the wind. I never believed it could be rebuilt, but now with Bridget, I'm wondering if maybe—

Stop it.

I duck my head with shame. I am not worthy of happiness.

Even Father Buck would agree, if asked. My eyes sweep to the side of the room, where he sits, pretending to study his sermons, but listening to my teachings.

Because for all its virtues, Catholicism is not a soothing religion. It's painful. And I am a glutton for its punishment. I've kept secret my unrequited crushes, believing foolishly that if I didn't acknowledge them, they couldn't be true sins—not really. *Sin is the act, not the thought*, Father Buck would say. But Catholic guilt knows no such boundaries.

My thoughts drift to Bridget, and I can almost feel her soft lips against mine. Hear the steady *thump, thump, thump* of her heart. My breath turns shallow with longing.

I have not only crossed well over the line into sin, but I have disobeyed my father by carrying on a forbidden relationship right under his nose. No question he would have me institutionalized for such a betrayal. Perhaps I deserve such punishment.

One of the children coughs, and I return my attention to the students. I grip the handout of Jonah and the Whale—it's one of the stranger stories of the Bible, but oddly, one of my favorites. It teaches obedience to God's commands, and tackling the impossible. Perfect for this group of six- to eight-year-olds, who act as though they'd never think of disobeying me. Perfect, perhaps, for the impossible life I know I can't have.

I can recite this story from memory, instinct drawing out the inflections of tone that will drive God's message home. With other students, we have cut and colored pictures of whales. Laughed. Sung.

I'm just not feeling it today. In truth, I've been distracted since Bridget first swept into the B and B, her every whisper, every touch, further chipping away at the foundation of my faith. What once brought me peace has become a source of turmoil. It *shouldn't* be like this—should it?

I've bragged about your cooking to Jesse. My throat swells at the memory of Emma's generous praise. *He's looking forward to trying your meat loaf. You're still making it, right, Izzy?*

I read between the lines. This is her subtle way of asking how much has changed in her absence, whether Father—or maybe Abigail—has finally broken my spirit. If I've given up my passion. The opposite is true. Being with Bridget adds fuel to it, motivating me to be more creative, more thorough. To strive for excellence.

To go to culinary school?

Every moan of Bridget's approval is like a direct line to my soul, lifting it further from darkness.

I smooth out the wrinkles in my new skirt. Silver and gold flecks glitter in the candlelight, like dancing stars. The material hugs a little close. It's too showy for church. Too tight for even my small frame, no matter what Bridget whispered in my ear as I twirled like a ballerina in the bathroom mirror.

I'm sure Father Buck was thinking all these things when he glared at me this morning—like an unfamiliar specimen he needed to classify, dissect, dismiss. As though I'd somehow offended God with my uncharacteristic—unworthy?—attire.

Abigail has worn far more revealing clothes in this church, and Father Buck barely lifts an eyebrow. Why am I open for judgment while she is safe from His disapproval?

My eyes flit to the lone wooden confessional rising up against the brick wall at the back of the church. *Forgive me, Father, for I have sinned.* But even I know that going to confession isn't a free pass for sinners—not even me, for as willful a servant I have become. I will remain, forever trapped, under the crushing weight of guilt, another obstacle on the path to any freedom I might hope to someday find.

A subtle cough pulls me back to my lesson.

"'This is what the Lord says,'" I say, deciding last minute to try a different sermon. "Jeremiah 29:10–11. 'When seventy years are completed for Babylon, I will come to you and fulfill my good promise to bring you back to this place. For I know the plans I have for you.'"

I reach for a glass of water and take a sip. The liquid coats my throat, thick like blood. I lick my lips, swiping clear a coppery scent so pungent it seems real, and swallow. "'Plans to prosper you and not to harm you, plans to give you hope and a future.'"

My students remain silent as the last of my words trail

off. Flickering candles pulse in tandem with my breath. I wait for questions. For commentary. For someone to tell me what I already know: this lesson is far too advanced for children of this age. *What was I thinking?*

I wasn't.

My thoughts are erratic and distracted, always hovering around Bridget. I am frantic, consumed with the idea of being with her, of feeling her skin against mine, her fingertips tracing patterns across my flesh . . . *Swipe.* I wince against the gut wrench of shame, wishing I could just wear a cilice as an alternative to confession. I'd rather endure the pain of coarse sackcloth than admit my feelings for Bridget, leaving them open to scrutiny and judgment.

A young girl, new to the church, to me, fidgets with the lace cuff on her pink dress. It's the shade of Pepto-Bismol, and my throat immediately constricts. "What if I don't like the future God has chosen for me?" she says.

The question hits too close to home. Not long ago, I too believed the Lord had chosen me as His faithful servant, that I was destined to do great things, to remain good and chaste and obedient. But my path is less clear now, muddled by the emotions I should not—am not allowed—to have. The consequences of betraying my father, the church, Him are too much—and yet, I have already begun my walk down this dark path.

A poignant, well-rehearsed answer to the girl's question

is severed from the tip of my tongue at the sound of the door swinging open at the back of the church. Bridget stumbles through the entrance, tripping on the upturned corner of the rug, the edge of her too-tall heel catching on the frayed fringe.

I muster a welcoming smile and finger my necklace. I expect the cross to ignite with my sinful thoughts, but instead the metal is cool to the touch. Bridget responds with a hesitant wave, looking small and perfect in this cavernous room where she does not belong.

Do I?

My stomach is a tornado of conflicting emotion.

Father Buck clears his throat, reminding me to focus on the unanswered question, alerting me also to the fact that he, like my parents, is never far from earshot, eyesight. Always watching. Listening. Seeing.

Even after all the years I've spent volunteering in this church, teaching Sunday school, participating in youth retreats, it's clear I still don't measure up here. Will *never* measure up—

Anywhere.

Bridget slinks through the pews at the back of the room. Warmth rushes to my hands, leaving them tingling and numb. The words in my sister's letter *tap, tap, tap* against my temples: *I think about you every day, Izzy. Are you healthy? Happy?*

I don't know how to respond.

I've been acting like my growing feelings for Bridget are normal, but all the while inside I'm beginning to unravel, slowly, like a thread being pulled painstakingly from its spool. It seems impossible, but it's as if my depression has begun to lift, replaced by a brightness that reflects from deep inside Bridget's core.

Seeing her here now makes my heart soar, and I smile despite the anxiety coiled around my chest. People *can* be happy and sad at the same time, I know—it's just that sometimes the sad parts just spiral out of control.

Would Emma accept this explanation?

"Miss Borden?"

I stare down at young Johnny, his cherub cheeks red from having spoken aloud.

"What if God wants me to be a doctor—and I just want to play soccer? What if our *plans* don't match up?"

A sad smile tugs at my heart. I've barely heard this boy say more than a mumbled "Amen" after prayer, let alone brave a question of such significance. My mind feels like cotton. How can I respond when I'm no longer sure of the answer myself?

I lift my gaze, focusing it on the image of another of God's martyrs. Light and darkness form the DNA of my religion, but in this cathedral—despite the stained glass—shadows are everywhere. Ghosts of the past swirl from beneath the floor, bringing with them the cloying scents of the burial ground on which this ancient cathedral stands. I am surrounded by old spirits, slowly becoming crushed under the weight of their wispy limbs clawing toward me, desperate to drag me under with them. Away from Bridget.

Far from sin.

Swipe.

Bridget finds a seat at the back of the room and crosses her long, slender legs. My students turn to follow my gaze, and Bridget gives them one of those "popular girl" finger waves that usually make me roll my eyes. Another, more increasingly common, feeling lingers there instead. An inexplicable giddiness that makes me flush and go cold at once.

The students don't acknowledge her—steadfast in their obedience to the church's teachings—and turn back to me with questioning eyes.

I silently beg Bridget to stay at the back, in the shadows and out of view from Father Buck's curiosity. We've kept our relationship secret, stealing time when my parents aren't home or have gone to bed. I help her clean. She watches me cook. In the evenings, we sip tea and scroll through her pictures, inching closer and closer until our skin just barely touches, while she shares tales of her adventures and we hold fast to dreams.

Every night, before one of us tiptoes back to bed, she kisses the tip of my nose, each cheek, and then finally my lips, imprinting her cotton-candy scent on my skin. I cherish each of those moments in private—but they can never become public, never be fully out on display, especially not here, in my church, where the gory and bloody images of saints offer stark reminders of what can happen to those who sin.

In my peripheral vision, I catch Father Buck as he raises a bushy eyebrow.

I speed through the questions from my students, fast-track my closing remarks—assuring each young face with superficial sincerity that yes, God *does* have plans for them all, perhaps some that even involve soccer—and then usher them out with their parents, whose judgmental eyes zero in on my too-tight, too-short skirt.

All except Johnny's mother, who always takes time to thank me for sticking it out with her son. For not giving up. She folds my hand into hers. "You're so kind." Her fingers are like ice, and a shiver ripples down my spine. I put a smile on when all I want to do is pull away. Run. "So very kind."

I try to shrug it off, but she keeps thanking me and it's awkward. I don't deserve her compliments today. I'm off balance. Out of focus. Unsure in my faith.

I've stopped going to church, Izzy. I'm sorry if that hurts you.

Jealousy prickles against my flesh. Why was Emma allowed to leave, to explore the world, while I remain tethered not only to the church, but to my family? Bound to the expectations and responsibilities imposed on a child chosen by God.

If *I* am the chosen one, as Father Buck suggests, why am I unable to do as I choose?

"You're very good," Bridget says as I approach her, her voice a bird chirp in this giant cage with its open beams and intricate windows. She reaches out to hold my hand, threading her fingers through mine. "You almost made me a believer."

I glance over my shoulder, spotting Father Buck as he winds his way through the pews toward me. My pulse ratchets up. He can't find Bridget. I pull my hands free and stare hard into her shimmering eyes, shocked to see pride. My voice catches. "You can't be here."

Father Buck's footsteps *tap, tap, tap* to signal his looming presence. Adrenaline rushes through my veins.

Bridget's face darkens. "Why?" She peers around me, craning her slender neck like a bird's. "Because I'm not religious and your God wouldn't approve of us? How about I have a chat with your priest right now?"

My throat seizes with panic. Father Buck is the most perceptive man I have ever met, and with just one look, he will *know* what's in my heart. "He'll tell my father," I whisper harshly.

Bridget tilts her chin upward. Sunlight beams through the skylight and narrows in on her head, creating an incandescent halo around her hair. The freckles across her nose and cheeks twinkle like bright new stars. *Please don't fade.*

"You're afraid," she says softly.

Tears gather in the corners of my eyes. I squeeze her hand.

"Go," I say, my voice hushed. "Please. Before it's too late."

"Lizbeth," Father Buck says, his voice reverberating like the church bells out front.

I turn around to face him, praying that I will block his view of Bridget, offering my most sincere smile, though my hands tremble with fear.

His lips curve into a frown. "Is everything all right, my dear?"

No. Unable to speak, I nod.

He comes closer, piercing me with his stare, his eyes the color of the startling oceans in Bridget's travel photographs. I long to be transported there now.

"Who were you talking to?"

My heart pounds like a gong. "I'm sorry?"

Annoyance flickers across his weathered face. "I could swear you were talking to someone."

I follow his gaze, preparing myself for the inevitable introduction to Bridget, already forming the excuses that will explain her presence, our relationship, my feelings. But as I turn, breath caught in my throat, I realize the seat she once occupied is empty.

Like a ninja, Bridget has slipped away, once again leaving behind only the faint trace of her cotton-candy scent, and an inexplicable hollowness in my chest.

CHAPTER

8

An ear-shattering electric shriek startles me awake. I bolt upright and stare wide-eyed into the darkness. The air is thick, like a steam room.

My father's terror-stricken voice bellows through the hallway. "Lizbeth? Lizbeth!"

I scramble out from under the covers, tripping over cotton sheets that tangle at my feet. The faint scent of smoke drifts under my door. *Fire*. My house is on fire.

"Dad?"

Panic turns my voice to a tremble. I yell again, but the steady trill of the alarm drowns it out. Footsteps thunder in the hallway and my father starts banging on doors, shouting for people to "get up, get out! Quick!"

Bridget. I have to get to Bridget.

I throw an old cardigan over my pajamas and gather a few items into a small suitcase—a change of clothes, the Bible, my noteb—wait. *Where is my notebook?* My nerves knot in my chest.

My father continues to bellow down the hall.

"Daddy?" I shove my bare feet into a pair of winter boots, but they're too big, and each step toward the door feels like I'm trudging through quicksand. I scan the room, fear and madness inside climbing across my bones in search of a way out. *Swipe.*

I will not succumb. But the incessant screech of the alarm grates under my skin, and my mind is numb with terror.

I press my hand against my bedroom door, checking for heat. With trembling fingers, I pry it open and peer into the hall, shielding my eyes from the billowing smoke I expect to find. The air is cool, clear. No stuffier than the ever-present musk that even repeated spritzes of Febreze can't erase. Lord knows Bridget has tried.

My feet shuffle along the carpeted hallway as I make my way to the maid's suite, my small suitcase trailing behind. I bang on the door. Bridget swings it open and her shoulders slump with obvious relief, her annoyance from our interaction at the church overshadowed by fresh fear. She's wrapped in my great-grandmother's patchwork quilt, shivering and tense.

She drops the blanket and gathers me in her arms, squeezing me tight enough to force out a gasp. I can feel her heartbeat against mine. Her lips skim my earlobe. "Thank you."

My stomach flips.

"We have to leave," I say, voice rising over the steady ring of the alarm. The fire seems contained so far—though I can't pinpoint its exact location—but I've taken enough safety courses to know how quickly flames can spread.

I nudge my head toward the suitcase. "Follow me."

For a split second I forget about the fire, the danger. Pretend it's just me and Bridget making our escape. Me, saving her. Saving us. Sneaking off into the sunset. My voice drops to a whisper. "Don't worry. I'll keep you safe."

I'll always keep you safe.

Bridget's eyes watch my lips like she's trying to read them. She runs back to her bed and grabs her backpack off the mattress. Moonlight streams through the billowing lace curtains at the window, blanketing the room in a haunting bluish tinge.

I slip my hand in hers, and together we tiptoe down the hallway, eyes and ears and nose on alert for any signs of the fire. At the end of the hall I spot one of the guests on all fours, crawling toward the stairway. The white of his robe glows red under the dim EXIT sign hanging above the landing.

He turns and spots me. "Is it safe?"

My father grunts from the lobby below. I imagine him

yanking the extinguisher from its case, trying to put out the flames while Abigail fans them with her fur-lined nightgown. *Swipe.* A mischievous grin curls up her lip. *Swipe. Swipe.* My mother's face emerges from the smoke, her eyes wide with alarm. *Swipe. Swipe. Swipe.* Her mouth opens. *Get out, Lizbeth. Run away....*

I blink hard, trying to ignore the visions, the sound of the alarm.

Bridget tugs on my sleeve. "Where do we go?"

Any second now the Fall River police and fire departments will be dispatched.

It's going to be okay.

I keep telling myself that as we hurry to the staircase and join the other guests at the landing. Four of them, faces pale, concern and fear weathering their skin. We huddle together, peering into the darkness below.

"Dad?"

My small voice gets lost in the blare of the siren. I squint but there's still no sign of flames. And now the faint smell of smoke I imagined earlier is replaced by the foul scent of someone's BO. I cover my nose with my arm. "We need to get downstairs."

The front door calls to us like a beacon, but there's no sign of my father or Abigail. Terror rips through my core. If something has happened to them—

Swipe. Abigail's skin bubbles, boils, drips from her charred skeleton. The stench of burnt hair makes me gag. Bile crawls up my throat. Across the room, my father's body puddles on the floor, his flesh liquefying under the heat. *Swipe. Swipe.* He turns his face to me. I recoil. *Swipeswipeswipe.*

"Lizzie, we can't stay here," Bridget says, snapping me out of the horrifying vision. "Do something."

I square my shoulders and take a deep breath. Bridget, the guests—their safety is my first priority, nothing else. Not in this moment. "Is everyone ready? We're going to make a break for the door."

I lead the group quickly down the stairs, glancing over my shoulder to make sure no one is left behind. I recite the emergency procedures in my head, again and again. A thump draws my attention and I turn just in time to see Bridget stumble. She hits the wall midway, regains her balance, and quickens her pace.

Be careful, I mouth.

I throw open the front door and a rush of fresh air swirls into the lobby. One of the guests shoves me aside to launch himself out the door, the others following him blindly into the dark. Their voices fade into the night. I focus on getting everyone safe, on keeping calm, when suddenly the alarm comes to an abrupt stop.

The ensuing silence sends a ripple of unease up and down my spine.

"Lizbeth."

My father's voice has a dangerous edge to it, and fresh terror stirs in my gut.

I pivot, heart racing, and his stern face emerges from the shadows. In his right hand he holds the fire extinguisher, in his left, the charred remains of what looks like a journal. He lifts it to eye level and his glare sharpens—he stares at me like I'm a black widow spider in need of extermination. "I believe this belongs to you."

In the haze of my confusion, I feel Bridget's presence, the weight of her questioning stare. "Your diary?" she says, so quiet it's almost a whisper. "What happened?"

Swipe.

My stepmother steps out from behind my father and snatches the notebook from his hands, her thin lips twisted in disgust. "You burned your journal."

My eyebrows knit together. "That's not mine." *My* journal is somewhere in my bedroom, hidden from these prying eyes. The messages and recipes, the observations and dreams, my prayers and confessions all stitched together in hurried penmanship, words meant only for me. That journal—*my journal*—is not in Abigail's fist, and certainly wasn't set on fire.

Was it?

Abigail thrusts her hand forward to reveal a single sheet of paper, ripped as though torn free from a binding. "It most certainly is." She pushes it toward my chest. "Who else would write such vile, immature things?" My eyes skim over the words. *Bitch. Slut.* Guilt slides under my skin. I've never said those words aloud, not even in a hushed whisper.

"For God's sake, Lizbeth," my father says, arms folded across his chest. "When will you stop behaving like a petulant little girl?" He grabs my wrist and whirls me toward him. His searing eyes penetrate right through to my bones. "Start acting your age. And apologize to your mother—"

Step. Mother.

"—for your disrespect." He presses the paper into my hand and scowls. "I thought you were better than this, Lizbeth."

Better than what?

He sneers. "Your medications were supposed to curb this kind of impulsiveness."

My eyes trail along each written sentence, processing, assessing. Memories begin to emerge, like snakes charmed from wicker baskets. Every name Abigail has called me. The insults, the put-downs. The lies. All cataloged.

I recognize the script, my penmanship. I'd know that anywhere. It's the same lettering I've used to draw hearts next to Bridget's name, looping it with swirls and swirls and— My throat tightens. Has Father seen those pages as well?

"Childish," my father says again, tsking with disapproval. "You will apologize. Abigail deserves far more respect than this."

She doesn't, but I can't say this to him. Can't tell him

that Abigail is cold and mean, not maternal in the least. She wears her armor like the scales of a lizard: patterned, impervious, perfect. Her smiles are tactical, and her voice is used only to get what she wants.

And what Abigail desires more than anything is to lock me up in a white-walled prison, for me to leave—but to also never be free. For Abigail, tears are nothing more than a sign of weakness, and for that reason, I have never cried in front of her. Not one tear.

But dang it if I'm not close now.

The dull wail of a fire-truck siren echoes in the background. Close, but not enough to release me from the thick weight of accusation. Everyone—even Bridget, so silent she's almost invisible—waits for an explanation.

This *is* my journal, and I recall in vivid detail the arguments that led to me writing each horrible word, to capture Abigail's disdain and cruelty. There can be no room for debate. No one lingers on details when it's easier to move forward as if they're the ramblings of a mad little girl, instead of memories and truths.

It's just . . .

What I don't understand, what doesn't make sense, is how this diary—these confessions—went from my bedroom to burnt.

"I didn't start a fire," I say, my voice hesitant and quiet. "Why would I do such a thing?"

My anger, my hopes, my wishes and dreams—now all nothing more than a pile of ash. Even my near-perfect meat-loaf recipe is burned to a crisp. My head spins, reeling from the loss of what I can never get back, and I can feel the tentacles of madness slithering up my throat.

Snippets of déjà vu—or something close—cloud my vision.

Swipe. Me, hovering over the bathtub, tears streaming down my face, the questions asked by my students echoing in my subconscious. *Swipe.* Flames licking the side of the mint-green porcelain. The paper catching fire, smoke drifting to the stained ceiling, taking with it my guilt. *Swipe.* I catch my reflection in the mirror, broken and dark. *Swipe. Swipe—*

—I barely recognize myself—

Swipe.

My heart feels like it's in my throat, beating a scream of denial from my mouth. "I didn't do this."

"Explain that to the fire department," Abigail snaps. She closes her robe over her nightgown with a theatrical huff. "If you'll excuse me, I need to put on something more appropriate. Andrew?"

My father nods, but he doesn't look at me. That's the thing about him these days. He never keeps eye contact for long. It's as if looking at me too long hurts, or disgusts him in some way, a constant reminder that I'm a disappointment, an utter disgrace. He threads his arm through his wife's and leads her away.

I stand, tears threatening to spill, and stare at the cruel words written by my hand. Humiliation washes over me.

"It's okay," Bridget whispers. She closes her hand over mine, and the paper crumples into a ball. Her thumb caresses my wrist. "We'll sort it out, babe."

"I didn't start the fire," I say again, louder.

But I know how things look. I want to blame Abigail, pretend she framed me for this. I convince myself to believe it, and ignore the inconsistencies in my theory, make excuses for the gaps in my memory, the insurmountable evidence.

A chill seeps into my bones. I wrap the cardigan tight around me and stuff my hands into the deep pockets.

Bridget pulls me close to her chest.

"I didn't burn my journal," I whisper.

But even as the words trickle from my lips, my trembling fingers dig deeper into my sweater and curl around the charred tip of a match. I pull it from my pocket and hold it up into the light. Ash smears across my fingertips.

Bridget tenses, and it's like the air is sucked from my lungs. I don't turn to look at her. I can't. I'm terrified to see the disbelief that I'm sure now mars her angelic face.

9

I push the meaty maggot onto the end of the hook with a soft pop. Guts squeeze onto my thumb. I smear them against my cargo shorts and finish tying the knot on my fishing line. In my peripheral vision, I catch Bridget's expression—total disgust.

A shiver of revulsion makes her muscles tense. "Jesus, how do you even handle the stench?"

I glance over my shoulder, eyebrows narrowed. "Of what?" Bridget nudges her head toward my rod and I grin. "Aw, they're not so bad." I thrust the pole toward her face. "Here, smell."

She sticks out her tongue and staggers backward, holding up her hand as though to ward off bad spirits. "Fuck that." Her leg knocks against the tackle box. Hooks, bob-bers, and fishing line spill onto the side of the muddy river-bank.

Bridget crouches to gather the items, her bare feet pre-cariously close to one of the hooks. "Careful. You don't want to accidentally stab yourself," I say, trying not to panic. "I can do that if you want to take over here."

She makes a face. "I'd rather jab myself in the eye."

"And ruin such perfection?"

She allows a grin. "True. I'd miss seeing your beautiful face every day."

A ridiculous blush creeps up the side of my neck.

The maggot squirms on the end of my hook and Bridget's skin goes a little green. I bite my tongue to stop the knee-jerk teasing that always comes when we hang out, the back-and-forth bantering that stuffs the madness deep down under my bones. Being with Bridget makes me forget all the things I can't be, the things I can't tell her. I forget everything and just let myself . . . be.

"I can't believe I'm doing this," she mutters, pinching some of the tackle between her fingertips before dropping it into the box.

She perches on the balls of her feet, keeping her balance. Her shorts are so short the insides of the pockets flap against her smooth thighs. The pads of my hands itch and I look away in an attempt to curb the longing. Spring has barely sprung and Bridget's already dressed for the beach—not that I'm complaining.

She holds up an oversize hook. "What's this for? Megalodon?"

I feel my eyebrow rise. "Isn't that a shark?"

"A big shark," Bridget says. "Possibly extinct, but that's what they said about the Loch Ness Monster."

I finish securing my bait, reel up the line, and grin. "Let me guess, you saw Nessie in the flesh when you were in Ireland?"

"Scotland," she says, deadpan, and I think she might be teasing me. Bridget is a fast study of one of fishing's cardinal rules—the ability to tell white lies. "Anyway, that's what keeps me from swimming in oceans and lakes. Sea monsters, giant sharks."

I turn toward the water. "There's nothing like that in Cook Pond. I promise. Some bass, perch. Maybe a few tigers."

Bridget's eyes go wide.

"Tiger muskies," I say, and wink. Goodness, she's so easy to make squirm. "They can get pretty big—"

She holds up the oversize hook again. "This big?"

"That's for pike." I pull my arm back and cast. The lure drops with a light splash in the middle of the pond. "Didn't your dad ever take you fishing?"

"You've seen pictures of my parents," Bridget scoffs. "Do they look like they fish?"

"One picture," I say, and then shrug. "You said yourself they're free spirits. Nature types."

Like my mother. Ems says our parents didn't like the outdoors much, but when she was at school and Father was at work, Mom took me fishing. Mostly at the reservoir, and occasionally in this very spot. I still try to feel her presence, but any lingering aura from her time here was stripped the second Abigail discovered this place. I breathe out a sigh. Far too many of my sanctuaries are graffitied by my stepmother's presence.

Maybe that's why I resent her. She never let me heal. The black hole of grief that should have bloomed when my mother died was overshadowed by a more ominous sense of dread, the crushing weight of entrapment the second Abigail entered my life. While my mother tried to help me work through my condition—cradling me after my first blackout and ever after until the last smiled faded from her face—my father never believed in the diagnosis. "Ridiculous woman problems," he'd say, though over the years his voice grew harsher, thicker with disgust.

And Abigail took his side, abandoning feminism in exchange for my father's adoration, however dubious.

Father wasted no time bringing Abigail into our lives either, as if she could somehow replace Mom. Or as if we could pretend she never existed.

Maybe it's for the best, because Mom would have hated

this, the dysfunction that our family has become. What happened to us? What made my father so bitter? A wave of sorrow sweeps across my chest, leaving me breathless with yearning. If only I could travel to the past.

I still come to this fishing hole once or twice a year in search of answers, but it's getting hard to even find the good memories, any semblance of life before the abuse, the sadness, before . . . Abigail.

Bridget coughs out a laugh.

I push the lip of my hat farther up onto my forehead to scratch at an itch. "What's so funny?"

"This," Bridget says. "I mean, you have a fishing net hanging out of your back pocket." She bites her lip in that not-so-innocent way that makes my stomach flip. "And you're wearing plaid. *Plaid.*" She settles into a lawn chair. "I guess I never pictured you as a fisherwoman."

"I haven't been out here recently." The tip of my rod takes a quick dive and I yank upright. I turn the reel a couple of times, but the line goes slack. "We used to bring home some nice rainbows, though." At Bridget's raised eyebrow, I laugh. It's so easy to laugh when we're together, away from the B and B and Abigail, away from everyone but each other. "Rainbows are trout."

She holds her hands about a foot apart. "Were they this big?"

Her smile is all mischief.

"Bigger," I say.

She doubles the length and her eyes burn with anticipation.

My voice is low and breathy. "Even bigger."

She holds her arms as wide open as they'll go. "This big?"

"Yeah. That's about right."

It's an absolute lie, and I'm almost positive Bridget knows it. But that's why I love fishing—it's acceptable to fib. Even Father Buck says an occasional tall tale is fine, so long as it isn't hurting anyone. My saliva turns sour. That should be the basic rule for everything, as far as I'm concerned. Like the way Bridget and I feel about each other. Who are we hurting? No one. So then why is our relationship a sin?

I watch Bridget's profile, my gut roiling like ocean waves in a storm.

A seed of sudden fear burrows deep in my belly. What if this relationship somehow hurts Bridget? My shoulders tense. I'd rather hurt myself instead.

Bridget grabs a soda from the cooler, wipes off the top, and hands it to me. I pull up a lawn chair so we're parallel, and sit. The bank's a bit rocky, and the uneven ground gives my chair a bit of a lean. I'm practically propped up against Bridget, aware of the current that runs between us, alive like static electricity.

Bridget rests her cool hand on my knee. "Tell me a story."

It's so intimate, the way she says it, and my pulse leaps.

That's the thing about nature—the silence, the peace, it can amplify everything else. Especially feelings. My cheeks flush hot.

Bridget reaches over and folds a wayward strand of hair up into my hat. I tense but don't pull away. Her fingertips are soft, smooth. Heat buzzes through my veins despite the coolness of her skin. "What kind of a story?"

"A love story." Her voice drops to a throaty whisper. "I want to know you, Lizbeth. The good, the bad. Everything. Tell me . . . everything."

"Ah, a novella, then," I say, trying to make light, even as a dark shadow begins to creep over my heart, as though the sun has slipped behind a cloud, casting everything into varying shades of gray. "My mom died when I was young. Cancer." A sharp pain stabs into my chest. "She loved Fall River. The town, the people, the shops. Even our house." I swallow hard and blink back a tear. "We could have lived up on the hill—we were *supposed* to live in a mansion. But Mom didn't care about money. She just wanted to stay close to her friends."

Bridget traces the pattern of a heart on my knee. "Abigail seems an odd choice for your father, then."

I blow out an unsteady breath. "That's an understatement. My father basically married her out of convenience. Love was never part of the equation." My voice stutters as I realize that my feelings for Bridget are already so deep.

Why would anyone marry for anything *but* love?

"I guess I'm not one to talk. I've made a lot of mistakes looking for my Princess Leia." Her smile is more a wince. "Sorry. *Star Wars*." She shuffles closer and trails her finger farther up my thigh. Goose bumps rise along my arms. "To me, the most important part of a relationship is the connection. Don't you agree?"

It's like there's a whole fish stuffed down my throat, making it hard to talk. I nod.

Her fingernails lightly scrape against my skin. "And when I get married, it will be . . ." Her shimmering eyes lift to mine and my breath catches. I'm overcome with an emotion so intense it leaves me light-headed. "For love. No matter who doesn't agree with my choice. It's nobody's business anyway." She kicks at a rock. "Love is love."

My throat feels thick, the gold chain pulling so tight around my neck that the edges of the cross wedge into my flesh. It's so easy for her to say things like that, make bold proclamations without having to worry about overstepping God's boundaries or my father's rules. The concept of Catholic guilt may sound like a cliché, a joke. But it's real. And in this moment, it leaves me breathless.

Hopeless.

Being here, with Bridget's fingertips dancing across my skin, and my mind twisting with impure thoughts, has given that guilt a buffet from which to feast. I want to scream at her to stop touching me, stop *looking* at me with her beautiful emerald eyes, to just STOP! But my willpower has given way to blinding need, and I won't—can't—walk away.

Forgive me, Father.

Bridget leans over to kiss me, but before our lips connect, she loses her balance in the chair. We both topple over, crashing onto the hard ground with a painful crunch. I'm sure my back must be broken, my limbs have gone numb, but then Bridget peers at me through the curtain of her hair and her mouth closes over mine. All pain disappears. She kisses playfully at first, and then with more passion. A sigh gurgles softly from my throat. Bridget nibbles on my bottom lip, and then pushes her tongue inside.

The tip of my rod takes a nosedive, and I realize it's still gripped tightly in my fist. My arm jerks. Bridget's eyes open and go wide. "Shit," she says with a giggle. "Is that a bite?"

"Fish on!"

We scramble to stand and I start to wind in the line. One hand holds the pole steady while the other spins the reel. Bridget's camera *click, click, clicks* beside me. I can feel the lens zooming in on my face, and then I watch as she snaps shots of the water, the rod, my hands working in tandem. Her clicks fire so fast they echo like mini fireworks. *Click. Pop. Click. Zzzzt.*

I reel faster. My palms go clammy under the weight of the fish—it's two pounds, at least, probably a trout.

Bridget bounces on her toes. "Bring it in, babe!"

The rod goes slack. I should be disappointed, but her sultry voice echoes at the back of my mind. *Babe. Babe. BABE.* I will *never* grow tired of that—

This.

"Lost him," I finally say, and finish reeling in the line to pull up the empty hook. "Sucker robbed me of my bait, too. Can you hand me the maggots?"

"You're serious?"

We're back to teasing again, and I quickly step into that role. "Worried they might bite you through the container?"

Bridget side-eyes the clear plastic tub. "They have teeth?" She holds it up into the light, and several maggot silhouettes writhe up against the lid. "Jesus." She squeezes her eyes shut. And dang it if my heart rate doesn't pick up speed. She's so cute when she's scared.

Never mind. She's always cute.

I tilt my head. "What are you doing?"

"Using the Force to will these fuckers away." She hands me the container and shudders. Our fingertips touch.

Trembling, I pop off the lid and root around for a fat maggot. Dirt wedges under my fingernails, black and earthy. I finish threading the bait onto the hook and cast, this time farther out. The sun's warmth seeps into my skin, which means the fish will swim deeper in search of food. My mother taught me that our first time out.

"I'm still waiting to hear more about you," Bridget says.

"Your stories are more interesting than mine," I say, licking my lips. "Tell me more about Ireland. Or Scotland."

"Not Scotland," Bridget says. "That place was a total bust."

"Except for that close encounter with the Loch Ness Monster."

She grins widely. "Yeah, except that." She picks at the tab on my soda can, flicking it with her long fingernail. *Tap, tap, tap.* "I've already told you everything about me."

"Tell me again." I clear my throat. "More about the Duomo, maybe." It's my favorite picture of Bridget's, the spiraling cement staircase somehow symbolic of this. Us. An impossible relationship, stretching toward unparalleled heights. Ironic, perhaps, that it too is steeped in Catholicism, a religion that would find our relationship abhorrent.

"Italy," she says with a smile.

I duck my head, embarrassed. "Religious stuff, I know. Blech. It's just . . . fascinating."

"Lot of steps," she says with a wistful sigh that tugs at my heartstrings.

A sharp yank on my line pulls my attention. I reel in a few times, and confident I've snagged a real fish, I hand Bridget the rod. The color drains from her face.

"Don't panic," I say, sliding in behind her. My arms go around her waist, and I hold the bottom of the rod to keep it in place. Her warmth nestles against mine. "Just keep the line tight and reel in. Nice and steady."

"It's heavy."

I nod with way too much enthusiasm. A shot of adrenaline shoots through me and my chest fills with pride. The tip of my rod is almost bent in half and I'm sure this fish will be a monster. A foot long at least. "Keep the tip up!"

Bridget continues reeling, her knuckles white, muscles tense.

I squeal when the fish boils on the water's surface. Its face emerges, reptilian skin slick with slime, eyes large and bulbous. *Swipe.* It opens its giant maw. *Swipe. Swipe.* Thick rows of sharp teeth drip red, splattering the muddy bank. *Swipe.* The giant fish shakes its head, spraying me with blood. It covers my skin, my face, coats my lips. Bridget screams.

Swipeswipeswipe.

I blink to reset my irrational panic, relieved to see the small pike skimming the surface, its yellow scales glinting like gold flecks under the sun's sharp rays.

"I'll get it with the net!" I say, and scramble down the side of the bank, glancing back to make sure Bridget is still reeling. Her face is set in determination, and it does something weird to my insides. I'm sure I'll never forget how beautiful she looks in this moment, my beautiful fisher girl.

My eyes well up and I glance away.

The melodic sound of Bridget's laughter makes me turn again. "What's so funny?"

"Just this," she says. "I guess I never pictured myself as a fisherwoman."

There's a lump in my throat that makes my words kind of choke out. "Welcome to the club."

Bridget grins. "Besides hanging out with you, any other perks to tell me about?"

"None that I can think of."

Her smile is radiant. "Perfect. All I need is you."

10

K nead. Roll. Knead.

Repeat.

Chef Emeril says the trick to making great bread is the pressure. How hard you *push, knead, press* with your palms. Not the amount of flour, or yeast, but the subtle manipulation of the dough.

Aim for elasticity. Not too sticky. Not too dry.

Just *perfect*.

I add a scoop of flour to the metal mixing bowl and punch my knuckles into the ball of dough. A cloud of white puffs in my face and coats my lips. I lick them clean. A noise outside grabs my attention. I pause, listen. *Nothing.* Glancing up at the window, I see my reflection peering at me through the murky glass. Distorted. Too tall. Too thin. I use the edge of my palms to draw the blinds closed.

"Izzy?"

My spine stiffens. *Swipe.*

"Pssst. Izzy . . ."

I dig my fingers into the soft dough, stomach clenched in disbelief. I'm obviously hearing things, hallucinating or something, because only one person in this entire world calls me Izzy and that's—

A rubber band snaps across the middle of my back. On instinct, I pinch off a piece of the bread mix, whip around, and fling it at my sister's chest. Emma dodges left and the dough hits the wall. It sticks for less than a second, then drops to the floor with a *thwack*.

"Perfect consistency," she says, winking.

My heart shoots up into my throat as I realize that Emma is *here*. In the kitchen.

Home.

I launch myself into a tackle hug that nearly takes us both down, choking back my tears. "Is this real?" I untangle from her embrace and stare at her cheeks, her eyes, like I'm memorizing every feature on her face. Her hair is longer, blonder, and she's lost a bit of weight. It seems like forever since she's been gone. "What are you doing here?" I squeeze her tight, feeling her rib cage against my arms. "They're starving you at college, aren't they? You're here for sustenance. Food. I can do that."

I'm good at that.

Emma laughs. "It's spring break. I told you I'd visit."

My eyes dart to the calendar swinging from a pushpin on the door of the pantry. There are no marks on today's date, no hearts or exclamation points. Nothing to remind me that my sister would be home. My throat clogs up. *How could I have forgotten?* "I should have written it down."

Why didn't I write it down?

I begin to pace. "Ems, I'm terrible. Horrible. I can't believe I've forgotten—"

Emma grabs my arm. "Izzy, relax." Her eyes scan my face, and I work hard to disguise the rising panic. I've begun to wean myself off the medications—my heart is so full, how can I possibly be depressed?—but my anxiety feels like it's cresting at the base of my throat. I glance at the bottle of pills, hoping she won't see them and ask me about them. They shouldn't even be in the kitchen, in the same place I've hidden the pills I don't take.

"I never gave you an official date because I wanted to surprise you," she says.

My pulse eases off. "Well, mission accomplished." I grab her cool hand and drag her to the kitchen table. "Sit. I'll get you something to eat—meat loaf? You want meat loaf, right?—and you can tell me everything. I want to know *everything.*"

I'm rambling and I know I should stop, but my mind is

like a Tilt-A-Whirl in sixth gear, spinning out of control.

Emma licks her lips. "Honey, there's something I need to talk to you about first. . . ."

I freeze, hand on the counter for stability. Pinpricks of unease ripple across the back of my neck. I tilt my head up and take a deep breath. A black spider scampers across the ceiling—*rat-a-tat-tat*—and disappears behind the light fixture veiled with its web.

Emma clears her throat. "I didn't come alone."

My tongue runs along the bottom of my lip, my mind playing back her words at slow speed, searching for comprehension. I turn and stare at her face. "What do you mean?"

There's a shuffle in the hallway and my sister averts her gaze. Her smile brightens. A blush creeps along her cheeks. I follow her glistening eyes and *BAM!* There he is.

Jesse.

At least I think it's Jesse, the way he stands all tall and rugged, with his sweater sleeves rolled up at the elbows to reveal a geometric tattoo that wraps up along his muscular forearm. Shaggy blond hair sweeps across his forehead and covers one hazel eye.

"Izzy, this is . . ." She pauses. "This is Jesse, my boyfriend." She practically glows.

Jesse saunters toward me—his walk cocky or just confident, I'm not sure—and extends a hand. "Nice to meet you, Izzy."

I stare at his calloused fingers and chipped nails a beat too long before choking out a response. "Lizbeth," I say. "Or Lizzie." Anything but Izzy; that's Emma's special name. A swell of fresh panic rises up into my chest, filling like a helium balloon. My sister knows I'm no good with new people, with socialization, not without warning. This boy is a stranger. An unknown. My heartbeat thumps in my eardrums.

"Would you like some . . . meat loaf?"

There's an awkward silence as Jesse tilts his head. I get it, it's an odd question to ask. My sister jumps in, resurrecting her role as savior with ease. It seems forever since she's rescued me. "Izzy is an incredible cook."

Chef.

A soft vibration buzzes in my ears, and I busy myself to stop the rising paranoia that feeds off my unease like a flesh-eating zombie. I can feel the madness pushing against my veins and I shove it back, hiding it deep inside, where I hope one day, even I won't be able to find it.

That day isn't now.

Not in the presence of this stranger, without Bridget here to calm and soothe me. I'm nervous around new people, afraid I might say the wrong thing, reveal family secrets, struggle to answer questions with responses that won't have me committed.

Even though it's clear that Jessie is more than my sister's boyfriend—he is a symbol, another indication of my sister's freedom from the life she left behind. A status I can't achieve, may never achieve, if I can't get it together. Father will keep me here forever unless I can convince him I'm able, stable—sane. Or until Abigail succeeds in sending me away, to a facility far, far, far from home, from Fall River, from Bridget.

My palms go clammy.

Bringing Jesse here—to this house—is Emma flaunting her independence, and for a second, my jealousy flares. I curl my hands into fists at my sides.

Jesse sits next to Emma and kisses the top of her forehead with a *smack* that raises the hair on the back of my neck. Envy continues to simmer under my skin. How dare they be affectionate in public, without His eyes ever watching in disapproval. I grab plates, cutlery, napkins, allowing the cupboards to slam, the dishes to rattle, the noises to build and grow until I block out the white noise of their conversation, their sweet kisses and hushed whispers.

Tears spring to my eyes, and I *swipe, swipe, swipe,* them away with the back of my hand. I can't even look at Jesse, or the way he's staring at my sister with utter adoration. My God, if anyone deserves such happiness it's Emma, but I'm overcome with a jealousy that *peck, peck, pecks* away at my skin like it's carrion.

"Is this a new recipe?"

Emma's voice snaps me back to the present and I turn, slowly. Carefully. Her smile is a beam of light into the darkness threatening to overwhelm me. I breathe it in. Remind myself that this is *still* Emma. She hasn't changed. "I've added a couple of new ingredients," I say, deftly avoiding the incident with my journal as I set the meat loaf on the table. Emma would ask too many questions, stare at me with those wide, knowing eyes, wonder aloud if I've remembered to take my pills. I glance away, but the scent of burnt paper drifts under my nose, strong enough I almost believe it's real.

Emma waves her fork at me. "I thought we talked about this—why mess with perfection?" The sternness in her eyes clouds over with obvious affection, and my heart does this weird *thump-thump* thing that always happens under her praise. I forget all about the journal. "I suppose in this case it's okay," she says. Her eyes burn with ridiculous pride, and I'm drowning in happiness. "It's divine, Lizzie. Don't you think, Jesse?"

He moans in agreement.

I watch his expression for lies. His lips for dishonesty. A subtle hint that he doesn't like the meat loaf, is only pretending to for my sister's sake, a blatant attempt at earning her approval. My trust.

Much to my shock, he seems sincere.

Emma reaches for her water glass, and something flickers under the overhead light.

I blink. Then watch carefully as she lifts, sips, swallows.

A small gold band encircles her finger, an oversize

diamond plunked at the center, as out of place there as it is on my sister's left hand. My stomach pulls into a tight ball of denial and I'm sure my face pales, drains completely of blood.

Emma catches my eye and I know she knows too.

I turn away to catch my breath.

A fat teardrop hits the countertop and splatters across the granite. I rub, rub, rub it clean with the back of my hand until my skin is raw and red. "Izzy, I'm so sorry. I swear I was about to tell you. . . ." Her voice catches, betraying the lie. Emma was nervous to share her news with me—and why wouldn't she be? She knows how unstable I can be. "It just happened yesterday."

I struggle to match her enthusiasm, but the knot between my shoulder blades won't let up. "I'm happy for you, Ems." My shoulders stiffen. "It's fine, really."

My words cough out like a steam engine fighting for air, and I feel a shortness of breath as my heart starts to race. Questions bubble at the tip of my tongue but I stuff them back, push them to the bottom of my throat where they're tangled up with disbelief, hurt, and a disquieting sense of dread that hangs on with the strength of a cinch. I am free-falling into darkness, grasping for the light. *Bridget. I need Bridget.*

But Bridget isn't home right now.

Emma's voice softens. "I'm glad. It's important to me that you approve."

My eyes wander to Jesse, more a boy than a man. Light

stubble peppers his jaw. His hazel eyes twinkle. By the expression on his face, it's clear he's misread the moment, thinking I'm pretending to be hurt instead of writhing in pain.

I exhale slowly, as though deflating a helium balloon. "Have you set a date?"

"Not without consulting you, of course," Emma says.

And I'd believe her too if the sharp stab of duplicity wasn't pushing against my stomach. I squeeze my eyes shut, not trusting myself to meet their gazes head-on. My sister will see through my reservations. "Have you told Father?"

Jesse clears his throat. "I'm going to ask his permission tonight."

The tremble in his voice suggests he knows it won't be easy. Our father straddles the line between not believing anyone is good enough for his daughters, and not believing anyone could want them—though I often wonder if that's just how he feels about me. My thoughts turn to Bridget, and I ache for her closeness. For the chance to show him I *am* wanted. That someone needs me as much as I need—

Her.

"And I was going to tell you first," my sister says again. I jump at the closeness of her voice. When did she leave the table? Her hand settles on my shoulder, the warmth finding its way to my bones and easing off the chill, her touch so different from Bridget's, yet somehow comforting, too. "You distracted me with your meat loaf."

I force a grin. "You're an easy mark."

I've never been able to stay angry with my sister. And not just because she's older, wiser. But because no matter how hurt or betrayed I may feel, her presence calms me, somehow quiets the paranoia and tames the beast that hovers—always—just under my skin. The medication is supposed to stanch the madness, but maybe Bridget can help with everything else—Father, Abigail, this new development with my sister. Is that too much to ask?

I close my eyes and imagine Bridget here now, soothing me with her words, erasing my fears with her magical fingertips. The hair on my arms stands erect, and for a split second I think about confessing to Emma.

No. This isn't my moment in the spotlight. Despite my reservations, my sister deserves this.

Emma rests her head against mine. "I'm glad you're not mad at me."

"Only enough to smother you in your sleep," I say with a light laugh, reminiscing of pillow fights that lasted long into the night.

Jesse coughs out a surprised, "Whoa."

Emma giggles, oblivious to how my words might have sounded to someone outside our family sphere. "You'd have to come to the Holiday Inn, because that's where we're staying for the night."

My shoulders slump. "Why so far away?"

Emma's eyes dim. "You know why."

A shiver ripples down my spine.

"Leaving this place was hard," she says, her voice cracking. "It took strength, determination, careful planning." She lowers her tone. "It's dark here, Izzy. I know you feel it too. And I can't come back . . . not now. Things haven't been the same since Mom—" She swallows. Her spine visibly stiffens. "After dinner, Jesse and I will go to the Holiday Inn. That's how it has to be. I got out, Izzy. You should too."

A halo of sadness circles my heart.

Emma knows the only way I'm leaving Fall River is in a proverbial straitjacket—Father will never let me go on my own. But the way she says it, it's almost like she thinks I have a choice. I stare into her eyes and it's just like I thought—neither of us truly believes I do.

CHAPTER

11

My sister's fiancé stares at his dinner setting, recoiling at the things on the plates before him. A human leg, the skin cracked, pink sinew shining through charred flesh. An arm, bubbled and blackened like burnt cheddar cheese, with its fingers curled tight into a fist, a sprig of rosemary protruding upright like a flag. Beside it, half an intact rib cage with the pulsing lungs still inside, draped with coils of intestines and surrounded by lettuce and kale, garnished with a ripe tomato carved into the shape of a heart.

My father tucks his linen napkin into his shirt. "The pigeons will be nesting soon," he says, lifting the lid off the silver platter at the center of the table.

There, Abigail's head, severed at the neck, nestles on

a sticky bed of rice, artfully drizzled in scarlet blood. Her blue-tinged lips part and a whisper croaks from her throat. "Pigeons. Such vile creatures."

"Don't say that around Izzy," Emma says, laughing. She sips her wine, the crimson color staining her teeth, and smiles. Maggots ooze from between her lips. "Isn't that right, sis?"

My heart feels like it's in my throat, blocking my scream. I blink—*swipe, swipe, swipe*—blink. The strong scent of tuna casserole swirls under my nose, bringing me back to reality.

"Lizbeth?" I crane my ear toward Abigail's voice, strangely relieved to find her head securely attached to her neck. The horrific images of severed body parts disappear like smoke. "What is wrong with you?" she says. "You're practically a ghost."

Swipe.

"She's afraid Father will start talking about killing the pigeons again," Emma says, leaning toward me so that our shoulders touch. I pull away to break the connection, angered by how easily she mocks me.

Jesse's eyes flit to mine, Abigail's, back to me, and then finally rest on his blushing fiancée. She pats his hand. "My sister has a soft spot for birds."

"Any animal, really," my father cuts in. He raises his glass in a fake toast. "But the birds, especially."

An uneasy quiet settles over the room; the calm before the storm. My attachment to the flock of pigeons that nest in the pear tree out back is a constant source of tension in this house. At first I only wanted to protect them as a way to annoy Abigail, but it's become more than a childish game now that Father is involved.

Jesse clears his throat. "Did you know that carrier pigeons were used by Julius Caesar to relay messages?" At everyone's blank stare, he shrugs sheepishly, his voice wavering slightly. "I wrote an article on them last year."

Abigail curls her lip up. "That's about all they'd be useful for. Such ugly creatures."

My father runs his tongue over the top row of his perfectly polished teeth and washes down his casserole with a splash of wine. "I've got no use for them," he says. "Nuisances."

I flinch at how easily he dismisses them, barely giving them a second thought. My skin prickles, as though hundreds of feathers form ridges along my skin.

Jesse swirls his wine, the bright liquid sloshing up the sides of the glass. "I find them fascinating, actually."

Emma elbows my rib cage. "Look how much you and Jesse have in common."

I smile thinly. What's he playing at here?

My father dusts off the front of his napkin. Bread crumbs sprinkle his casserole, camouflaged against the excess of baked cheese. "These insolent birds insist on eating the pears."

Forbidden fruit.

"Lizbeth makes quite a delicious pear pie," Abigail says.

My flesh ruffles. This might be the only compliment I've ever received from her, and I struggle not to call out her insincerity.

Jesse holds up his fork, layered with cheese, and smiles. "If this casserole is any indication, I'm not surprised."

I jab my tongue into the inside of my cheek, still unsure of Jesse's endgame.

A shadow in the hallway pulls my focus. Bridget, sneaking by the dining room as she makes her way to the kitchen, where I've left her a generous slice of tuna casserole and a chunk of strawberry shortcake. I imagine her swiping a layer of whipped cream onto her finger and sucking it clean, hiding in the small staff room that is only a fraction bigger than a broom closet. My mouth parts and a soft sigh escapes.

"She can only make pie if there are pears," my father goes on, oblivious to the rising discomfort in the room. "Which is why when the pigeons become a nuisance this year, I'll have to kill them." He smiles without humor. "I saw one just the other day, in fact."

I saw her too. A mama, looking for a place to lay her eggs. Sometimes I watch her through binoculars from my bedroom window, her tiny beak bobbing for scraps. *Peck, peck, pecking.*

I envy her freedom, the way she flits around the yard as though no one is watching. Building a home, a life, without judgment.

"I should poison them all," my father says.

A tightness pulls in my chest. "What did you say?"

Jesse's sympathetic eyes land on me just as the blood begins to drain from my face. I set my fork down and fold my hands on my lap, looping my pinky through the lace edging around the bottom of my dress. My knuckles are white with tension.

"That would be a shame," Jesse says, his voice soft and soothing.

Curious, I lift my gaze.

"Pigeons are quite symbolic." He dabs at the corners of his mouth with his napkin, transforming from tattooed jock to college professor in the blink of an eye. "Some people believe that the pigeon symbolizes determination and the ability to overcome obstacles."

Abigail squirms. "Hogwash."

Jesse shrugs.

"Preposterous," my father says. A string of cheese hangs from his beard. I imagine a mama pigeon *peck, peck, pecking* it off, twisting it around and around her beak, feeding it to her young.

My spine straightens. "Pigeons are renowned for their navigational skills." All eyes turn to me. I lick my lips. "They're known for their ability to find their way home—which is why they are a symbol of house and home."

Jesse lifts his glass and offers me a discreet wink. "Indeed."

Some of my reservations about him begin to fade.

My father pushes his plate forward. "I think we've talked enough about pigeons for one night." He gives me a warning glance, quietly dismissing me, and then shifts his gaze to Jesse. Elbows on the table, he steeples his fingers, pressing the tips so tightly they turn light pink. "I understand there is something you'd like to discuss with me."

My intuition hums like an overloaded electrical wire. I stand, gathering the plates and cutlery, the empty glasses. My sister puts her cool hand on my arm. "Stay," she says softly. Her eyes plead, but I look away.

This conversation won't go well—and I would rather hide from conflict than face it head-on. Emma knows this. "You'll be fine," I say, and it's true. Emma is always fine—her menstrual cycle isn't irregular she doesn't black out or need medications to be normal, isn't tethered to the church by her calling or still grieving the loss of our mother.

No, Emma is free from all that.

And when this is all over, Emma and her fiancé will leave and I'll still be here. Stuck. Trapped.

Jesse's voice fades as I quickly make my way out of the dining room. I set the dishes in the sink and inhale. Exhale. Bridget's portion of tuna casserole remains untouched. Was her appetite suppressed by the conversation in the dining room, or—?

Outside, the moon hovers high in the sky, peeking at me through the window. Fresh blades of grass in the backyard appear iridescent under the light. In the distance, branches from the pear tree are silhouetted against the old barn, their shadows twisted and gnarled like monstrous arms, beckoning me closer.

The pigeons will be nesting soon, my father whispers over my shoulder.

Vile creatures. Abigail's scratchy voice zigzags up my spine and buries itself at the base of my neck.

I should poison them all.

No. I can't let my father do that. Can't let him destroy the joy I find while watching them fly free, oblivious to the dangers that lurk only a few feet away.

I shrug into the sweatshirt hanging on the back of the pantry door and pull the hood up over my ears. My head throbs at the temples. In bare feet, I tiptoe to the door and ease it open, silent as a rat.

Vile creatures.

I jerk my face back to look over my shoulder, my spine electric at the thought of someone standing behind me. But there's nobody there.

Just as there is no one to watch as I creep across the damp grass to the barn and slip inside.

The pigeons will be nesting soon.

But only if I get to them first.

12

Bridget brushes up against me, her breath a whisper across my neck. Tiny goose bumps ripple across my flesh. "You're sure this is safe?" she says.

I put my finger to my lips and then lift the metal bar that latches the barn door closed. It opens with a loud *creaak*. For a split second, I freeze.

Moonbeams spill into the room, casting light over the film of dust that covers everything from the floor to the soiled boxes stacked in the corner. Tools are propped up against the side wall—a shovel, rake, two hoes, and a headless ax. A smaller hatchet leans up against the workbench.

Something small scampers at our feet. Bridget jerks closer to me as the creature darts into the darkness. Her hand tightens around my arm like a vise. "Rat?"

"Most likely a mouse."

"Christ," Bridget says. She exhales hard. "And you're sure it's safe?"

I flick the light switch and a pale-yellow glow fills the barn. "Promise."

Bridget follows me inside, flinching as I close the door. I stand on tiptoes to peer at the house through the small round windows, relieved that everyone seems to have gone to sleep. My gaze lingers on Emma's empty room, its vacancy now luring me into the past. The memories we've shared—the fights, the laughter, the tears and whispers. She'll never come back now, not after the things Father said to her. I squeeze my eyes shut to hold back the tears.

I'd rather die than see that abhorrent man again. A sharp pain of regret stabs me in the gut, and I shake loose the sadness that follows. I'm not surprised Father didn't approve of the marriage, but my sister's venomous response—a series of hisses, strong words, and thinly veiled threats—plays back in my mind like a tape recorder on slow speed. That isn't her, isn't the Emma I know and love.

"Why are we whispering?" Bridget says, startling me to the present. "Abigail is passed out by now, and your father . . ." Her voice trails off, and I know what she's thinking. Not even Bridget's and my laughter can wake him, especially in the dead of night. His snores often echo through the vents in the house, as though the walls themselves are groaning.

Bridget and I spend our evenings alternating between her

bedroom and mine. We play cards and board games, watch reruns of Emeril, and challenge each other to Truth or Dare. Mostly truth, I admit, but I don't think I'm good at either. It's hard to be "bad" when you're suffocating in air so heavy with judgment you can barely breathe.

Each night as Bridget tiptoes down the hall, I thumb through the weathered copy of my Bible, reinforcing the tenets of my faith—and how I am failing it. But as a child repeatedly reminded of her inadequacy, her dirtiness and worthlessness, I'll never shed these feelings of guilt and shame, not even if I confessed every last sin. Do I need forgiveness? Or is Bridget enough? These questions plague my dreams, spilling over to my waking hours, deepening my confusion.

Bridget says it's up to me to decide. "I don't know if I believe in a higher power," she says. "But if I did, I wouldn't side with someone who thinks I need His approval of who I can love."

That's the thing about Bridget—she's never believed she's anything *but* worthy.

I slip my hand into hers and tug her toward the far end of the barn. Her palms are slick with sweat. She stumbles after me, tightening her fingers, squeezing so hard I almost cry out. A light fluttering begins in my stomach and funnels toward my heart. It's still like this every time we touch.

"Stay close," I say. "There's stuff everywhere. I don't want you to trip."

"Define stuff."

I cup my hand over my mouth to trap a giggle at her fear.

We stop at the base of a ladder, the rusty rungs shimmering under the faint glow of the overhead light. The paint is chipped and scuffed. There's a cluster of my muddy footprints on the floor. "You go first," I say.

Bridget glances up, her eyes wide with alarm. "You're kidding, right?"

I shake my head.

"Not happening." She drops my hand and stuffs both of hers in the pockets of the gray *Star Wars* hoodie that she's slipped over her skirt. *Swipe.* Han Solo slings his arm around Princess Leia's shoulder and winks.

"I've got this thing about heights," Bridget says.

"You hiked to the top of the Duomo."

She licks her lips. "That was different."

"What about bungee jumping in Thailand?"

Bridget kicks at something on the floor, and a cloud of dust spirals like a mini tornado. Her foot barely misses a splat of bird poop.

"Or diving out of a plane?" My throat gets a lump at the thought and I shudder. "You can do all that, but climbing a ladder scares you?"

She kind of snorts. "I'd rather swim with sharks."

My mind zips back to Cook Pond, where Bridget admitted her fear of maggots and open bodies of water. "I doubt that. You've hiked Mount Everest," I say, winking. In our·

games of Truth and Dare, Bridget has admitted that not all her adventure tales were . . . truthful. I'm okay with that, since we share so many of the same dreams. It's easy to think maybe she's saving those real adventures for when we can do them together. "You've had dinner with a Japanese mob boss. Where's *that* girl?"

Bridget pouts. "I'm allowed one weakness."

"Fine." I grip the ladder handles and put my foot on the first rung. "I'll go first, but you should probably follow me right away. There's a chance that wasn't a mouse earlier."

Bridget tugs on my shirtsleeve. "What do you mean?"

I glance over my shoulder and grin like a Cheshire cat. "Rodents of Unusual Size."

"You're horrible," she says through a smile, and I'm surprised all over again at how easy it is for us to play.

At the halfway mark, I sense her weight on the base of the ladder. I continue my ascent, ears pointed toward the loft overhead, listening for sounds that are both familiar and foreign. My heartbeat thunders in my temples. What will she think when she sees what I have done?

I reach the top rung and crawl onto the wooden loft floor. My knees hit the edge of the thin mattress, and a bird coos overhead. "You're almost there."

Bridget grunts. "This had better be worth . . ."

Her voice trails off as a sharp chirp freezes her in place. I peer down at her, grinning. "Birds," I say. "Just normal size."

"Bats?"

I chew on the corner of my lip, weighing the pros and cons of fibbing. One look at her pale skin and I decide to tell the truth. "Not even of the vampire variety."

Her shoulders visibly slump with relief.

When she finally reaches the top of the ladder, she folds herself onto the mattress and splays out on her back next to a fleece blanket, sucking in deep breaths as though gasping for air. Her movement stills. "Fuck. Is that a spiderweb?"

I follow her gaze. "Conceivable. They're normal-size too, though."

She sits upright, the top of her head just barely missing the low-hung overhead beams. "An insect of any size is too big."

A small chirp from the corner of the loft draws her attention. She tilts her head. "What in the hell is that?"

I curl my finger, motioning for her to follow, as I crawl across the mattress to a corner of the loft floor, where a coil of blankets forms a makeshift nest for a family of pigeons. I've been creeping into the barn late at night to ensure Mama's babies are feeding, breathing. Safe from my father. But this single act of rebellion sends a shiver of unease up my spine.

Bridget leans in close and gasps. "They're so little."

I lift one into the palm of my hand and stroke the downy feathers on its fragile back. Abigail says pigeons are ugly, but I love the silver-gray shade of their feathers, the way they look blue in just the right light. I lean up against the slightly open window and hold the chick up to the overhead glow. "Mom is around somewhere."

"You made this for them?"

The awe in her voice creates a stir in my belly. No one else—not even Emma—could understand what I've done. "Everyone deserves a sanctuary." I set the baby pigeon back in the nest with the others. "And if I don't keep them safe, I'm sure my father will kill them." I nudge my head toward the small window. "They scavenge the pears."

Precious pears for Abigail's pies.

Forbidden fruit.

Bridget presses her face up to the glass. In the lightly blowing wind, tree branches tap at the window like long, thin fingers, calling for our attention. She points into the darkness. "I think there's an owl in the tree right now!"

I know without looking what she means, but my reflection stares back me, urging me to explain. In the spring, I hang plastic owl and hawk ornaments from the branches to deter the pigeons—though, admittedly, it doesn't always work. "They're meant to scare them away, but once a pigeon has made its home, they aren't easily deterred." *They always come back.*

"I can't believe you did this," Bridget says, her voice so soft I have to strain to hear it. The pride in her words is like a secret language speaking straight to my bones, and I lap it up. "Actually, I can. You're basically an angel."

My denial comes out in a sharp laugh. "Remind me to dig out my halo."

There's an awkward beat of silence before Bridget reaches into her backpack to pull out an iPad. She presses the power button. "Well, maybe not perfect exactly—but we're about to fix that."

The screen comes to life.

"You won't scare me. I've seen *Friday the 13th*," I say with sarcasm. *"Chee-chee-ha-ha . . ."*

Bridget leans back on the mattress and rests the tablet on her stomach. "But you've never seen *Star Wars*."

A familiar orchestra tune bellows from the speakers and Bridget's face relaxes, as though every ounce of tension is released with this music, this moment. Her eyes sparkle in anticipation.

I curl up next to her, my skin alive with the electricity that dances between us. A script rolls across the screen, and Bridget mouths the words. She catches me staring and jabs at the iPad. "Watch this, not me."

It takes all my effort to concentrate, and then at some point near the end of the opening credits, she belches out a guttural animal sound that ratchets up my pulse. "What on earth was that?"

"Wookiee call," she says. "Don't worry, you'll get it soon."

I inch closer, my hand brushing up against her hip. The edge of her shirt has lifted to reveal a thin band of warm flesh.

She flinches when I touch her but doesn't pull away. My heart rate picks up speed.

"Bridget?"

Her voice is hoarse. "Yeah?"

"I'm sorry for not introducing you to my sister." I wait for her to say something. When she doesn't, I keep talking, an attempt to lessen my guilt. "I wanted to, but—"

She squeezes my hand. "You don't need to explain, Lizzie. I already know." She curls closer and taps the iPad screen. "So, this is technically episode four."

I clear my throat, understanding that the conversation about my sister is done. "Why aren't we starting with episode one?"

She rolls her eyes. "Lucas screwed up—that's the director. He tried to reboot the series and—" Her cheeks burn bright red. "Wow. I am full-on geek. It's not important, trust—" And she's gone again as two guys with glowing wands face off against each other. Bridget's breathing goes shallow.

My fingers creep across her stomach and flatten against her belly button. I sink my teeth into my bottom lip, trying hard to focus on the movie, but my thoughts are everywhere except on *Star Wars*.

Later, I poke at her arm. "Those guys in white are Stormtroopers, right?"

She grins. "You've heard of them?"

I snort out a short laugh. "People have been dressing up

like Stormtroopers for Halloween since I was a kid." I don't say it, but I'm familiar with Luke Skywalker, Darth Vader, and Princess Leia, too. Especially her.

"One year I went dressed as Han Solo," she says. "But then, only as Princess Leia ever since. She's pretty much the most beautiful woman in the world." Her lips brush against my cheek. "After you, obviously."

My words tangle up inside my esophagus. "I've never dressed up for Halloween," I say, stammering.

Her eyes go wide. "You're shitting me."

"My father considers it a waste of time."

Bridget scoffs, "Cheap asshole."

For some inexplicable reason, the dig stings. I force a shy smile, deflecting the blame to my stepmother. "Abigail hates kids ringing the doorbell, so she and my father go to the pub. I hand out candy."

"Do you give extra to the Stormtroopers?"

"Maybe a little," I fib, knowing it will make her smile.

I've come to rely on her smiles—the slight curl of her lip, those toothy grins. They lift me, soothe me, sometimes even take my breath away. I fall into her happiness, like Alice through the rabbit hole, anxiously anticipating each new adventure, always hopeful they'll lead me far from Fall River, millions of miles from this place.

But that dream always ends in reality, and it's enough to darken my mood.

Bridget senses my sadness—she's so intuitive that way. "Hey, we're going to get out of here someday."

"How?"

I have to convince my father that I can make it on my own, without medications and curfews, without an ever-watchful eye. It's an impossible mission, because even if he loosened his grip, the church would tighten its.

She snuggles in close, wrapping the blanket around us. Even still, goose pimples form on my skin. "I don't know yet. I'll figure it out. I just need some time."

I don't say it aloud, but I'm beginning to think it's already too late.

Bridget's hand slides under my T-shirt and rests on my hip. I can feel her mouth pressed against my arm, lips slack with awe, and my skin tingles like it's on fire.

A man in black comes onto the screen.

"That's Luke's father, right?"

Bridget's breath hitches. "So you *have* seen it."

"It's not exactly a spoiler."

Bridget sighs. "It's iconic, really."

I don't disagree. In fact, I say nothing at all. Bridget presses her chest tight against my side, and just as I remember to start breathing again, her hand moves from my hip and gently slides into my palm.

As ridiculous as it seems, I've already memorized the way her heart beats against mine.

CHAPTER

13

*S*cratch.

Scratchy, scratch.

My pen skips across the paper, etching words, letters, symbols. Ink bleeds onto the page. A collection of hearts and broken hearts, famous quotes and infamous sayings, things that won't make sense later and don't make sense now. A jumble of thoughts.

Feelings.

I shrivel into myself, pulling my knees to my chest. Wrapping my arms around them to rock back and forth, back and—

Stop!

The fresh pages of my new journal whisper to me.

I balance the notebook on my knees and push the pen

onto the paper, pressing so hard my fingers go white. Invisible.

I am a ghost.

The pen slides across the paper. *Scratch. Scratchy, scratch. Riiiiip.*

The page tears, shredding one of the hearts in half. Pain spiderwebs across my chest. I drag the torn paper to the edge of my notebook. It curls. Unfurls. Falls onto the carpet, disappearing into the stains, burrowing itself deeper and deeper until it's—

Gone.

Everyone leaves.

A recent argument flits through the fog of my madness, like slashes of lightning through storm clouds. My father, his fist *thump, thump, thumping* against my bedroom door. Bridget curling up against me on the bed.

"Lizbeth, who are you talking to in there?"

Swipe.

Abigail's shrill voice, mocking and cruel. "She's always talking to herself." I hear her cackle, imagine her throwing back her head to howl. I shrink onto the bed next to Bridget, begging her to be still.

So. Still.

"Just open the door, Lizzie," Bridget whispered, and my skin cooled so fast a shiver rocked through my core. "You don't need to be ashamed of me."

Not ashamed, scared. Frightened that if Father caught us

together, intertwined on the bed, our legs and arms wrapped around each other—

No. I can't let him take her away.

"I'm going to Boston," he announced. "I expect you to be available for your mother."

Step. Mother.

His voice hardened to cool steel. "And for God's sake, Lizbeth. Take your fucking medication."

"I am taking my pills," I whispered, voice raw. "They're killing me."

Bridget wiped her thumb across my cheek. "No they're not, Lizzie," she said, so softly I had to strain to listen. "Sometimes you just feel like you're spinning out of control when you bring yourself up instead of down."

Father knocked again, and again, until the sound pinged off the walls and *tap, tap, tapped* against my skull. "Do you hear me?" he bellowed, in a thunderous voice that still, hours later, vibrates through my core. "You have one damn job. Serve Abigail—"

Abigail.

I etch her name into a fresh page now, drawing each letter in bold red ink, so thick it is an artery that leads to her invisible heart. I press harder on my pen, drawing over each symbol again and again. Swirls loop around the letter G, and I add drops of blood that trail

down

the

paper

Pooling at the bottom of the page.

A.B.I.G.A.I.L. is bleeding out.

A shrill laugh billows in my throat. I close my mouth to tamp it back. *Shhhhh.*

Scratch. Scratchy, scratch.

Scratch.

I swipe—*swipe*—the notebook off my legs and curl myself into a ball. I tuck my calloused heels up against my underwear. They are cold, too cold. A muted gasp escapes as my ankle caresses my naked thigh. I tug at my shirt, pulling it over my bare knees and legs, trying to yank it all the way past my toes.

Cocooning.

The thin cotton rips at my sleeve. Cool air seeps in and blankets my chest.

I shuffle deeper into the closet, ducking my head under the skirts and dresses and aprons that hang like puppets on hangers laden with dust. I am safe in this morgue of memories, laughter, and tears. No one comes here, cleans here, looks in this room where my mother once slept, dreamed—

Died.

I am death.

My tongue slides along my bottom lip, catching on cracks of dry skin that peel, stick, peel away. I pick at the scab with my teeth and it breaks free, falling between my lips and into my mouth. The skin lingers at the back of my throat, *scratch, scratch, scratching.*

I swallow the slimy, squishy scab and my gaze returns to the notebook. To Abigail's name. I study the letters that are etched onto the page with such force they've become three-dimensional. Alive.

There is still not enough red.

I drag my tongue across the paper, scraping at the letters, coating my lips with ink and pulp and spit. My saliva bubbles the paper, deepening the red. Spreading it thinner.

Still unsatisfied, I grind my teeth against my lip, aggravating the open wound. It grows. Bleeds.

I am a vampire.

Fat tears carve their way through the grit on my face and splatter on the paper. I tear it from the journal, crumple it into a tight ball, and stuff it in my mouth, coating it in saliva and blood. *My blood.* A.B.I.G.A.I.L. begins to dissolve.

I chew.

Suck.

Roll the soggy paper around and around in my mouth with my tongue.

I resist the urge to spit it out. I want to swallow her, erase her from my world, this house, from her entire existence. I am empowered. Unhinged. I am—

Swipe.

Free.

You can never be free.

A knock outside the closet door makes me freeze. I suck in a breath and stay still. So still. *Quiet as a mouse.*

Another knock. Softer. Tentative, almost. I slide farther into the closet, covering my face with clothes. Camouflaging myself so that Abigail cannot find me. Hurt me.

"Lizzie?"

Swipe.

My heart crawls up into my throat at the soft melody of Bridget's voice. I inch toward the closet door and peer out through the thin slats in the frame. Watching. Waiting.

Bridget is there. Cheeks, nose, eyebrows all scrunched and pinched with concern. She reaches up to caress the scarf wrapped around her neck. I tilt my head to stare.

I'm here.

My hand covers my mouth to block the whisper.

"Lizzie, are you . . . ?" Her voice trails off. "I could swear I heard a noise. Something. Where did you go?"

Bridget begins to pace. She looks over her shoulder before stooping on one knee to look under the bed. *I'm not there.* She stands and peers behind the door of Mother's en suite bathroom. *You're getting warmer.* She pauses at the closet. Hesitates. *In here,* I want to scream. I'm sure she can hear the *thump, thump, thump* of my heartbeat.

I scurry backward, hunching on my hands and knees, crouched and ready to pounce, poised to attack.

Stop! Bridget is not the threat.

The first pinpricks of fear drip down along my spine. I can't let Bridget see me like this. Frightened and vulnerable. The madness uncoiling at my feet, pooling like fresh blood. What would she think?

Creaaak.

My stomach clenches.

Breath hitches.

Bridget's hand is on the closet door.

A noise in the hallway startles her, and she scurries behind the dresser just in time to avoid Abigail passing by in the hall. I inch closer to peer out through the slats and recoil when I catch Abigail staring into the room, at the closet, at me. She *sees* me.

A smirk curls her lip up.

I swallow hard, forcing every bit of paper down my throat, every minuscule piece of her name. She is *in* me—and out there too.

She is everywhere.

Fear turns my blood to ice.

I'm scared that she'll discover Bridget hiding behind the dresser. That she will find me in the closet. Terrified that she will *sliccce* me open and uncover the sticky, pasty ball of her existence dissolving in my stomach, breaking into tiny little pieces.

My eyes flit between Bridget and Abigail.

Neither moves.

Abigail flicks off the light. She pulls the door closed and traps me within darkness, with Bridget. I will Bridget to smile, to bring warmth and sunshine. To ease the ache of loss that swirls in my chest. But even though I can't see her face, I *feel* her sadness.

"Where are you, Lizzie?"

Here.

"I need to know you're okay."

A dull ache spreads across my abdomen, forcing out a muted gasp. I am dying.

"I found blood. . . ."

On the bedsheets, the carpet, the bathroom floor. *Swipe.* A drop trickles down my thigh and hits the floor outside my bedroom door. *Swipe, swipe.* I drag my feet across the carpet, digging my toes in as I stumble toward the bed, my stomach bloated and sore. *Swipe—*

"I know you're not well," she says, voice cracking. "It's more than your period though, right? Let me help you. We can get through this. . . ."

A tear runs down my cheek and splashes onto my hand. I rub it into the floor of the closet, burying it with stains and memories, the ghosts of the past, the present. My future.

All of it here. For now. Forever.

Her tone drops to a whisper. "I'm sorry you're hurting. . . .

I didn't mean to make things awkward. . . . I know you're not ashamed of me."

It's not your fault.

The words don't come out. Not even as Bridget casts one last longing glance at the closet door. Not as her shoulders slump, her thin body trembling. Not even as she creeps toward the front of the bedroom, her shadow silhouetted in the soft light of the stars shining in through the window. I am frozen. Immobile. Bridget peers out into the hallway and closes the door behind her with a soft click.

Everyone leaves.

Reeling, I grip the pen and drag it across my thigh. I push so hard, a vein bulges.

Pops.

Blood bubbles out through the opening, trickling along my skin and onto the carpet. My mouth opens. Closes. I can't force the scream out. Dizziness buzzes through me and my eyes grow heavy, weak.

Music drifts in from the bedroom. I stare through the slats at my mother twirling across the carpet. *Swipe.* Her dress rises and falls as she spins and laughs. I call to her, but no words come out.

She turns and smiles. I flinch so fast my head slams against the back of the closet. The coppery taste of blood fills my mouth. Maggots squirm from between my mother's lips and out from her black, vacant eye sockets.

Swipe. Swipe.

Swiiiipe.

I slump down on the carpet and drop my head.

My eyes catch the glint of something metal. A knife, not a pen, its serrated edge outlined in my blood.

A wave of nausea rolls through my body and turns my world black.

14

Bridget's camera *clicks, whirs, clicks*. I shift left, right, take two steps back at her soft command. When she moves in closer, I freeze, carefully sliding my hands across my stomach.

"Stop covering up," Bridget says. "You're beautiful."

I lick my lips, go very still. Pretend I'm focused on this moment, when I'm still thinking about the other night in the closet, the visions, the madness, the loss of control. That madness is the elephant in our relationship, both of us tiptoeing around it.

How long before one of us snaps?

Click, click, click.

Bridget pulls the lens away from her face. "I get it. Cameras make people anxious." She grins. "Don't believe the myths, though—they don't strip your soul or add ten pounds."

My left palm caresses my belly. "That's a relief."

Bridget shifts on her hip and studies me. "You're a natural, you know?"

I choke on a laugh. My arms move like spaghetti noodles, limp and lifeless. Every pose is awkward. *Un*natural. Like a mannequin trying to do advanced yoga. "You keep saying that word. I don't think it means what you think it means."

Click.

"Nonsense. My lens is Jedi. It sees straight to the goods."

Bridget is always saying stuff like that. The kinds of things that make my stomach flip and my heart flutter.

"Lean up against the tree," she says, as though I haven't tried that pose a half-dozen times. I step through a patch of daisies and press my back against the rough trunk of what I'm sure is the biggest maple in Massachusetts. "Like this?"

She shakes her head. "Too stiff. You're like a plank."

I turn sideways and wedge my hip against the tree. "Better?"

Bridget picks a daisy and tucks it behind my ear. "Good. Now tilt your head down."

I do, and gasp. My shirt is unbuttoned at the top, and the black lace of the bra I lifted from Emma's old room peeks through. It's like my breasts have grown a full size in one day. A rash of heat creeps up the side of my face.

"Excellent," she says, in a low gravelly voice that makes

my knees go weak. Her gaze lingers on my chest, and I stiffen under her scrutiny. It takes every ounce of willpower not to cross my arms over my chest. What would Father Buck—*God?*—think of such brazenness?

Bridget ducks behind me and holds the camera so that the lens faces us. "Selfie time," she says, and tilts her head toward mine.

Sunlight streaks through the clouds and hits me in the eye. I squint, make a face. "A little warning next time?"

Bridget snaps off a few more candid shots—she scrunches her face, sticks out her tongue, throws her head back and laughs. "I like being spontaneous." She kisses my cheek so fast I barely have time to blush. "You should try it more."

A light breeze blows through the branches, and a few leaves trickle down around me. I reach up to dust off my shirt, but Bridget holds up a finger. "Don't move. Don't . . ." *Click, click, click.* "Okay, now you can move."

I lift my eyebrow. "Something interesting on my shoulder?"

"Caterpillar," she says with a wink.

My spine stiffens as I see the insect's green-and-black body in my peripheral vision. Bugs don't skeeve me out, but this thing is perched near my collarbone, precariously close to falling into my cleavage. I clench my fists at my sides.

Bridget leans forward and zooms in on the caterpillar. "I wonder what kind of butterfly this will become."

"Monarch." Another symbol of the resurrection, Father

Buck often says. But to most people they're just butterflies, famous for their orange-and-black-patterned wings. "We get a lot of them out here."

Bridget shudders. "I saw a TV show about them once. . . ." She peers at me over the lens. "Kinda creepy."

"I think they're pretty." A cramp in my leg makes my knees buckle, and Bridget steps forward, hand out to steady me. I resume position, still tingling from her touch. "This photo shoot is taking forever. Rigor mortis must be setting in."

Bridget smiles like she knows the secrets of the world, and somewhere deep in my heart, I believe that she does. If not the world . . . me. No one has ever taken time to get to know *me* before, and I cling to the idea that she'll stay with me, even once all my secrets are revealed. "Art takes patience."

The leg cramp tightens and I stumble forward, losing balance before Bridget can react. My foot gets caught on a root, and I start to fall. The ground comes at me in slow motion, punctuated by the *click, click, click* of Bridget's camera. I hit the grass hard on my wrists. A stinging vibration runs along my forearms. "Dang it!"

"Jesus, that was magical."

I glance up at the sound of Bridget's voice. Her eyes are all watery, like she can't help but laugh.

"You kept taking pictures?" I say, incredulous. At her half-apologetic nod, I crumple to the grass and roll onto my back. A daisy petal tickles my ear. I shield my eyes from the sun. "Delete them at once."

Bridget clutches the camera close. "You'll have to pry it from my cold dead hands first."

"Happily." I reach up, and she twists away. Her strawberry hair twirls over her shoulder and cascades down her chest. The sun hits her golden highlights, forming a halo over her head. The image is in stark contrast to the devilish grin that splits her cheeks in half.

"Give up now, baby," she says.

I blink innocently. "Can you help me stand?"

Bridget eyes me with suspicion, so I fake a light moan to indicate that I'm in pain. She takes the bait. As soon as her fingers curl around my wrist, I grab her forearm and yank. Bridget falls forward, crashing down on her knees with a curse. "Motherfucker."

She tries to stand, but I push her over so she lands on her hip. Her hair gets lost in the weed-choked grass. She coughs out a laugh. "I suppose I deserved that."

I clap my hand over my mouth to stop from giggling and lie beside her. Light clouds drift across a deep blue sky, almost too dark for this time of year. Warmth spreads over me, but I'm not even sure it's from the weather. Bridget is so close, I can almost touch her. Every cell in my body snaps awake.

"We should learn to ride horses," she says, threading her fingers through mine.

I turn my face to her, cupping her hand to my chest. Can she feel my heart beat? "Didn't you ride one across the Sahara Desert?"

Her eyes glisten. "Okay, I've never been to the Sahara Desert."

"I know." I reach with my free hand and push aside a strand of hair covering her cheek. "You're quite a mess."

My beautiful disaster.

She arches an eyebrow. "Yeah? You're not exactly *Teen Vogue*-ing it yourself."

I stretch across her to grab her camera, my chest resting on her torso as I turn on the screen. The image on display stops me cold. Heat flushes my cheeks. The picture is of me, but I barely recognize myself—I look different. Relaxed and happy.

Not me.

Swipe.

"I told you," Bridget says, her voice a near whisper. "You're beautiful."

"Stop it." My eyes get watery. "That isn't me."

"It is, Lizzie. It's the real you. The one I see every day."

The lump in my esophagus grows to the size of a softball. I can't breathe.

Anxious, I scroll through some of the other pictures until I find the series of selfies. It's me again—still relaxed, still happy—but Bridget is blocked by a ray of sunlight that hits her lens at just the wrong angle. Everything else but me is washed out. And for some inexplicable reason, I'm overcome by sadness. I set the camera down with trembling fingers. I blink to try and stop a tear from falling. I'm too late.

Bridget brushes her thumb across my cheek, the light touch igniting the burn on what's left of my latest bruise. She pretends to ignore them now, understanding that her silence means I can somehow move on. Not forgive—*never* forgive—but forget. If even for a few hours. "You're perfect, Lizzie. Just the way you are."

Uncomfortable with her praise, I swallow, and try lightening the mood. "So, we gonna lie around all day, or shoot some pictures?"

Grinning, Bridget lunges toward me, but I'm too quick. I leap up and take a giant step back. She's on her feet now, reaching for my skirt. Genuine laughter rumbles from deep in my chest, and I stumble backward. My foot catches on the same root and I pitch backward, landing faceup in a cluster of daisies. I prop myself up on my elbows and crawl backward, eyes wide as Bridget dives on top of me and pins me to the ground.

Her eyes glint with mischief. "Whatcha going to do now?"

I take advantage of her confidence and flip her over onto her back. In seconds, I straddle her, trapping her wrists with a viselike grip. She's stuck.

Just like the lump in my chest.

I bend forward, hair falling across her face, eyes locked on her lips. She runs her tongue along them. My chest fills like a helium balloon as her mouth moves toward mine. Her breath is hot on my skin. The energy between us *snap, crackle, pops*.

Our lips touch.

Gently, so soft it's almost nothing—

And everything.

Her tongue darts between my lips. A soft moan purrs from my throat. Bridget curls her hand around the back of my neck, pulling me closer. My stomach is a roiling mass of butterflies.

Bridget's teeth scrape against my lip.

"Shit," she says. "Did I hurt you?"

Emotions swirl around my heart like a dust devil, but pain isn't among them. "I'm stronger than I look."

Bridget's complexion pales and she looks away. The tips of her ears have gone pink, and I realize she's upset. When she finally meets my gaze, there is a sadness in her eyes. My heart skips a full beat.

"You shouldn't have to be so strong," she says.

The conversation shifts to less comfortable ground. I try to change the subject, but Bridget stands firm. "Where did you go the other night, Lizzie?"

I swallow, stalling.

"I *felt* you in the room with me and—" She inhales a shaky breath. "And I couldn't do anything. Why wouldn't you let me help you? We need to tell someone about what's going on. Your father should be reported."

I swallow hard. "Calling child services won't do anything. It's my word against his." The logic makes sense, but somewhere beneath it, a much more confusing emotion lurks. A sense of love and loyalty that's woven into my DNA and refuses to let loose, coupled with the realization that I *need* him. As easy as it is to pretend with Bridget, the reality is I'm *not* well. "It's complicated. . . ."

"Not if you showed them the bruises." Bridget blows out a slow breath. "They'd put you in a foster home or something."

"I don't want to live with strangers," I say, but that's only a fraction of the truth. The only reason Abigail hasn't had me committed is because my father is worried about how that might affect his reputation—what reason would foster parents have to keep me? I'm sure they'd just send me away.

"I hate your father," Bridget says, her tone thick with venom. "I fucking hate him with every fiber of my being." Her hands curl into fists. "I want to kill him for hurting you, Lizzie. Him and his fucking wife."

My heart grows heavy. I crawl off her and sit, curling my knees up to my chest. Across the horizon, the setting sun silhouettes the barn against a red-and-orange-streaked sky. It's picture-perfect, but this new tension has ruined the shot.

A shadow flickers in the distance and I flinch. "Someone's out there."

Bridget puts her hand up to her forehead and squints. "I can't see." She reaches behind to grab her camera and adjusts the lens. She sucks in a breath. "Shit."

The hair on the back of my neck stands on end. "Let me look." I zoom in and gasp. My stomach twists into knots.

A line of trees marks the edge of the field where the Borden B and B sits. In front of it, Abigail stands, hands on her hips, staring off into the distance.

Staring . . .

At us.

15

Welcome, child. How long since your last confession?"

The question startles me, or perhaps it's Father Buck's voice, solemn and muffled behind the thick screen of the confessional, that raises the hair on the back of my neck. His face is all shadows and soft angles. Though there is nothing anonymous about this.

"Six months, Father."

Since just before Bridget arrived. The significance of that isn't lost on me, but even still, I hadn't exactly planned on confession today. Perhaps not ever. Circumstances had other plans.

Despite all my teachings—and God's ever-present disapproval whispering in my subconscious—I've clung to the belief that somehow, I can have both. My faith, *and* Bridget. An impossible wish, now that Abigail has seen us together. I'm sure she saw us in the field. She had to have.

Fear is a low humming buzz in my veins. Why hasn't she said anything? What is she waiting for?

I didn't imagine her standing there, staring at Bridget and me as we rolled around on the grass, laughing, kissing, pretending to be free. Abigail *saw*, and before she tells Father, I must repent.

The confessional bench presses against my thighs, and I'm grateful the church decided years ago to do away with kneeling. I tug at the hem of my skirt, pulling it down to my shins, as though it can ward off the chill that winds its way into my bones. It must be below zero in this place. Restless spirits in the burial grounds below have begun to move.

I'm frightened.

But of what?

I've avoided confession until now, fearful of the consequences, both inside and beyond these walls, once I have bared my soul to Him. But listening now to Father Buck's heavy breaths echo within the confines of this small space, I'm not sure what I'll say. How much I'll reveal.

This isn't my first confession—I've always considered myself a good Catholic girl—but it's perhaps ironic that here, where I should feel most safe, I've never been able to fully spill the contents of my heart. Maybe it's because the feelings that truly haunt me are not *my* sins to confess.

Until now.

A bead of sweat trickles down the back of my neck.

The flickering candlelight does little to soothe my nerves, and for the first time in all my years at this church, the booth feels too small. Cramped. As though the walls themselves are caving in on me, and will somehow force the words out that I am too nervous to share on my own, suffocating me beneath them.

"I sense your hesitation," Father Buck says. I have been silent for too long, uncharacteristically so. "You are safe in God's house."

My breath comes out in a huff that I worry he'll interpret as sarcasm. Father Buck is perceptive, if not perfect. I've often wondered what secrets he keeps beneath that thick robe, whether he is as pure in spirit as he leads our community to believe. Fall River is a community of make-believers.

But again, I'm shifting blame and guilt, because it's not Father Buck who will be asked to perform Hail Marys at the end of this session. And what does it matter whether he's blemished? None of us is absent of sin, none worthy enough of God's true acceptance. Isn't that what my father always says? Certainly in his eyes, I am not worthy.

A candle inside the confessional flickers. I focus on the wax that slides down its side, dripping like tears. It awakens something in me and I begin to cry. I swipe at the sides of my face, unable to mask the sniffle.

"Lizbeth, if you'd prefer to speak outside the confessional, we can start there," Father Buck says, his voice etched with concern. He would argue that he is not only a priest, but also a friend, a confidant.

But there's so much I've never confided to anyone, not even Father Buck—what reason would he have to believe me? Money may not buy happiness, but influence is an entirely different story—and my father is a man of considerable wealth.

"I've developed feelings . . ." I choke on the words, forcing them out in a burst of false courage. It's not that I have found sudden trust in the process, in God's will, but rather the idea of *confessing*, of saying this aloud to Father Buck's unmasked face is more terrifying than the act of confession itself. At least here, I can pretend the privacy screen conceals my true identity. "These feelings . . . they're for someone I should not have feelings for. Not in this way."

Father Buck shifts closer, as though he's adjusted himself in his seat, leaning in to listen to teenage gossip.

I've never sat on his side of the booth, and I wonder if his seat is as hard as my bench, or if he pads his chair with cushions and pillows to soften the edge. What color is his candle? How do *I* appear through the screen, if at all?

The scent of lavender incense whispers through the

cracks in the wooden door. I breathe deep, allowing it to soothe me.

"Is this an older man?"

I smile in silence. If only it were that easy. "No."

"A boy in the church, perhaps?"

It's cruel to keep Father Buck guessing, but I'm not yet ready to reveal Bridget's identity. While I may be able to conceal her name, keeping her gender anonymous isn't possible—not if I'm truly going to confess.

I exhale hard. "Not a boy," I finally say.

There is an extended pause before Father Buck sighs. "I see."

I should leave now, slip through the giant front door and run out of the church. But that's the problem with small towns—Father Buck knows it's *me* in his confessional, and even if I divulge no further information, I can't take back what I've already confirmed.

There are sins for which I much atone.

I raise my chin, straighten my posture. Try to convince myself that there is nothing wrong with these feelings, that I have no reason to be ashamed. The act is the sin, not the desire, I remind myself. That's what the Bible teaches. But what acts, specifically? I squeeze my eyes shut and think of Bridget's fingers trailing across my cheek, her hip pressed against mine. I ache for her touch, for her lips to claim me once again. Are those the sinful acts God speaks of?

"And does this . . . person . . . have feelings for you?"

I lick my lips, dry despite the humidity in the air. "We are in love."

A brief hesitation. "Do I know this young lady?"

I've kept Bridget sheltered, tucked safely within the confines of the B and B—but now that Abigail has seen us together in that way, I worry our time may be running out.

A knot forms in my chest. "You do not."

Father Buck sighs. "Tell me about her."

The simple command snaps away any hesitation, and my voice fills with childlike enthusiasm. Adrenaline flows like spring rivers. "B—I'll just call her that—is well traveled. Adventurous. Oh, Father, you should hear of the places she's been, the experiences she's had."

Father Buck chuckles. "I suppose you would be drawn to someone like that, someone who is—"

Not lame, I think. It's not what Father Buck means—at least not what he'd admit aloud—but it's as though he's dismissed my confession as nothing more than the childish ramblings of a lovesick schoolgirl. My feelings are so much richer, more mature, than that.

But of course, this is what he would see. Father Buck envisions me as a modern-day spinster, pouring my passions, wants, and needs into the church and its beliefs. Not long ago, I saw this too. The seed of doubt rooted upon Bridget's arrival has sprouted new branches.

"—a person so well-traveled. A free spirit," Father Buck finishes.

"It's not just that. . . ."

"Of course not," he says, undeterred in his preaching. His inability to listen is something my Sunday school students complain of weekly. "But you must realize, Lizbeth, that your life is much different from hers."

More structured. Controlled.

"You were destined for other things, perhaps *greater* things."

I can't think of anything more enlightening, more free-ing, than traveling with Bridget. Exploring culinary hot spots, trying new things. To see the world with my eyes wide open, rather than how I often see them in the mirror after one of my father's beatings: swollen shut.

I resist the sudden temptation to out my father for his violence, my stepmother for her mental abuse. It would be easy to use the sympathy card here, but I'm afraid it would fall on deaf ears.

And, while my dysfunctional family situation is certainly at fault for many things in my world, it isn't the reason I've fallen in love with Bridget.

My breath hitches.

I still stutter on the word, as if it's part of some secret language.

I don't know the meaning of love, not really, truly. Only

that being with Bridget renders me light-headed and giddy, that her touch makes me forget the abrasiveness of my father's hands, or that her laugh can erase the high-pitched *screech, screech, screech* of my stepmother's voice. Our love gives me a sense of freedom, however false. Isn't that enough? Should my skin not tingle when she brushes her hand against mine? Should my whole chest not fill with yearning when she walks into a room? I shake my head, now grateful for the cloak of darkness the confessional provides.

"This girl . . . she will move on from Fall River," he says. "Few with that kind of spirit stay in one place."

Though I know it's true, I'm struck with resentment that he would say it aloud. "And if I go with her?"

Father Buck clucks his tongue, a first sign that he's annoyed by my persistence. Perhaps he thought dismissing my feelings would void the confession altogether, bring me back into the fold, no Hail Marys required. But I'm not letting him—not letting myself—off that easily.

"You know that isn't an option," he finally says, softly.

My spine goes rigid. "I love her."

Father Buck bangs his fist on the screen partition that separates us. The force of it makes me jump, and I question whether this was a mistake. Whether I should confess this—or anything—to this priest ever again. Rumors of his temper have always been quashed, but here, now, I'm starting to realize he isn't quite the man we've all been led to believe.

In that way, he has much in common with my father.

I press my hands on my knees, prepared to stand and leave. But then I'm struck with worry. If I go now, pretend that he's right and I'm no more than a lovesick fool, can I trust him to keep this secret? Or will he run straight to my father to share what he knows?

My face goes hot at the idea that Father Buck may betray the sacraments of the church. I have nothing to substantiate these theories aside from the ember of fear and doubt that burns in the pit of my belly. Still, it's not a risk I can take.

"'Every human being is called to receive the gift of becoming a child of God by grace,'" Father Buck quotes from an unknown text. "'However, to receive this gift, we must reject sin, including homosexual behavior.'"

His voice is somehow ominous and soothing, low, calm— the vocal push and pull of both rationality and stark judgment. "'Homosexual desires, however, are not in themselves sinful.' You have not acted on this desire, have you, Lizbeth?"

"Of course not," I say, shocked at how easily the lie slips from my tongue.

My butt cheeks have gone numb from the hard seat, and the candle has burned a quarter of the way through its solid base. Overhead, the patter of steady rain hitting the stained glass morphs into something that sounds a lot less like rain pattering over a window and more like nails scratching on a chalkboard.

"I don't understand why homosexuality is a sin," I say, surprising myself with a candor that doesn't come naturally. It's perhaps the first time I've challenged the Bible and its teachings in this holy place. I grasp the cross around my neck with one hand and squeeze hard enough to create indents in my palm.

For years, I have recited God's words to young students seeking truth in their faith. I have led youth groups and Sunday school sessions, volunteered at every church event. It's within these walls—within the house of the Lord—that I have often felt safe and pure and innocent.

Today, that innocence is replaced with shame.

It shouldn't be like this.

"Feelings are sometimes difficult to interpret," Father Buck says.

I know this, but it doesn't change how I feel, and it won't convince me to forget about Bridget, about me and Bridget, the idea that we can be together despite—or perhaps because of—the obstacles.

Who am I kidding? I'm stuck in Fall River while Bridget, as Father Buck has just reminded me, will . . . leave. *Everyone leaves.* This isn't a place for her. She doesn't belong here, just as I am an outsider in her world. I swallow hard.

It's conceivable, probable even, that she won't remember me or our time together, the laughs and tears we've shared, the pictures she's taken of me. I suck in a breath to stanch the pain of this new reality.

Love hurts.

"I don't know what to do, Father."

Tears fall in symmetrical lines down my cheeks, but I don't wipe them away. I need them to remind me, ground me. I need to face this pain head-on.

"You must ignore these feelings, Lizbeth," he says. "Resist temptation. Do not succumb to sin."

My voice cracks. "And if I can't?"

"There will be consequences."

Swipe.

"Spiritually, of course, but also in other ways. . . ." He takes a deep breath. "Resist, Lizbeth. It is the only way."

16

Oversize sunglasses rest low on the bridge of my nose, way too big for my face. They're new, pocketed from Mr. Bentz's grocery and department store just last night while gathering other supplies for three days at Father Buck's annual church retreat.

Except, that's not really where I'm going.

Bridget bounces on her tiptoes beside me at the bus stop. She's a restless ball of energy, while my stomach flip-flops like a fish out of water. I'm so queasy I have to sit. She clutches her hands together and grins. "Can you believe we're doing this?"

I can't. At first the idea seemed preposterous—running off to Boston to interview at Le Cordon Bleu, one of the premiere cooking schools in the whole state. But now I wonder if this time away from Fall River isn't exactly what I need to find context, to mull over Father Buck's words, figure out my next steps.

It's as though fate intervened, giving me both motive and excuse.

"I'll go with you," Bridget said, and the next thing I remember is hiding in the closet with the phone tucked up to my ear while I lied to Father Buck, my voice husky and raw to convince him I was sick. I added a theatrical cough—the kind even Abigail might have admired—and then sat very still, my stomach roiling with guilt.

The fluttering kicks up again, but I'm not sure if it's my nerves or the thought of going away with Bridget that has my guts twisted into knots.

I clutch my small black suitcase with white knuckles and adjust the rim of my hat so it rides low on my forehead. The letter from the school's top instructor—he's almost as amazing as Emeril!—is tucked in my inside pocket, pressing up against my heart. "I'm nervous," I whisper, but the truth is I'm terrified.

This is the first time I've been outside Fall River, a whole three days without Abigail or my father telling me what to do, how to act, when to take my medications.

My breath hitches on another betrayal. The half-full bottle of pills is tucked under my mattress, hidden from

Abigail's view. I've purposely not brought them, choosing to wean myself off medications that are clearly not helping. I'm not *depressed*—I'm happy. Deliriously so.

Bridget grins. "I can hardly believe this. We're free."

Not quite.

At any second, Father Buck could cruise by in his rented van, or worse, my father could drive past on his way to work. Either of them could make me—my disguise isn't exactly covert. I roll my fingers under the hem of my skirt, twirling it around my thumbs until it stings.

Bridget notices and swats my hands away. "Stop fidgeting," she says. "You look suspicious. I promise, it will be okay."

I want to believe her, but across the street, the gray brick facade of the church rises into the sky like an ominous sentinel, trapping us under its massive shadow. Wispy clouds above the steeple beckon like crooked fingers, daring me to confess.

I spot Father Buck's van at the far corner of the parking lot and slink behind a bush to spy on the teens loading up their suitcases and instruments and prayer books. "There he is," I whisper, heart pounding.

"Okay, *now* you're being ridiculous," she says, and then giggles. "He can't hear you." She cups her hand to her mouth and yells, "Over here!"

Eyes wide, I yank on her sleeve. "Please, Bridget . . ." I'm sure every gossip on the street is peering through their curtains with curiosity or annoyance. If one of them recognizes me, they'll call Abigail, or my father. My pulse *tap, tap, taps* against my skull. "Don't draw attention to us."

She laughs, louder now, and shakes her head. "No one is looking at us. I promise."

Except someone *has* already seen us together, maybe not today, but before. Abigail. It's always tense when I'm around her, but these days the air is thick enough to suffocate. I watch her eyes, her expressions, every subtle shift of her body, trying to predict the exact moment she'll confront me about what she's seen, how she'll leverage it in the most painful way.

The anticipation is killing me—and maybe that is her intent.

Father Buck's van pulls away from the church and turns up Second Street. I stare down at the pavement, counting the cracks, watching a black spider as it scampers across the top of my foot and down along my big pink-nailed toe. The polish is bright, almost neon, so totally not me. Bridget insisted.

"To our first adventure," she said, adding color to her toes as well. We are twins, but not really, because she is a sun-kissed butterfly and I am a gothic freak. My heart swells, panic rising as I realize how dangerous—ridiculous—this all is.

Bridget shuffles closer. "Okay," she says, after what seems an eternity. "We're in the clear."

I release the breath that's pinched between my ribs and glance up, just in time to see the vehicle's taillights disappear into the early morning mist. Before I can even finish my sigh of relief, our bus pulls up to the curb and the door swooshes open with a soft *hiss*.

"This is it," Bridget says, adjusting her rainbow backpack high on her shoulder. "You ready?"

Unease shakes through me, and still, I nod. "I shouldn't do this," I say under my breath.

The words repeat like radio static at the back of my conscience until something inside me snaps. Dang it. I'm sick of being the good girl, the one always following the rules. That's all I've ever done, and what do I have to show for it? Bruises and scars. A crippling lack of self-worth. The constant knowledge that no matter how hard I try, how *good* I am, it isn't enough.

I *am* enough. At least that's what Bridget always says.

Head down, I climb the steps into the bus, drop in enough money to take us to the main depot where we will catch an express coach to Boston, and wind my way to the back row. A half-dozen pairs of eyes land on my back. The hair on the nape of my neck goes rigid, and again I wonder if anyone will recognize me, rat me out.

Bridget places her hand on my waist to guide me. Her touch—in public!—turns my insides out. I trip over a bag left halfway in the middle of the aisle and stumble forward. My hat falls off and lands in some kid's lap. He hands it back to me with a snicker. "Watch your step."

A terrifying anger begins to unfurl from inside me. I stuff it away and continue to my seat. Bridget slides in next to me. Her hand rests on my knee. "You're fine," she says. "You've got this."

I breathe *in, out, in.*

My eyes skim the backs of heads in the seats ahead of us. I count fifteen people, most of them adults, and only one I think might recognize me if she lifted her gaze from the book cradled in her hands. Satisfied I'm safe, for now, I stare out the window as we turn down Second Street and pass the Borden B and B. My heart skips a beat. I place my face up against the glass and crane my neck, positive the ghostly image staring at the bus from the foyer is Abigail. She *sees* me. Us.

Swipe.

Bridget squeezes my knee. My leg kicks up on reflex and knocks against my suitcase. Her eyes twinkle with mischief. "It's like you packed for a month."

I chew on my lip, embarrassed that my indecision is so obvious. This is the farthest from home I've ever been—may *ever* be—and I want everything, every last detail, to be perfect. "Some of us don't have magical backpacks."

She shakes her head. "Oh, the Force is strong with this one today, folks."

Despite my nerves, I laugh. I fold my hands on my lap

and continue staring out the window, watching as the familiar scenes of my hometown begin to fade. With each passing blur of a street sign, the knots in my chest begin to unwind.

I steal a glance at Bridget, who looks at me with rosy cheeks and an impish grin.

My face goes hot. "What?"

"You're adorable," she says, and leans over to kiss my jaw.

I thread my fingers through hers and slump in my seat, trying to pretend that this indiscretion—this enormous act of rebellion—doesn't glow from my skin as though I'm draped in neon.

CHAPTER

17

Parallel forests flank either side of the highway, which stretches far into the distance. I focus on staring straight ahead and not looking back. I don't want to go back, not now, not ever. I think of my suitcase stuffed next to Bridget's rainbow backpack and wonder how long we can survive with just this. Just us.

As the coach bus turns onto Highway 24, I feel my tension drain like a slow-leaking tire.

Bridget leans in close and whispers, "Holy shit. We're totally doing this."

Her breath is hot against my neck, and I'm flushed. The woman in the aisle seat next to us glares at us through her thick-rimmed glasses, curling her lip in disgust. Bridget says

I should ignore her—"let them judge"—but my eyes keep flitting back, her disapproval seeping into my rapidly darkening soul.

I inch my fingers closer to Bridget's. She grabs my hand and smiles. "We're heading to Boston, can you believe it?"

Emotion swells in my chest. I shake my head, unable to speak. The trees, cars, and road signs all pass in a continuous blur. I shift closer to peer through the window and take off my hat. It doesn't even matter that my hair's a mess, that it's disheveled and imperfect.

This.

This moment is what matters.

A slow smile creeps across my face and I fall back against the seat in a sudden burst of soft giggles. Bridget joins in until we're laughing out loud. I force myself not to look at the judgmental woman in the seat across from us.

"I wish the scenery was better," Bridget says, when the laughter finally dies down.

"It's perfect."

Bridget scrunches up her nose. "It's Massachusetts, aka boring as fuck."

My voice catches. "Why did you come to Fall River, then?" I ask, not for the first time. It's questions like this she refuses to answer, and I'm afraid she finds me too invasive, too needy. But her phone never rings, there's never any mail. I understand her parents are traveling, but don't they even want to know how she is? "I mean, you've been to so many amazing places. . . ."

"I needed a change, I guess." She shrugs like her response makes all kinds of sense, but it doesn't. Not to me, at least. If I'm ever able to travel, I don't think I'll ever come back. "Being on the road all the time can get lonely."

That's okay too—I'm used to feeling alone.

Half an hour passes where we say nothing, giving root to my insecurities. I feel the madness, tight like a guitar string, urging me to tell the bus driver that we need to go back. Guilt eats away at me, leaving black streaks of doubt across my heart and my flesh. I'm wound up so tight that when Bridget speaks again, I actually jump.

"Twenty Questions?" she says.

"Yes!" I nearly gasp in relief that things are on their way back to normal. *This* is our game. "Only if I can go first."

Bridget nods.

"Most beautiful place you've traveled to?"

She groans. "You know the answer. Italy."

Bridget's right—that's always my go-to question, because I know she loves to talk about her adventures. She's like an artist, painting pictures with her words, bringing to life the sights and sounds, the tastes and smells of places I can only dream of going.

"Venice, if you want me to be more specific," she says, echoing Father Buck's sentiments. I've heard many stories about Italy, but the water traffic in Venice is by far what he talks about the most. "The architecture in Rome is stunning, but the river canal that winds through Venice is . . ." Her voice trails off and she sighs. "Breathtaking."

"Is it true that you have to get around by boat?"

Her eyebrow rises above the top of her sunglasses. "Is that an official question?" She laughs before I can respond. "Gondolas, actually. The water system in Venice is quite intricate. Like a liquid maze." Her fingers flex, release, and tighten on my knee. "My turn."

I wring my hands together on my lap.

"Most trouble you've ever gotten into with your sister?"

My heartbeat stutters. I chew on the inside of my cheek, stalling on my response. "I never got into trouble with Emma."

After Mom died, Emma's role changed. She stopped treating me like her baby sister, started nurturing me as if I was her own child. I used to be the good girl. Obedient. A prodigal daughter, our parents said. But then the trifecta of trauma blew through my life—my irregular menstrual cycles, Mom's cancer, Abigail's grand entrance into our lives—and something inside of me just . . . snapped. Emma got the brunt of that.

Dr. Driscoll says I'm still grieving, that I'm simply depressed. Even if that were true, it's not as "simple" as he makes it seem.

I haven't said it aloud, not even to Bridget, but I know there's something else wrong, because even when I was taking the full dosage, the medications haven't been working the way they should. There's a darkness that lives deep in my heart.

Some people can find the silver lining in a storm cloud. Not me. When I black out, I can't see, can't hear, can't find anything but madness.

Except when I'm with Bridget. That's when everything seems clear.

And maybe, if I take this trip without an episode, without medications, I can use it as evidence to convince my father I'm not crazy. That I *can* make it on my own.

The bus shifts down a gear as we pull up behind a slow-moving tractor. "I didn't get in trouble with my siblings either," Bridget says, her lip curling into a mischievous smirk.

"Because you don't have any," I say, smiling. I learned that the last time we played Twenty Questions. The bus moves around the tractor and we pick up speed. "Maybe you don't have to act out because your parents aren't strict."

Bridget rolls her eyes. "Mom has rules, trust me. Like, no boys in the house. I got around that, though." She winks. "I invited my girlfriends over instead."

My cheeks go pink. "Did she ever figure it out?"

Bridget shrugs. "I guess so, but my parents never made a big deal out of it." She rubs her thumb against the top of my hand. "Like I always say, you love who you love."

She makes it seem so easy, but I know it's not.

Fresh guilt washes over me. Father Buck's voice rings in my eardrums, unspooling each lie until it thickens into a web. I am a fly trapped in its deceit.

Bridget twists in her seat so she's facing me, her expression solemn.

"What is it?"

She caresses the edge of my hand. "We don't have to go back."

"Of course we do. Where would we go? What would we do?" The questions pop out of my mouth like firecrackers, my tone turning incredulous. I breathe in and out. It's like I'm drinking my father's Kool-Aid, starting to believe that I really couldn't make it without them. "We have to go back."

Bridget nods. "Maybe this time, but you're going to get into that school, Lizzie, and when you do, you can give Fall River the big old middle finger." She demonstrates to prove her point, and the woman across from us scowls. "It's going to happen for you, Lizzie. You believe that, right?"

I glance away to mask the tears gathering in my eyes. In the distance, the sun hangs high over endless fields of grass. The beauty of it sucker punches me in the solar plexus, and I realize with sadness that I've never truly *seen* the beauty that surrounds me.

Could Bridget be my silver lining in the storm that is my life?

My voice softens. "I'm not sure about anything, really." I tuck a strand of Bridget's hair behind her ear and swallow. "But for the first time in my life, I can see more than Fall River on the horizon."

18

Bridget flicks on the overhead light, and I pull the thin duvet up over my eyes to dial down the brightness in the hotel room. She yanks the blanket off, crouches so that her face is inches from mine, and tilts her head. "Wake up, sunshine."

Sunshine.

A distant memory snakes through my groggy haze. My mother hovers over me, smile welcoming, the promise of adventure twinkling in her eyes. "Rise and shine, sunshine," she said, her melodic singsong twisting under my skin. "There is a whole world waiting for us out there."

Looking back, I must have known something was off. Ice cream for breakfast, skipping school for a hike through the reservoir, s'mores for lunch and waffles for dinner. I should have felt something when she took my hand and led me through the forest, should have realized we were chain links of desperation, attached to each other, trying to hold on to something that by the next week would abruptly end.

Mom hid her cancer from me, from Emma, from Father, too.

None of us knew until the tumor had leaked into her blood and burrowed its way to her bones. Sometimes when I squeeze my eyes shut at night, I search for her face, for the sunshine in her heart. But all I've ever found is darkness.

I blink. See Bridget. And remember that with her in my life, some of that pitch-black has begun fading to gray.

"What time is it?"

Bridget flops down on the bed next to me, and the mattress sinks, making me roll into her. "Early."

I perch on my elbows and yawn. "Is there coffee?"

Bridget shakes her head, fanning me with the scent of strawberry shampoo. Her eyelashes are long and thick, lips freshly glossed, hair pulled back into twin braids that fall in parallel lines down her chest.

My fingers tangle in the knots of my bedhead hair. "What is this fresh hell?" I sit upright, conscious of how I must look, and rub the sleep from my eyes. "Got anything else to offer in exchange?"

Bridget makes a face. "Nothing that can replace caffeine. But I do have . . ." She hands over a slip of paper with a theatrical flourish. "This."

This is the bus route from our hotel to Le Cordon Bleu, along with a list of Boston tourist attractions ranging from the Museum of Fine Arts to a pond apparently named for its abundance of frogs. Bridget has numbered each item in order of preference, ranking the Boston Symphony Orchestra at the bottom of the list, while the Boston Public Garden is circled in red, starred, and numbered with an oversize *2*.

"They have swans," she says, when I trace my finger over the blue lettering. Bridget's penmanship is atrocious, an odd mix of cursive and printed letters similar to my own. "Like, giant ones that you can actually ride in."

"I can see why it ranks so high," I say, eyebrow raised. "But you're missing a number."

Bridget leans in. "Nope."

I count off the items on the list—nine—and then follow the random pattern of numbers. "You've clearly forgotten one."

"Turn it over," she says with a wink.

I do, and my pulse quickens. In bold ink, framed with hearts and stars, Bridget has written *EMERSON COLLEGE*. Tears burn my eyes. I don't look up, afraid she'll ask me what's wrong and I'll snap.

"We could meet your sister for lunch," she says, oblivious. "Before your interview. I know it's short notice, but I'm sure she'd skip class. Don't you think?"

"I don't know if she would," I whisper. Or if I even want her to.

Because the truth is, we've barely spoken since Emma's last visit. And for the first time in our relationship, I'm the one coveting secrets and breaking rules. It's me who's clammed up, shut her out. I keep pretending it's because of Jesse, but deep down I know that's not the issue.

Bridget is.

I've never been able to lie to Emma. She can decipher every facial expression, knows every beat of my heart. Two seconds in a room with me and Bridget, and Emma would *know*. She'd know how Father hasn't stopped hurting me, how I'm *mad* at her for getting engaged to Jesse and abandoning me, how I feel about Bridget. She'd know—

Everything.

No, I cannot go for lunch with her and Bridget. I'm not ready.

"I thought maybe you'd want to see her," Bridget says. "She'll be excited for you."

"Can I think about it?" I say, an attempt to explain why I can't—won't—see my sister.

"Absolutely." She spreads the list flat on the bed. "Anything else here of interest?"

"Maybe I could go for giant swans?"

"Excellent choice." She stands and smooths her hands over her hips. "How about I scare up some java while you get ready?"

"I can get behind that plan."

The words come easy, but the second Bridget steps out of the room, I'm struck by a wave of panic. It hits me like a tidal wave, pummeling my chest with doubt. Who do I think I am, pretending I have a chance of being accepted to culinary school, thinking I'll ever be able to leave Fall River, my father, that house stuffed full of darkness? I yank open the blinds and allow the sun to stream into the room. My breathing steadies.

For a brief second, I wish for my medications, and then remember that they don't calm me. I have to learn to do that on my own if I'm to ever truly be free. *You've got this.*

Yes, I've got this.

I change into a knee-length pair of shorts and a fitted T-shirt with black lace on the collar and sleeves. Apply a thin layer of mascara and a clear sheen of gloss that makes my lips feel like they're covered in snot. I smile, and the girl in the mirror smiles back. I lift my chin, and she does too.

Bridget knocks on the bathroom door. I ease it open and she shoves a Starbucks cup through the opening. *DRIZZIE* is scrawled across the side in black Sharpie. I tilt my head in confusion.

She shrugs. "I think coming up with alternate names is like a game for baristas. Don't worry, I'm 'Legit.' Which"— she scrunches up her nose—"I suppose could be a compliment based on how hard the ginger was hitting on me."

I swallow the bitter taste of jealousy in my mouth and take a sip. "The coffee's good at least."

"Substandard," Bridget says.

"Next to Italian espresso, I'm sure."

Bridget grabs my hand and tugs me out of the bathroom. "I looked up the Boston Public Garden while I was waiting for our coffees, and if we want to hitch a ride on a giant swan, we should hit the road. We can grab breakfast on the way, maybe do a picnic lunch before your interview if you don't want to see your sister?"

My stomach makes a loud gurgling sound and I cover it with my hand.

Bridget drops her gaze. "Seth?" She crouches so her face is eye level with my stomach. "I thought we told you to stay home."

"Clever guard dog," I say, grinning.

Bridget slings her backpack over her shoulder. "And ferocious. I guess we should feed him, since he's already made himself a third wheel."

I shrug into my sweater and stuff my wallet into my back pocket. A gift bag on the bed catches my attention, pink tissue paper poking out of the top. Bridget sees me staring and nudges my shoulder.

"Oh yeah, I almost forgot, that's for you," she says.

I point at my chest questioningly.

"No, the other you," she says with a slight eye roll. She grabs the polka-dotted gift bag and holds it out to me. A small card dangles from the side, where's she's written

Happy Day of Birth, Lizzie. I Love You. Every *I* is dotted with an imperfect heart, two hastily drawn arcs that join to form the perfect symbolism for how I feel.

"How did you know it was my birthday?"

"July nineteenth," she says, rocking back on her feet. "Remember when I asked you? Back when we were fishing?" She taps her skull. "I've got a memory like an elephant."

I lick my lips. "You shouldn't have . . ."

"Of course I should have." She leans in and lightly kisses my lips. My face tingles as every cell in my body ignites.

"Open the present," she whispers, her breath warm against my mouth.

My heart feels like it will beat straight through my rib cage. With trembling fingers, I untie the bow and peer into the bag. I reach in and withdraw a hot-pink citrus peeler.

"It's for your kitchen," she says, blushing. "I mean, when you get your own place. You always say you want one." She lifts my hand to her lips and kisses the inside of my palm. "You're always cutting yourself."

A teardrop trickles down my cheek. "This is the most thoughtful gift anyone has ever given me."

She smiles softly. "I don't like it when you're in pain, Lizzie."

The words seem light, but I know they're just skimming the surface of feelings that run far deeper than the superficial cuts by my kitchen knife.

19

There's something kind of creepy about a bunch of boats shaped like swans drifting down a river. Like I've fallen into Wonderland, which maybe isn't a terrible analogy, since the whole of the Public Garden is kind of a tribute to children's literature.

I perch at the edge of the bridge, staring down at a pair of real swans floating by and a cluster of tourists whose cameras blink and flash, click and snap. Beside me, Bridget leans over the railing, her feet dangling off the ground.

"Hang on to me," she says.

I grab onto her hips and brace against the railing. She clicks through a series of shots, her lens pivoting along the riverbank. The hum of her camera thrums against my chest, as though imprinting the memories from her lens through to my heart. White and purple blossoms reflect off water that ripples under a light breeze.

Bridget tips forward, her torso bent almost in half, and my breath catches. "We're not quite equipped for bungee jumping," I say, eyeing the drop below. It isn't far—maybe six or seven feet—but the sun turns the surface of the river dark, making it difficult to see the water's depth.

"An artist must make sacrifices," she says.

She flips upright and uses my shoulder for balance to readjust her shirt, and tug at the bottom of her denim skirt. "Though admittedly, flaunting my booty wasn't exactly part of the plan." She double-raises her eyebrows. "Not that I don't have an impressive booty."

A nervous giggle seeps out. "I won't argue that."

Bridget grabs my hand. "Come on, let's get in line."

We kind of half run, half stumble across the bridge, and even as I will my ankles not to break, my knees not to give out, my feet not to trip over a wayward pebble, stick, discarded tissue, the pit in my stomach begins to shrink. I am lighter. Happier.

Free.

It's the most amazing feeling in the world. And for the second time in just a few hours, I convince myself I *can* do this, escape from my father's clutches, leave Fall River behind. My stomach flutters with hope. I can't remember the last time I felt like this.

And I'm without medications!

"Come on," Bridget says, tugging on my hand. We line up behind a group of teens around our age, watching as a giant swan boat winds its way toward us. Bridget grabs a bag of licorice from her backpack and hands me a stick. "Here, for our guard dog."

My mind locks in on a single word: *our.*

Maybe I shouldn't cling to hope like it's a lifeline, but when Bridget slips her hand in mine, I get this weird tickle in my throat. I'm sure I'll never get used to the way it feels when we touch.

I steal a glance at the line of people behind us, and my hand goes clammy. Are they watching? Judging? What are they thinking? My heart flutters a thousand beats per minute, and the first inkling of paranoia creeps up onto my shoulder. It digs its claws in with a force that takes my breath away.

This will never be your life.

The words whisper across the back of my neck, so real I can almost hear Abigail's voice. Her cackle sends a shiver up my spine.

Swipe.

Bridget leans close and lowers her voice. "We're next."

Anticipation coils around my chest. "I need pictures of everything." When I get back to Fall River, I want to remember this, us, everything about this trip. In time, the memories will fade, drift behind matters of more urgency and importance, but in Bridget's snapshots, I will always find truth.

Comfort.

Bridget turns the camera so it's facing us, and we tilt our heads together. She snaps off a series of pictures. My eyebrows rise, her tongue sticks out, we laugh, we frown. The *click, click, click* goes by in a blur.

The line slinks forward, and we all spill onto the boat. Bridget and I settle into spots at the back. Beside us, our captain perches on a chair behind the swan's enormous plastic neck. He tips his hat at me and smiles.

My grin is brilliant. Radiant.

"Bridget," I whisper, as our boat begins to float across the water's surface. "I really love you."

A ghostly smile lifts the corner of her lips. "I know."

20

Bridget's finger trails across my knee.

I suck back a gasp. Exhale slow, steadying. My head is still light from this afternoon's amazing interview at Le Cordon Bleu, and the feeling intensifies alone with Bridget in our hotel room.

Her hand slips onto my upper thigh and traces the thin line of an old scar.

"What's this from?"

Our game of Twenty Questions has taken a new twist. My skin tingles beneath her touch and I try to focus on the question. But then her fingertip drifts to a new scar. "And this one?"

I swallow unease. "Shaving accidents," I lie. The truth is,

I'm not sure where they came from—only that they emerge after each episode, as though counting down through an invisible time line. The one that's most fresh is from the night I spent in the closet, desperate to contain the madness from rearing up in front of Bridget. She can never see its full extent. *Never.*

Bridget shifts on the mattress and gently slides my dress up over my thigh. I take a deep breath, nervous under her scrutiny. Her eyebrows pinch, and she purses her lips together with concern.

I can tell she's counting the number of thin lines that have been carved into my skin with a sharp blade. Fifteen—plus five that are too faded to show. "That was a lifetime ago," I say, though it's obvious more than one of the scars is less than a year old.

"I can't imagine how much pain you must have been in to do this," Bridget says. Her voice is choked with emotion, and her sadness gets under my skin, burrows deep into my bones. "Does your sister know?"

I look away, embarrassed. I try to laugh, but it comes out more a snort. "She'd have me committed too."

Isn't that where you belong?

I blink to block out Abigail's face. She is here, with me, even when she isn't. Bridget squeezes my hand. "You're not crazy," she says. "You're . . ."

"Sick," I say, and sink lower into the mattress. We've never talked about my condition—conditions?—and even now, I'm not sure how much to explain. Will my honesty keep her with me, or cause her to run?

She squeezes harder. "Don't say that."

My fingers ache, but I don't pull away. "It's true, though. Something is very, very wrong with me. There's this"—I swallow the lump lodged at the back of my throat and feel it inch down my esophagus like a slow-moving snail—"darkness inside of me. And I don't know where it comes from."

I've tried to rationalize it, blame it on my menstrual cycle, or my father's abuse, the loss of my mother. But how do you explain something you can't prove? It's like trying to explain God to a child—you can't *see* Jesus, can't speak to him, at least not literally. You just *know* He's there. If you believe, you can *feel* His presence.

That's how it is with my madness and the hallucinations that come with it—even those I try desperately to swipe clear.

None of it can be explained away by depression, erased by medication. At least not when the pills don't match my symptoms. Maybe if my parents were honest with Dr. Driscoll, he'd have a different diagnosis, a more effective cocktail of drugs.

Another impossible wish, because in order for that to happen, my father would have to admit to what he's done, continues to do.

"It's because Abigail says things to you," Bridget says, her voice clipped. These days, talking about my stepmother makes her angry.

"My father thinks I'm not well too," I say quickly. The question of my mental health is an ongoing debate in the Borden household. Emma doesn't say it aloud, but sometimes I can see it when she looks at me, the sadness in her expression, knowing that something isn't quite right about me.

"You can only hear something so much before you start believing it," Bridget says, shuffling closer. "Don't listen to them. They don't know you, not the way I do."

The truth cuts deeper. Lately Bridget has asked more questions, pushing for answers about the black holes in my memory. She clings to incidents and episodes, like my burnt journal, trying to come up with excuses and explanations.

"Maybe you have PTSD," she said once.

I laughed, even though it wasn't funny, and changed the subject like I always do when the feelings get too real. Maybe I'm taking a gamble by opening up to her now, but I can't risk losing her altogether. Can't bear the thought of her leaving.

Everyone leaves.

"Why are you here, Bridget?"

She scoots down so we're lying next to each other, our faces only inches apart. Her hair splays out on the pillow, framing her porcelain features made whiter by the soft moonlight leaking in through the windows.

"Because there's nowhere else I'd rather be."

My heart pulses. "Not here—in Fall River. At the B and B. With Abigail and my father. With me."

Her smile slips. "Because there's nowhere else I'd rather be," she says again louder, as though that should be explanation enough.

I want to believe her, but my chest squeezes with unexpected doubt. I roll my thumb along her hand, trying again to draw out an acceptable response to the question she keeps dodging. "Of all the places you've traveled . . ."

"I like Fall River the best," she says. "Because that's where you are. Can we drop it?" Her voice softens. "Please?"

Our gazes meet, and in her eyes, I see what is reflected in my own: need. I thought I was the one with all the secrets. What could she be hiding from *me*? She cups her palm to my cheek and I whisper, "I'll stop asking questions."

"Good, because I'm going to kiss you now."

My skin ignites. "Okay."

She finds my lips with hers, warm despite the cool air that surrounds us. Her mouth presses against mine softly and slowly, like stepping into a wide, unknown ocean, one foot at a time. It's not the first time we've kissed, but something about this feels different.

Bridget's hand slides over my hip, and beneath my thin cotton T-shirt. Her thumb hooks under the waistband of my underwear, and I suck in my stomach. I inch closer, as if drawn by an electrical current. Her purr deepens. Every inch of me feels like it's on fire, tingling with anticipation of her touch.

Bridget's tongue darts between my lips. I gasp, pull back, and reconnect.

The hair on the back of my neck prickles. My flesh is peppered in goose bumps.

Bridget kisses the corner of my mouth, the tip of my nose. "Lizzie, did you burn your diary?"

Yes. I resist the knee-jerk reaction to lie—but the truth is, I'm not sure. "Maybe. I guess." I wait for her to say something, to *do* something, expecting the confession to scare her away. I should have known Bridget was too strong, too *brave*, to walk away from this, from us, from—

Me.

"Thank you," she says, touching her forehead to mine. "For being honest."

Bridget kisses me aggressively, scraping her teeth against my mouth, biting at my lips. By morning, I'm sure they'll be swollen and bruised.

She pulls back a little. "Too much?"

I weave my hand into the back of her hair and pull her mouth to mine. "More," I say, breathless, weightless. Every cell in my body begs for more of this, more of her.

Bridget curls her hand around the base of my neck and presses our foreheads together. The air between us crackles.

"This . . . ," I say, voice quivering. "It won't be easy. I'm . . ." I breathe out a sigh. "I'm messed up, Bridget."

"We all are, Lizzie," she says. "In some way or another."

"But . . ." My heart feels like it's beating through my chest. At any second, my rib cage will shatter into a million tiny pieces. "What if my family is right? What if my madness can't be controlled?"

"We're not so different, Lizzie."

My mouth opens in surprise. "How can you say that?"

"Because I love you," she says, and a ghost of a smile curls up her lip. "And love is a kind of madness, isn't it?"

CHAPTER

21

I spot Emma weaving her way down a sidewalk clustered with early-morning traffic. Her blond hair is piled under a newsboy cap that matches the rustic material of the messenger bag slung over her shoulder. Camouflaged among the crowd as though she's belonged here her whole life.

My body hums with restless energy. I fold my hands on my lap, threading my fingers together to stop from fidgeting, but it doesn't stop the *tap, tap, tap* of my shoe against the laminate floor.

I take a sip of coffee. It scarcely eases the dry itch at the back of my throat. My mouth is so raw, I'm afraid to speak. Excuses and explanations flip through my mind like a film reel, pausing to catalog each frame. *Click, click, click.*

I'm still not sure of my decision to meet with Emma. Bridget thinks my sister will be thrilled to see me, to hear about my interview at Le Cordon Bleu, but one look at her furrowed brow, the slight redness to her cheeks, and I know I've worried her sick. And yet somehow, her distress fills me with relief, gives me comfort that however she feels about Abigail and our father, she hasn't fully abandoned me.

I scratch at the edge of my skirt.

Emma swings open the door, our eyes connect, and the tension drains from her face. I stand, knocking over my cup, spilling coffee onto the Victorian tablecloth.

"Izzy," she gushes, part surprise, part annoyance at the scene I'm creating. I launch myself at her, wrapping her in a hug she returns with such force, my breath blows out in a raspy gasp. We hold on for what seems an eternity before she pulls back and places her cool hands on either side of my cheeks, staring deeply, curiously, into my eyes. "Happy birthday! What on earth are you doing here?"

Her voice is a prism of conflicting emotion, putting me on immediate defense. My spine stiffens. "It's kind of a road trip," I say, because I can't figure out how to explain the rest just yet. I blink, wishing Bridget would materialize with one of her tension-melting smiles. How silly of me to ask her to stay behind.

"Alone?" Emma says, her voice high-pitched and incredulous. I shrink lower into my seat while she scans the café, like she thinks she's been duped. Does she expect to see our father lurking behind the mug display with an apology and blanket acceptance of Jesse? No, Ems knows better than that.

Her eyebrows narrow. "Why do I get the sense this isn't a parent-approved adventure?"

"I'm eighteen, not twelve," I spit out, frustrated that I have to get through this part before I can tell her the good news.

Ems shoots me a look of annoyance and flags down a waitress. Her lips aren't moving, but I can read my sister's mind. She always says she wants me to escape Fall River, but sometimes, I think she just says what I want to hear.

"How did you get here?" She holds up her finger. "Wait. I need a coffee first."

I grin, trying to convey just how excited, how happy, I am. "Better make it a double."

Emma's eyes widen. "Start talking." She giggles nervously. "How long are you staying?" She lowers her voice. "Where does *Andrew* think you are?"

The way she says Father's name sends a chill up my spine. "At Father Buck's annual church retreat."

Fresh guilt slicks my tongue at the confession.

Emma's skin pales. She sets her elbows on the table and squishes her cheeks between her palms. "I think I need a cinnamon bun too. You?"

I shake my head. "We—I—had breakfast."

Ems catches my slipup and again scopes out the café,

straining her neck over the crowds gathered around tables, and at the line at the coffee bar. For a split second, I see Bridget, peering from behind the tall, spindly barista, and my pulse ratchets up. She gives me a thumbs-up. I blink. No. That girl isn't Bridget at all.

"Izzy, tell me what's going on." There's an edge to Emma's voice that lets me know that she's scared. Confused. "You're acting strange."

Strange or crazy? I wonder if she sees any difference. A low vibration hums in the pit of my belly. The accusation irks me, but I know how this must look. Emma used to be my best friend, and keeping secrets from her is the hardest thing I've ever done.

The waitress sets two coffee cups on the table and whisks my old mug away. I stir in two sugars, absently watching the heart-shaped foam blend in and disappear. My shoulders slump. "Or maybe you just don't know me anymore."

Emma's eyes harden. "That's not fair."

"You left," I say, choking out the words. It's not just that she went off to college, or got engaged to Jesse. It's not even that she stormed out of the house, vowing never to set foot in it again. Emma *knows* what it's like there. How it can be stifling and cold—and she still walked out that door. Leaving me alone. With them. "I needed you."

"Are you in trouble, Izzy?"

Yes.

Of course that would be her first thought. And dang if I haven't allowed my excitement to fade. I've always seen Ems as my savior, the only person who ever saw me for *me*—I was wrong. My eyes shimmer. "For the first time in my life, I think things are going well." I can feel my breath quickening, my pitch rising, the *thump, thump, thump* of my pulse. "I had an interview at Le Cordon Bleu and—"

"The culinary school?"

I nod, expecting to see pride, but her lips press together in a straight line. My fingers wrap around the porcelain coffee mug, trembling hard enough to make the liquid inside ripple. "I know it sounds impulsive, but Bridget—"

"Bridget? Who is that?"

I take a deep breath, forcing myself to slow down, to take things one step at a time. "My girlfriend."

Emma's pupils grow wide. I scan her face, trying to read her reaction, listening for the *click, clunk, chug* of the gears in her mind churning through questions. She cranes her neck over her shoulder. "Is . . . Bridget here?"

I lick my lips. "I wanted to tell you about her first."

Emma leans back in her chair. "Where do I even begin?" She leans forward and steeples her hands on the table. "You spent the night in a hotel?"

My teeth scrape against the inside of my cheek. "I'm eighteen, Ems." Why is she focused on this when all I want is to tell her about my interview?

She rubs the back of her neck. "You could have called me. Stayed with me."

"The hotel was close to the school, and it was even paid for by Le Cordon Bleu," I say, trying to steer the conversation back to my interview. The chef was intrigued with my meat-loaf recipe—"such a unique take on a classic dish"— and inspired by the way I described each of the herbs in my kitchen. "Your culinary descriptions make me salivate," he'd said, and I repeated those words the whole way back to the hotel, skipping along the sidewalk holding Bridget's hand.

I release a slow, nervous breath. "What is it, Emma?" A dull ache pounds at the back of my skull. Obviously I won't be sharing any of that until we deal with the issue that's pecking at her. "Are you upset because I didn't tell you about Bridget? Or that I'm dating a girl? Or—"

"Don't be silly," she says. "Of course I'm not upset you're with . . . Bridget."

I hate how she keeps stumbling on her name, like she can't quite remember the most important person in my life.

"It's just that the church—"

"Fuck the church," I spit out. Emma gasps and I cup my hand to my mouth, shocked at what I've said. New guilt begins to swirl. I'm not sorry I said it, but the anger I feel has tainted the excitement I *should* be sharing. Sisters share stuff, right?

"Izzy, you're acting so strange," Emma says. She closes

her hand over mine. "You're talking about going to cooking school, and leaving Fall River, and dating a girl. . . ." She gulps. "And you're swearing! Do you even hear yourself?"

I do hear myself. And it's the sound of my mind struggling against everything I'm supposed to feel. My bottom lip quivers. "How am I any different from you?" I press my palms tight against the table, steadying myself. Trying to keep calm. "You left Fall River. Went to college. Fell in love."

"It's not the same. . . ."

"That's not true." My anger gives way to tears. "I'm sorry that I'm not who you think I am, or that you're disappointed. I'm sorry that I'll never be enough. For you, for Father. I'm just sor—"

Stop saying sorry.

Bridget's voice feathers against the back of my neck. I spin around, but she isn't there.

The concern in Emma's eyes deepens. "That isn't what I meant. No one is good enough for our father." She pushes her coffee aside and sneers. "I hate that man, and I'll never forgive him for how he treated me or Jesse. I wish he was dead."

My throat clogs up. "You don't mean that."

Emma leans back in her chair. "I do, and don't tell me you haven't considered it." I blink, as if to reset this conversation. This isn't going at all how I thought. Thick cords of tension tighten across my sister's neck, and in her expression I see darkness, not a reflection of mine, but the outline of something living inside Emma, too. "I'd kill him myself if I could. So would you—"

I can't take it anymore. "Stop it!" I drop my gaze, working through my emotions. Today isn't supposed to be about Father, but her words bring back nightmares and memories, a sense of déjà vu. Is it possible she's right? That I have those feelings too?

I shake my head. "I came to tell you about cooking school. And about Bridget."

Emma sighs. "Does Bridget know about your episodes?"

My spine stiffens. "She accepts me. All of me."

Emma says nothing for a long while. Her eyes search mine, and I look away. I'm always the one to look away. "You haven't answered me. Does she know that you're . . . not well?"

The question is like a slap across the face. I recoil from the unexpected sharp stab of pain that *jab, jab, jabs* at my chest.

"Our father has beat me for the last five years." My voice is dangerously calm. "Did you know that?" My mouth turns down in a sneer. "Five. Years. And not once have you offered to help me."

Emma starts to cry. Mascara trails down her cheeks. "Because I was afraid they'd take you away."

I stand and push my chair back. "That excuse isn't good enough."

"Izzy, please." She grabs my wrist and hangs on tight. Her voice is embarrassingly loud. "Have you taken your medications?"

I consider lying, but for some reason the truth seems to cut deeper. The weight of a thousand stares land on my back, at us, and I don't even care. My limbs go numb, my mouth feels like cotton. "No, and you know what? I've never been happier." I pirouette, almost stumbling after the spin, and Emma's eyes grow wider. I throw my head back and laugh. "You think I'm crazy, don't you? That I'm unstable?" I lean in close. "Unhinged."

"You're scaring me," she whispers. "Let me take you home. I know you hate them, Izzy, but you *need* Father and Abigail."

I grit my teeth and seethe. "You're wrong, Emma. I don't need them anymore. If anything, this trip has proved that I can do just fine on my own."

The truth of my words hits me and I almost smile. Like a baby pigeon, I was no longer content to open my mouth and have my parents fill it—I was ready to feed myself.

22

russic acid.

"I haven't heard it called that in years," Mr. Bentz says. He shifts his thick-rimmed glasses onto the bridge of his nose. "Do you mean hydrogen cyanide?" At my nod, he raises his voice. "That's poison, Lizbeth."

The words echo off the empty shelves in the storage room. My shoulders tighten and I glance over my shoulder, half expecting Sheriff Dunby to be lurking in the shadows, handcuffs dangling from his pudgy fingers.

Mr. Bentz uses a razor knife to slice open one of the boxes on a pallet stacked four deep. He unfolds the flaps and starts putting the cans of vegetables on the table. I pick up the pricing gun and adjust the sticker tape to read $0.89. That's standard for corn, peas, and carrots. When he gets to the asparagus, I'll raise the cost fifty cents.

I don't work for Mr. Bentz, but I've been coming here for years. Helping out today will soften him up for the favor I'm about to ask—plus it keeps me out of the house, away from Abigail's hawk eyes. Ever since Bridget and I returned from Boston a few days ago, Abigail is everywhere—in the bathroom mirror when I brush my hair, in the after-fog of a deep sleep, the aftertaste lingering under my tongue. It's as though she can sense something in me has changed.

She's not wrong.

I've been flushing my medication down the toilet to make it look like I'm taking the appropriate dosage. It's been days since I've even thought about the pills at all, as though my resolution in Boston, coupled with Bridget's support, has freed me to do whatever, whenever I want. I feel lighter, happier. Cautiously convinced that freedom is within my grasp.

I price a can of asparagus and set it on the shelf. "So, do you have any?"

Mr. Bentz wipes the sweat off his forehead with the side of his hand. "If I did, I couldn't sell it to you." At the sound of a noise out front, he stills. "Did you hear the bell?"

I shake my head. He shrugs and keeps pulling out cans of corn. Creamed. Sweet. Mixed with carrots. He should charge extra for those, but what he prices things at is none of my business.

He stands and puts his hands on his hips. "What on earth would you need poison for anyway?"

The forced smirk doesn't quite mask the unease in his voice.

I pull the trigger on three more cans of corn—*click, click, click*—and set the gun down. "Have you ever eaten corn out of a container? I mean, like by itself?" I pick up a can of creamed and curl my lip. "This stuff is pretty much one step away from baby food." I make a gagging noise. "Emma made me eat it on a dare once."

My jaw twitches as I say my sister's name aloud, but I doubt Mr. Bentz is paying attention. By now, I'm certain he's tuned out my voice, which is how I know it's safe to ask again about the poison.

"Is hydrogen cyanide something you'd keep behind the counter?"

Mr. Bentz snorts. "Well I certainly wouldn't leave it out in the open."

I hand him the last of the canned corn and wait as he slits open another box. Tomatoes. Crushed, diced, halved. Is it a fruit or a vegetable? The debate continues. Me and tomatoes have a lot in common.

"I wouldn't need a whole lot of it," I say.

Mr. Bentz doesn't bother pricing the tomatoes. The smaller ones are $1.50, but the bigger containers—the kind I use for making chili and lasagna—are almost three. Unless you get them on sale, two for five bucks.

Five bucks, five bucks, five bucks.

It makes me giggle a little when Mr. Bentz says it. His voice drops and he rattles off the price like an auctioneer. Except there's no haggling with Mr. Bentz. Not even for my father, who's been buying his cigars here for more than fifteen years.

Mr. Bentz lifts another box onto the table. This time, I slice it open. The knife slides along the crease and shoots off the cardboard, narrowly missing Mr. Bentz's meaty hand. He pulls away with a curse. "And that is why I can't sell you hydrogen cyanide."

"Because I'm terrible at box cutting?"

His eyes dart to my bruised cheek, the result of another of my father's rampages. "You're clumsy."

"I'd be more careful with the poison," I say with an innocent grin, ignoring the reference to my repeated stories about falling down the stairs. He doesn't believe me—though it's not enough to prompt some kind of action. Call the police, child services, Father Buck. Is the price of my father's business worth the guilt of turning a blind eye?

The truth is, I'm being evasive on purpose about why I want the stuff. I've decided to turn the barn into a darkroom for Bridget—a place she can develop the images from our trip or our photo shoots without worrying that someone will rat us out to my father.

And actually, it's the rats I'm worried about.

I wasn't completely honest with Bridget when I told her about the mice in the barn. Oh, they're there too, but the rats are bigger. Not quite Rodents of Unusual Size big. Just big enough.

"You haven't even told me what it's for." Mr. Bentz glances at his watch. "Never mind. Go on, get out of here. I promised my wife I'd be home for dinner on time for once."

"Just one bottle," I say, my voice straining a little under the desperation. I've tried distraction, being helpful, stooped to near begging. If Mr. Bentz doesn't cave this time, I'll be forced to take alternative action.

He waves me off with a flick of his hand. "Forget it, Lizbeth," he says. "I'm not selling poison to a minor."

I'm not actually sure there's an age restriction on prussic acid, but arguing that won't help my case. It's my father he's afraid of. I chew on my lower lip, contemplating my next step. The problem is, I'm not sure where Mr. Bentz would *keep* something like that.

"Okay, maybe I'll just take a look and see if there's something else that might work."

Mr. Bentz scans the packing order, concentration making everything else around him fade to dark. I take advantage of the distraction to slip into the front of the store. I'm careful to avoid mirrors and cameras, weaving through the aisles in a strategic pattern that ensures there's no proof I'm anywhere near the cash register.

Ducking behind the counter, I crouch in front of the cabinet and carefully open it. A familiar thrill makes my skin pimple like sandpaper—I know it's a sin, but stealing stuff gives me an adrenaline rush. Maybe it's because I can control it, make conscious decisions, without the influence of my madness or putting the blame on my blackouts.

I shuffle around the items in the cupboard, pushing the fireworks and gun ammo to the back for a closer look at the labels on the bottles.

A noise behind me makes my stomach flip, but when I glance over my shoulder, there's no one there. The first pinpricks of unease ripple along my spine. Resuming my search, I locate the hydrogen cyanide and hold the bottle up toward the light. There's maybe a quarter cup, but that's enough.

I'm sure a couple of drops will take care of the rats.

Take the bottle and go.

With a racing heart, I tuck the poison into the waistband of my shorts, adjust my oversize T-shirt to hide the bulge, and creep from behind the cash counter. A wooden clock over the ice cream freezer tells me Mr. Bentz will close up shop in two minutes. It's now or never.

Go!

I go back to the storage room and poke my head inside the door. "No luck," I say. Mr. Bentz looks up, eyes glassy with confusion, and I keep talking. "I guess I'll need to figure out another way to deal with the rodents."

Mr. Bentz nods. "Traps," he mumbles. "They're in aisle four. Across from the kitchen gadgets."

23

B ridget wields her Swiffer like a glowing lightsaber, hold-ing it at arm's length to swat at the cobwebs and dust bunnies gathering in the corners of the sitting room. Her lips purse and a noise vibrates from between them.

"*Zzzt. Zzzt. Zzzt.* Take that!" she shouts, thrusting the handle at the bookcase. She spins, twirls the Swiffer, and jabs it at the ceiling. "And that!" Sweat glistens on her forehead and neck, but still she quickens her pace. Ducking, thrusting, manhandling the duster like it's a weapon of mass destruction. Dust particles swirl like tiny stars in the sunbeams that stream through the windows.

My pulse quickens. Bridget likes to think she's from *Star Wars*, but she's more like a fairy, sprinkling magic throughout the room, this place, inside my heart.

"Whoa there, young Skywalker," I say, reluctantly emerging from the shadows. I tuck my hands behind my back and rock on my heels, amused by her wide-eyed expression of shock. "I'm sure those spiders have turned to ash," I say, grinning.

Bridget recovers quickly, flicking her shoulder with a wink. "The Force is strong with me today." Her head tilts. "Hey, I thought you had a church function."

My stomach twists. I've managed to avoid Father Buck for more than a week, faking the flu to get out of teaching Sunday school, and extending my illness by two days to skip youth group. I'm unprepared for his questions about my absence, scared he'll also ask about Bridget. I shrug with as much non-chalance as possible. "Didn't feel like it."

I finger the cross around my neck and silently pray for forgiveness. Not long ago, missing a church function would have caused me to break out in hives, but I just keep thinking about the life I could have with Bridget. If I'm forced to choose, God won't win the battle for my heart. "Do you want to hang out?"

Bridget blows out a breath, curling the ends of her hair upward with the air. "Can't. The entire inn needs a dusting. I should do that before your father and Abigail get home—I don't want them to fire me."

A cloud of disappointment hovers over me. Now would be the perfect time to sneak to the barn and finish the surprise darkroom, but the thought of being away from Bridget leaves a gaping hole in my chest. The project can wait. "I'm not bad with a Swiffer."

Bridget hands one to me. "I think you mean lightsaber." She grabs a wet rag from a bucket on the floor and wrings it out. Water *drip, drip, drips.* "You swiff, I'll wash."

We work our way to the bookshelf, where I lightly run my finger along the spines of the classics: Dante's *Inferno, Romeo and Juliet,* a slew of Jack Kerouac. My father's private collection. There's a weathered copy of Stephen King's *It* tucked between Shakespeare's *Macbeth* and *Hamlet* that gives me a little thrill. Commercial fiction is forbidden in this house, but hiding that novel in plain sight was my first act of rebellion, however wasted. I doubt Father knows it's there.

"Who even reads these books?" Bridget says, wiping a shelf with the damp rag. "I mean, besides *Romeo and Juliet?*" She grins. "I'm a sucker for a love story." A pause, and then, "No matter how tragic."

My stomach does a slow roll.

At the fireplace, I dust the cobwebs from the rusty gate, skimming the Swiffer over the fire poker. *Swipe.* The pointed tip glistens, razor sharp. *Swipe, swipe.* I hold it over my head, staring down at Abigail's crown of graying hair.

"Lizzie?"

Swipeswipeswipe.

Bridget's stare is frank, concerned. "I asked if anyone had ever been stabbed with that thing." She points to the sharp utensil and grimaces. "You could skewer someone with it."

Swipe.

"I'm sixty percent sure it's been used only for firewood," I say, and then smile at my joke.

Bridget scrunches her nose. "Pity the other forty."

She stands on her tiptoes to wipe the mantel, swooping all the dust balls onto the carpet. Something gold glints from the pile of dirt. A key? I crouch down to pick it up and hold it at eye level, twisting the jagged edges between my fingertips.

Bridget's eyes glisten with mischief. "Maybe it unlocks some kind of treasure."

"Not in this place." My father collects nothing of true value, and even Abigail's meager jewelry is kept behind closed doors. She demands diamonds, and Father often complies, but it's his family heirlooms that she covets. "It's probably the key to Abigail's soul."

At this, Bridget laughs. The sweet melody cuts through the tension of my guilt, that persistent black aura that seems to follow me everywhere that Bridget isn't. She is the reason I don't succumb to its powerful pull, I know that now.

After a quick glance over my shoulder, I pocket the key and continue to clean. Bridget hums or dances. I'm trying to lighten up, but our discovery weighs heavy in my cardigan, piquing my curiosity. "Come," I whisper, and Bridget follows, though not without notable hesitation.

We tiptoe down the hall to the back staircase that leads to the master suite. I've not been in Abigail and my father's bedroom since Abigail moved in. My stepmother doesn't trust me with her things. As though she thinks I might steal her silk lingerie and gaudy pearl necklaces. What use would I have for them?

The wooden staircase creaks under our footsteps. I hold on to the banister with one hand, keeping my eyes straight ahead so I can navigate the gentle curve. Slow and steady.

Turn around.

If my parents come home early, we'll be trapped with no logical explanation for this. Bridget will be fired and forced to leave.

Everyone leaves.

Shrugging off the voice of reason, I slip the key in the lock and turn the handle. The door opens with a soft click. My pulse ratchets up.

"Lizzie . . ." Bridget's hushed voice cracks a little. "What are you doing?"

I peer inside the room, deflecting the paranoia in Bridget's tone with my own curiosity. A puff of cheap perfume hits me square in the face. I cover my nose with my palm and cough.

"Shit, that's like stepping into Macy's," Bridget says with a small giggle.

My heart is pounding like a kick drum. "Do you have anything I can cover my hands with?"

Bridget lifts an eyebrow. She reaches into her pocket and withdraws a pair of latex gloves, the kind she uses when washing the toilets. "Something like this?" I nod eagerly and her eyes darken. "Bit creepy, Lizzie."

"We can't leave fingerprints," I say, stepping across the

threshold. The room's smaller than I remember. It's all wood—cherry armoire, oak headboard, an empty bookshelf that might be walnut. Any traces of my mother have been stripped clean, except the floral wallpaper Mom wanted to replace. I trail my fingertips along the wall, looping around the swirls in the pattern.

"How about we just leave?" Bridget says. She shudders. "This place gives me the creeps."

My voice drops to a whisper. "Just a minute more."

Something doesn't feel right, like I'm missing something, some kind of leverage Abigail must be hiding. My eyes fall on the dresser. The second drawer is slightly open, begging to be explored. My pulse stutters. I kneel on the floor and push aside Abigail's underwear.

Bridget's breath whispers along my shoulder blades. "What are you doing? You're invading Abigail's privacy."

Annoyance chips away at me. It's not like Abigail hasn't been encroaching on my life since the minute she came to Fall River. Pushing herself on my father to take his money, his spirit, his life. Abigail no more belongs in this house than I do in her dresser drawer—but there is nothing either of us can do about it.

My fingers deftly explore the back of the drawer. I lift out a small cardboard box and give it a little shake. Something rattles, like jewelry. Or bones. Tiny baby bones. *Swipe*.

Inside there's fifty bucks, a gold watch, two pairs of

earrings, and a necklace that sparkles with red jewels. Rubies? Maybe. The color looks right. I slide the watch over my wrist. It's heavy, ugly and old, totally not my style. But I know how much it means to Abigail—and that's enough.

The clock across the room *click, clacks*.

"Come on, Lizzie, we should go." Bridget tugs on my sleeve. When she sees the item in my hand, she frowns. "Put that back. It's not worth the consequences if you're caught."

"So then we won't get caught," I say.

Bridget's back goes rigid. "Stay if you want, but I'm leaving."

Everyone leaves.

"Fine, we'll go." The gray shadow of paranoia begins to fade from Bridget's eyes. I go to stand, but something else catches my eye. I reach farther into the drawer and pull out the items stuffed at the back—a pearl necklace, a rare gold coin, a lace doily that was crocheted by my grandmother. Items and their memories, stolen from my mother and tucked away with Abigail's things.

"Lizzie, they're coming home."

I shove everything back into place, and then tiptoe into the hall. We creep down the stairs, my hand in my pocket, *tap, tap, tapping* against the antique watch.

If Abigail can steal my mother's things, I have no problem stealing hers.

24

I coil my fingers around the small bottle, thumb brushing against the rough edges of the faded label, tracing the letters C and Y.

My mind fills in the blanks. C—*raz*—*y*.

No, not *my* mind. Dr. Driscoll's. Father's. Abigail's. It's what they all think. Pieces of conversation flit around in my brain. Abigail and Father were on the phone with the doctor. Carefully, I picked up the second receiver, cupped my hand over the speaker, and listened.

"If she isn't taking her medication, wouldn't her symptoms get worse?" my father said.

Dr. Driscoll paused, cleared his throat. "Sometimes it takes a while for the medication to leave the system." Another pause, and then, "The patient"—my stomach twisted at such an impersonal label—"may experience moments of euphoria, a kind of calmness before the storm."

I imagined my father licking his lips, processing, rationalizing.

"I saw the pill in the toilet, Andrew," Abigail said. "She hasn't been taking them."

"That is a concern," Dr. Driscoll said.

"Are you suggesting that my daughter is crazy?"

I hung up before hearing the diagnosis, foolishly thinking that if I didn't listen, I could pretend the conversation hadn't happened at all.

The end result is that Abigail is back to feeding me the pills again—waiting until I swallow, forcing me to stick out my tongue to prove that they're gone. The alternative is a mental hospital, where I may never see Bridget again. And I will do anything—*anything*—not to let that happen.

I hold the bottle of poison up to the light and tilt it on its side. Clear elixir slides up the side of the glass. I *twist, twist, twist* off the cap and draw the bottle close to my nose. *Sniff.* The slight scent of bitter almonds trails under my nostrils.

Hydrogen cyanide.

Poison for rats, spiders, livestock, for—

Abigail?

I touch my cheek, tracing the outline of a fresh bruise, the result of Abigail's accusations about pawing through her things. I neither confirmed nor denied it, but Father made up his own mind about my guilt.

Just once I'd like him to give me the benefit of the doubt.

I set the bottle on the kitchen counter and crouch low so I can read the words, the ingredients. Fingernails chipped, I *scratch, scratch, scratch, scraaape* at the label, tearing, ripping, bunching paper and ink under my nails.

They're dark. Black as a raven's wings. Black as pitch.

As black as Abigail's cold heart.

Swipe. I picture her in the garden, bending over her rose garden, skirt rising *up, up, up* the back of her thighs. *Swipe.* She cranes her neck and stares at me. At me and Bridget. *Swipe.* She points a bony finger. *Come.* We don't. Can't. The windshield wipers *swipe, swipe, swipe* the image clear.

A swarm of wings flutter up along my rib cage.

I tear the last of the label off the poison bottle in one long strip and crumple it into a ball, squishing it into a tight mound of paper wet with sweat. *Squish, squish, squish.* I imagine crushing Abigail's skull with my thumb, twisting and turning.

Madness presses against my chest, eager for release. Some of it begins to seep out. I push harder on the counter and the paper, ink, bones flatten and tear. Fragments pepper the granite like snowflakes, each itty-bitty bit so different and unique. I gather them into my palm and fold over my fingers, pressing, rebuilding—

The skull.

The label.

I open my palm and stare at it before blowing the pieces into the sink. They are everywhere. I crank the tap—

Leave no evidence.

Water swirls down the drain, taking with it the bits and pieces of my stepmother's paper skull. I watch until it is going, going

Gone.

I move the bottle to the back of the counter, holding it open over raw hamburger, eggs, a pile of saltine crackers. The liquid heats in my palm. The acid inside hisses and snaps.

One drop.

Two.

My knuckles knead into the meat, threading the herbs and spices, the salt and poison through my fingers, squishing against the metal bowl and up over the lip. A clump rolls onto the counter. I scoop it up and lob it into the sink.

I lean toward the bowl and sniff. The scent of almond mixes in with rosemary and garlic, egg yolk and cow's blood. I wipe my hands on my apron and add two more drops of cyanide.

BAM! Meat loaf to die for.

I am totally kicking it up a notch.

I snap my head back and cackle. Softly at first, and then louder as the madness takes over my body, my mind. I screw on the cap, wipe off the bottle, dry, polish, and buff the glass until my distorted reflection ripples back at me.

Erase the evidence.

I hold the bottle over the garbage bin, but something pulls me back. A whisper of warning creeps along the back of my neck. I root through the junk drawer, gathering pens, markers, two very sharp pencils.

With the Sharpie, I trace the outline of a skull. An evil skull with bulging eyes and giant angry teeth. I draw an upside-down heart for a nose. Color the eyes in black. The tip of the marker *squeaks, squeaks, squeaks* across the glass.

Shadows.

Bones.

The details swirl to life with each pass of the pen. My outline gets darker, bolder, a thick, black warning to stay back, KEEP AWAY.

My fingers unfurl and the Sharpie falls to the ground, rolling under the fridge. I get on my hands and knees and peer into the darkness. A spider skitters inches from my face, taunting. It is unfazed by me, and me by it. We stare at each other, eight beady pupils against my wide snake eyes.

I sit up on my knees and reach behind me to grasp the poison. Carefully, I twist off the cap.

The spider doesn't move.

Not a single millimeter.

I am the spider; it is the fly.

I grip the bottle in my hand and tip it toward the floor. A drop of liquid rolls off the lip. "Come closer," I whisper. The insect raises a leg, and I grin. "Yes. Come closer, my friend."

Pressing my nose to the ground, I inhale the elixir. I touch the liquid, just barely a dot, and my skin tingles, goes instantly hot. *Dot and hot. Hot and dot.* The rhyming words go back and forth across my tongue like a device used for hypnosis.

The spider turns away, unharmed, and scampers deeper into the dark. I press my face to the floor and wait for my eyes to adjust. There's an apple core, dust, years and years of neglect. I don't remember when anyone last cleaned under the fridge.

Isla.

My eyebrows arch with confusion. Not Isla. Bridget. Abigail sent Isla away, fired her without notice. She left.

Everyone leaves.

Panic grips my heart like a fist and squeezes tight. I won't let her take Bridget from me too.

Swipe.

I push Abigail's face down into the floor. The weight of my boot digs into the back of her skull. *Sw—* I shake my head and step down harder. Abigail's mouth hovers over the poison. Her lips touch down. An animal cry belts from somewhere in her chest. *Swi—* No! I watch as her skin bubbles, boils, burns. And I laugh.

I laugh so hard my stomach shakes with it.

My throat goes raw and dry.

I keep laughing until every last drop of poison is gone. Until Abigail lies lifeless, limp, on the kitchen floor. Her body shrivels, shrinking into the liquid. The bubbles turn black as ash and lift off the floor. They float *up, up, up* toward the ceiling. Float until they—

POP!

Dark residue rains down all around me. I *sweep, sweep, sweep* it into a pile and then under the fridge, pushing it to the back. It coats the apple core, the dust, the spider with its eight beady eyes.

A thump at the front door causes me to startle.

Swipeswipeswipe.

My heart slams against my rib cage.

Father is home.

25

Bridget's low moan floats through the kitchen and buries itself deep under my skin. "Jesus, Lizzie. This just keeps getting better and better."

Cooked meat maggots hang from the corner of her mouth. She licks it clean and closes her eyes, as though savoring each and every bite. Her lips form a crooked smile. "Seriously. You could sell this stuff." She stabs another forkful and holds it up by her mouth. "I mean not just at the B and B. Like maybe the farmers' markets or whatever."

My mind wanders back to Boston, where street vendors hawked hot dogs and burgers, kettle corn by the paper cone. "I can't see people lining up for meat loaf." My face goes warm. "It's nothing special, really."

"Bullshit." Bridget hops up on the counter and dangles her feet over the edge. No socks—even though the air conditioner has thrummed steadily for two solid days. She nudges her head toward the window. "What time are you expecting Dr. Jekyll and Mistress Hyde?"

I wring my hands together. "Any minute now."

Bridget stuffs what's left of the meat loaf in her mouth and chews. "Did you add a new ingredient?"

"I'm not sure." My favorite recipe was burned, the contents of my journal now fertilizer for Abigail's rose garden. Sometimes I look out my bedroom window and dream of her flowers wilting, their leaves going dry and brittle, the petals turning black.

But they remain a deep crimson, the stubborn color of dried blood.

Bridget wags a shaky finger at me. "You need to write this shit down again." She swallows. "Have you heard from Le Cordon Bleu?"

I busy myself with tidying to mask my unease. Bridget asks the same question every day, sometimes following me to the mailbox like a puppy without a home. We walk with light feet, optimism guiding each step, and back—empty-handed—our shoes like bricks.

"It's still early," Bridget always says, but I'm starting to think it's actually too late. Is it possible my interview didn't go nearly as well as I'd planned?

I lop off another chunk of meat loaf to put in a Tupperware

container. The scent of burnt almonds curls under my nose. Odd. I don't keep nuts at the B and B—too many people have allergies.

Bridget eyes the meat loaf with suspicion. "You shouldn't give me seconds. They'll notice it's gone."

"I made two batches. Trust me, it's fine."

"I do," Bridget says softly. "Trust you."

I pretend like there's something stuck in my throat as relief seeps through me. Bridget is like a drug and I'm holding on like a dog with its jaws clamped around a bone. But lately it feels like she's pulling away.

The seed of doubt in the pit of my stomach grows and spreads like cancer.

Bridget hops off the counter and peers through the kitchen blinds. Her voce goes leaden with disappointment. "They're home." Her shoulders drop a little, so subtle I almost miss it. "I guess I'll get to . . . cleaning."

Abigail hasn't complained, so I guess she must be impressed—and she should be. Bridget scrubs, dusts, washes the floors, and pulls the sheets so tight you could bounce a quarter off them. In fact, sometimes that's our game, as pathetic as it may seem.

Often I watch her—dancing, singing, twirling through the rooms with the lightness of a ballerina. I guess I don't really know what she has to be happy about. I just know that *I'm* happy she's here.

Still here.

Bridget rubs her belly. "Maybe I'll just go to bed. My stomach is feeling a bit queasy."

My own guts twist into knots. "Nerves?"

"Flu, maybe," she says, though I'm not entirely convinced. Something niggles at the back of my mind, an ominous cloud of impending dread. I glance at the second batch of meat loaf cooling on the stove. The hair on the back of my neck stands upright.

Bridget pulls me in for a quick hug and brushes her lips against mine. "Thanks for the contraband."

My laugh is dead-ended by the sound of the front door opening. Abigail's Jimmy Choos click across the foyer and down the hall.

"Love you," Bridget whispers, and then slips out the back, just as Abigail and my father enter the kitchen.

My father's suit is impeccable as always, the cuff links silver today, his hair combed to the side with a swath of the same brand of gel he's used for ten years or more. The intensity of his stare turns my legs to Jell-O.

"Meat loaf?" he says.

I listen for disapproval, but his voice is light, almost teasing. I inch forward, training my nose to pick up the scent of alcohol—there's none. "A new recipe," I say, folding my hands together and holding them at my churning stomach.

In my peripheral vision, I catch Abigail rolling her eyes and my spine stiffens.

My father twirls the end of his new mustache around his finger, a smirk playing on his mouth. It's more trimmed than the kind he wore when Mom was alive, back in the days it tickled my cheek when he used to kiss me good night.

"Tonight, we'll eat together at the table."

I don't know what's put him in such a good mood, but I won't risk upsetting him now, not when relief flows freely through my veins, making me light-headed. A low whistle vibrates from between my lips as I gather plates, cutlery, three wineglasses, and linen napkins. I move quickly through the kitchen to set our places at the dining table, and then carefully carry the fresh meat loaf to the table.

Steam rises up from the pan, bringing with it the scents that soothe, even when I am at my darkest. My father leans over the pan and breathes deep. "Rosemary?"

A genuine smile creases my cheeks, as I dish up everyone's plate. "And garlic."

Abigail stabs at her meat loaf and shoves the whole fork into her mouth. For a split second, I imagine the tines lodging in her esophagus, blood trickling from her lips. *Swipe.*

"Lizbeth, this *is* delicious," my father says, funneling more and more into his mouth. I must be dreaming, because I could swear I hear pride. "Don't you agree, Abigail?"

Abigail looks up at me, her face tinged with green. She doubles over, and then jerks upright, mouth opening to spew vomit across the table.

26

The second time Abigail opens her mouth, she screams.

My father's head snaps to me. "What the hell is going on here?"

Abigail hunches over her plate, heaving. Her hand goes to her throat. The scent of bile curls under my nostrils and in an instant, I'm queasy.

"She's choking," Father says, his face white.

Abigail shakes her head and moves her hand from her neck to her mouth. "Water," she says, voice raspy and raw. "I need water."

My father goes to her. He takes one of the linen napkins and I stand frozen, watching as he pats at her cheeks. Gently he pulls his hand away and cleans up her mouth. I'm transfixed by his sensitivity, but there's an undercurrent of jealousy that thrums through my blood too. I remember when he used to be this tender with me.

Abigail lifts her head. Our eyes connect. "I need a bucket."

I run to the kitchen and root through the cupboards. Pots and bowls clank together, reverberating off my temples. A dull ache throbs at the base of my neck. I can't find a dang bucket, and with every passing second, I imagine Abigail's spool of patience unwinding.

Bucket.

Where in the world will I find a bucket?

As the answer becomes clear, unease creeps across my chest. The cellar. I grab a flashlight from the kitchen drawer, walk to the basement door, and unhook the thin latch with my thumb. The door groans open. I stare down at the darkness, every hair on the back of my neck rigid with tension.

I take my first tentative step.

Breathe in.

Take another.

Exhale.

The flashlight beam passes over thick cobwebs that dangle from the low wooden ceiling and tangle in my hair. I swat at my face. By the time I reach the bottom of the stairs I feel like an insect, silken threads coiled around my neck. I pull at them, but the choking sensation won't go away.

From upstairs, I hear Abigail's high-pitched scream.

I pan the small cement room with the flashlight. Images flit through the beam—a rusted saw, an oversize hammer, a broken hatchet. Wooden crates overflow with discarded junk. Behind them, I spot two pails and stagger toward them. A shiver slips under my shirt and crawls down my spine.

Get out.

It's been forever since I've been down in the cellar, but the feelings are as fresh today as they were five years ago. My first blackout—first menstrual cycle—where my mother found me, broken and scared, a puddle of blood between my legs.

Tears spring to my eyes. Mom never told me I was unstable, didn't blame me for my condition. I never *asked* for this.

Holding tight to the handles, I carry the buckets up the stairs, each step bringing me closer to the light. To air that isn't dense with memory and pain. I close the door behind me and lean against it, gulping for breath.

Upstairs, the toilet flushes and the pipes creak and groan.

The noise is enough to snap me out of memory and into action. In the kitchen, I gather water bottles from the fridge and hurry to the dining room with one of the buckets and my supplies. Father and Abigail are gone. I run to the stairway that leads to their private room and bound up the steps.

"Lizbeth?" Abigail croaks, which I take as invitation to enter.

She lies on her side, staring blankly at the door. Her eyelids flutter. "Come closer," she says, and then licks her lips.

I inch toward her, repulsed by the smell. There's a patch of wet vomit on her pillow, and chunks of vomit cling to her stringy hair. I set the bucket down, holding my breath. She wraps her cold fingers around my wrist and squeezes. I'm shocked by her strength.

"You did this."

I shudder. "I'm sure it's just the flu," I say, though it's a lie I'm trying to convince myself of. Something about this doesn't feel quite right.

"Food poisoning," Abigail says, her voice cracking.

I shake my head. "The meat was cooked all the way through." Chef Emeril taught me all about food safety, and how to prepare every type of animal protein. I've watched those episodes twice. Steak can be rare, a little pink is perfect, but not hamburger. Ground meat must be cooked all the way through. The rules are ingrained in me.

Abigail holds her hand close to her throat. "Poison."

"No, it has to be something else." My hands tremble, and my stomach twists and roils. "One of the guests is sick too." It's a bald-faced lie but I'm grasping at straws, deflecting the accusation, which rings a little too true at the back of my mind.

Abigail turns her neck toward me, and her eyes flash with evil. "You will pay for this."

My blood flushes with anger and I stiffen my spine. "I won't accept the blame, Abigail."

I won't.

Not this time.

Even if it is food poisoning, it's nothing *I* did. I remember measuring the ingredients, cracking the egg, folding in the crackers, the spices and herbs. And still, a nagging sensation lingers, a loose thread that needs knotting. *Swipe.* I stand at the kitchen sink, an unmarked bottle in my hand. *Swipe. Swipe.* The bottle tilts downward. A single drop curls over the lip . . .

Swipeswipeswipe.

Dear God, is it possible? A chill seeps into my bones. I glance nervously at Abigail. Her face is so pale . . . it's almost ghost white.

Her eyes flutter closed and her breathing stills. My heart leaps. I press my fingers to her clammy temple and pray for a pulse. It's faint, but there. My shoulders slump with relief. If she dies . . .

I shake my head, clearing the fear, leaning on logic. *Food poisoning.* That's all. Something sour in the eggs, or maybe tainted meat. I pull the blanket up to Abigail's chin and turn off the bedside light, then tiptoe to the bedroom door.

A low murmur of distress from the en suite bathroom freezes me in place. "Lizbeth?"

Father? I blow out a slow breath and creep to the bathroom door.

"Lizbeth," he says again, louder now. "I hope you brought a second bucket."

His request is punctuated with a spine-tingling retch.

27

The stench hits me first. Metallic, like blood.

I press my hip against the barn door, one hand on the handle, and draw in a steadying breath. Something evil lurks on the other side. My heart *thump, thump, thumps* against my rib cage.

Go inside.

Instinct tells me to run, to wait until morning. But I'm drawn to the barn, in search of refuge, safety, the kind of absolution the church is no longer able to provide. Abigail's voice rings in my eardrums. *Poison!* My father levels an accusatory stare at me, his lips swollen from throwing up.

I'm exhausted, beaten down by their relentless accusations. Now that they've finally fallen asleep, I am free to sneak out to the barn, find comfort in the family of pigeons I've been nurturing.

Except something isn't quite right.

Heat from the sun, long ago set, warms the handle. And still, my hands are cool, as if ice runs through my veins. My entire body vibrates.

I inhale a deep breath. The smell of death is cloying, seeping through my pores. Almost as though the smell is emanating from deep inside *me*.

I blink to clear the image and press my ear up to the door. The silence is eerie. Unnatural. I knock, a subtle *tap, tap, tap*. Rodents don't scurry. The pigeons don't flutter or chirp. I should hear *life*.

The sound of dead silence is almost worse than the smell.

Sweat trickles down my spine. I should call Bridget, my father, maybe even the police. But who would believe me? What evidence do I have? And of what?

Go back.

My mind, ever the prankster, is playing tricks on me. I have nothing to fear in here. Steeling myself for whatever ghost lurks behind the door, I shove it open. The handle rattles with enough noise to entice the deceased.

And still, nothing stirs.

I step across the threshold and stagger backward at the weight of the smell. It's the stomach-churning rot that I imagine blankets most murder scenes left too long before discovery.

Bile rises up into my mouth.

I flick on the light switch and the room clouds in a hazy red glow. Photography equipment sits on the workbench, most of it still in boxes and bags. A stack of glossy paper in thick wrapping, bottles of chemicals and strange-looking tools the salesman claimed necessary, but only Bridget will be able to explain. I'd hoped to finishing setting up her darkroom tonight—a way to get my mind off the evening's chaos—but my eyes burn and my throat is on fire.

I brace myself against the door frame and hang my head to temper the nausea.

My eyes lock on a stain on the floor. A rusty patch of burgundy, the color of dried blood. I cup my hand against my mouth and double forward. My palm fills with sticky saliva.

Not blood.

It can't be. I'm hallucinating, suffering some kind of episode, another trick of my mind. What is happening? *Breathe.* I inhale air that smells like death, and it slithers down into my stomach. *Blink, blink, blink.* The puddle is still there.

Not a puddle, a drop.

A tiny speck.

Just a pinprick's worth.

Swipe.

I close my eyes again, as though to reset my vision, and look away. A silvery-gray feather catches my gaze. The edges are torn, stained deep red. My adrenaline jacks up. I stumble toward it, making excuses, rationalizing, trying to explain. A cat, yes, that's it. It's come into the barn and—

Kill the pigeons.

A muted sob escapes from somewhere deep inside of me.

I stagger toward the ladder, my feet leaden with grief. I grip the side with one hand, the other dragging behind me as I climb to the loft. With each step, the smell heightens, grows more pungent and dense. I pause on the top rung, terrified to keep going, to turn back.

To *see.*

I already know what's there. Dead pigeons, their sanctuary violated, the result of some animal attack. A fluttering in my stomach warns me not to look.

I must.

At first I see nothing, and relief turns my head light. The makeshift nest looks intact, not destroyed. But the smell won't go away, won't disappear.

Carefully, I climb across the mattress and lean over the nest.

Swipe—

Blink.

—swipe.

I suck in a gasp. *Swipe.* A silhouetted figure stands above the nest. *Swipe. Swipe.* The sharp edge of a hatchet glints under the moonlight. *Swipe.* My eyelids blink closed and I squeeze tight, as if I can *push, shove, push* the images away.

But when I open my eyes, the horror is still there: a

half-dozen baby pigeons, stacked neatly on top of one another, their necks severed by the bloody hatchet that lies at their side.

Swipe.

The silhouette turns so that I can make out the face.

My breath hitches.

Swipeswipeswipe.

It's me.

28

A guttural scream bursts from my chest.

I grasp the hatchet, raise it over my shoulder, and swing down at the thin mattress. The blade slices, hacks, tears through the surface. Tears stream down my cheeks and trail into my mouth. I chop away at the mattress, funneling my anguish, my grief, my feral anger into it.

Without even touching the pigeons, not one bloodied feather, their corpses are all over me, the decay and sadness—in the grooves of my thumbprints, threaded through my hair. The reek of evil and loss, creeping out from a disjointed memory and back into life.

Swipe.

I blink through my tears, try to *blink, blink, blink* the images away.

They don't fade.

Refuse to disappear.

Could I have done this?

Another cry belts from my lips. I crumple to the mattress and lay my head against the bloodstained hatchet. The cool blade digs into my skin. I cry out in pain, and then burst into tears.

My shoulders shake.

"Lizzie?"

The voice is so quiet, a whisper through the dark. I lift my head and listen. The thick silence makes my skin tingle.

"Lizzie?"

Bridget.

There is an undertone of fear in her voice this time, and my stomach begins to churn. I can't hide. I'm not able to disappear. But she cannot see me like this.

I peer over the edge of the loft, look to where she stands below, and hold my hand up to shadow my face. A thin night-gown billows at her feet. She looks up, our eyes meet . . . I am paralyzed by shame.

Bridget looks at me in a way that makes me feel like a thing that crawled from the sewers. Like I'm a decrepit, crooked, beastly thing, an evil to be feared. Is this who I have become?

"What have you done?"

The stark cruelness of the question takes my breath away. "My father . . ."

Her voice trembles. "Should I go get him?"

My head snaps upright and I feel my eyes go so wide, it's conceivable they may *pop, pop, pop* out of my head. My first instinct is to blame someone else, but this is not my father's work. "Please, no . . ."

Bridget moves to the base of the ladder, and my stomach twists and turns. I can't let her see this morbid scene.

See what I have done.

"I'm coming up there," Bridget says.

I slowly lift the hatchet.

She steps on the first rung, looks up. Her eyes lock on the weapon and she freezes midstep. The color drains from her face. "You should come down here," she says, working hard to sound calm. The tremble in her voice betrays her fear.

I shake my head. "Go away, Bridget."

Her spine goes rigid. "I won't leave you like this, not when it's clear you're—"

Not well.

My sister's words echo at the back of my mind and make my pulse race. "There is nothing wrong with me."

Bridget's response jumbles up in my head. Everything she says is like radio static, amplified as though I'm listening over a stereo.

. . . episode.

. . . we . . . get you . . .

. . . help . . .

"Enough," I say, covering one ear. "Just go, Bridget. . . ."

"Lizzie, you can trust me." A vibration of untruth cuts through her bravado.

"I didn't do this. . . ." A sob leaks into my voice, a touch of denial that doesn't quite ring true. "I didn't kill the pigeons."

See what I have done.

"Of course you didn't," she says quickly, but I can read the truth in her furrowed brow. Panic sweeps across my flesh as I realize she intends to come up the ladder. I can't let her—no one should ever see the severed heads of these poor pigeons. Bridget exhales a sharp breath. "But who would do this, Lizzie?"

I have no response.

"Maybe we should call the cops," she says. "Or . . . ?"

The question of my mental health hangs in the air, and I'm sure she'd call Dr. Driscoll if she had the number.

"No police," I say quietly, and then with more force. The madness inside me pulses like a second heartbeat, growing stronger, more intense. I have to get Bridget out of here. "No police!"

Bridget nods.

I shuffle forward and perch on the edge of the loft bed, dangling my feet. A bloodied feather drifts from the bottom of my shoe, somehow stuck there. My arm feels heavy, so, so heavy. I slump forward. . . .

Bridget screams my name and I jerk alert.

"You need to come down here right now," she says.

Numb, I climb onto the ladder. Step one rung at a time, *down, down, down,* until finally I reach the floor. I don't turn around right away, afraid to face Bridget's disgust, her disappointment, her *doubt.*

She puts a hand on my shoulder and spins me toward her.

I stare down at the floor so as not to look at her, but her thumb catches under my chin and lifts it so we're eye-to-eye. Her gaze flits to my forehead. She licks her finger and rubs at my skin, gently, erasing the blood I know is wedged in the creases.

"The pigeons—"

"They're dead," she says.

I swallow hard.

She leans closer. "Did you—?"

I choke on a sob and shake my head. "I don't know."

But I know Bridget will see through the lie. Fresh tears gather in my eyes. My chest feels heavy, weighted down by a torrent of emotions that rise and fall like tidal waves against a jagged rock cliff. I stand at the precipice, ready to jump.

"We'll get you help, Lizzie," Bridget says.

She sounds sincere, but there's something else in her eyes, and it makes my stomach sick. Bridget finally looks how she should in Fall River: scared to death.

CHAPTER

29

The pigeons are dead."

My father's jaw tenses, but he doesn't look up from his desk, doesn't have the respect to listen when I talk. Nothing new there.

"What are you going on about now, Lizbeth?"

A wave of nausea washes over me. It's been a week and I still hear their chirps in my mind. Their baby heads—or whatever was left of them—float behind my eyes at breakfast, in the kitchen, plucked from the middle of my dreams. It's like I'm carrying a chalice of those severed heads with me everywhere, their beady eyes following me from my nightmares into the waking hours of morning light.

I stiffen my spine and ball my hands into fists at my side. "The pigeons in the barn."

He glances up, his eyebrows pinched with confusion, and shakes his head. "For God's sake."

My father's tone nips at the last vestiges of my calm. Beneath the surface I'm broken and confused, still grappling with the belief that I could actually kill the very birds I'd sworn to protect. But it's the anger that simmers on top that scares me, turns my thoughts dangerous.

Murderous.

Swipe.

I brush away the tears gathering in the corners of my eyes. "I found them in the loft, their heads severed," I say, swallowing. "But then I guess you already know that."

Father tosses his pen on the desk and lifts his gaze. "Because you think I killed them?"

My voice chokes up a little. "You had motive." It's a weak argument, I know, but I need my father to confirm somehow that it was me, give me irrefutable proof that I could do something so terrible, so cruel.

Annoyance flickers in my father's dark eyes. The wrinkles on his forehead are more pronounced, his cheeks appear sunken, his complexion pale. When did his hair begin to turn so gray?

"I don't have time for this today, Lizbeth."

My stomach clenches. "Time for me," I say. "Isn't that what you meant to say? I suppose I should be used to that." A spark of irrational fury rushes up my esophagus, burning at the tip of my tongue. "You killed them, didn't you? Just like you promised." *Please, God, let this be true.*

But their tiny helpless faces peer up at me, pleading for me to save them, protect them. And seconds later, their tiny eyes bulge out with fear—of me. The truth is right in front of me, but I won't, can't, believe it. "It didn't matter that I gave them a sanctuary, a place to be—"

Free.

My father stands, pushing his desk so hard the front lifts off the ground. A picture of my mother topples off the edge and hits the floor with a *crack*. The frame splits, the glass spiderwebs across my mother's face. A sob catches in my throat.

I hate this picture, the sad look in her eyes, the way her brother's arm drapes across her shoulder with a kindness that he no longer possesses. I haven't seen my uncle since Mom's funeral. Not so much as a birthday card, a phone call, an obligatory check-in—just gone, erased, as though he never existed at all.

Everyone leaves.

"Now look what you've done," my father says, his tone choked with emotion.

See what I have done.

He comes around to the front of the desk and we stoop in unison to pick up the frame. His head knocks against my cheek, and I cry out in pain. My father's eyes go wide with alarm. He puts his finger to my face. "Jesus, Lizbeth. You're such a damn klutz."

Tears spring to my eyes, and I yank away from his touch. "Get away from me, murderer."

"For Christ's sake, Lizbeth." My father sets the broken picture on the desk and calmly, methodically, picks up his phone.

Panic swells in my chest. "Who are you calling?"

"Dr. Driscoll," he says. I lunge for the receiver and knock it out of his hand. His cheeks flush crimson. "This is out of control, Lizbeth. *You* are out of control." Hands on his hips, he begins to pace. "I'm at my wit's end here."

My voice drops to a whisper. "I'm not crazy." I take a breath. Exhale.

I squeeze my eyes shut, blocking the sheen of blood that clouds my pupils. Blood from the pigeons, the birds I was supposed to protect. Someone else had to have done it—because the alternative is terrifying and surreal.

My voice cracks. "Why are you always punishing me?"

Father's eyes go glassy and he tilts his head to the side. Behind his insincerity, I catch a glimpse of the truth—the subtle way he shifts the conversation to make this my fault, to try and convince me I'm unstable, fragile. A *psychopath*.

Is it possible they're right?

I'm so mad I could spit. "You don't believe me. *In me*. You never have."

He hangs his head. "Grow up, Lizbeth. You're acting like a little girl." He lifts his eyes to meet mine. "Is it possible . . . ?" He struggles a little to finish the sentence, but I know what's on his mind. "Your episodes have become worse."

Not a question. I shake my head. "No, I—" But the protest dies on the tip of my tongue.

My father licks his lips. "I spoke to Eli Bentz, Lizbeth," he says, and a chill skips along my spine. "His security cameras caught you stealing the poison—"

I hold very still.

"—and that damn kitchen gadget or whatever it was."

I cock my head. "What are you talking about?"

"There's no point denying it," he says. "I paid Eli so he wouldn't charge you, but you're going to pay me back. I hope that citrus peeler was worth it. Probably paid extra for that godforsaken color," he scoffs.

Confusion shakes through me. I've been stealing from Eli Bentz since the summer after Mom died. A pack of gum, a chocolate bar, a small toy that could fit in my pocket. Ever since he found out I have been stealing, my father deals with it all under the table, paying for my indiscretions without making a fuss. Maybe it started out as a way to get Father's attention. I'm not even sure anymore. But obviously Mr. Bentz is confused—or lying. Because I didn't steal a citrus peeler—that was a gift from Bridget.

For my birthday.

She bought it when we were in Boston.

My father runs his hand through his hair. "I can't protect you if you don't talk to me."

My heart pounds and my mouth turns dry. *"Protect me?"* I laugh without humor. "All you've ever wanted is to keep me here, trapped in this house."

His eyes darken. "Where else would you go? You should be

grateful you have a job, a roof over your head. It's more than a woman—"

My pulse ratchets up. "Don't you dare make this about gender," I say through gritted teeth. Mom used to say my father believed men and women had different roles because he was a traditionalist, but I know better—he's a misogynist, and there's a very big difference. "You think I won't leave, but I will. Just watch."

My father reaches out to put his hand on my wrist. I yank away as if burned. "Don't touch me." His eyes widen in shock, and for a split second, I feel shame.

A flash of anger crosses his face and I know I should stop, quit while I'm ahead, but I can't. I'm prodding, poking, forcing some kind of reaction, to be punished for the acts I commit when the madness takes over and spirals out of control.

My father doesn't disappoint. "Are you out of your mind?" His temples pulse, pupils cloud over. I take a step back. "I've had enough of your disrespect." He lifts his hand, and I stare it— him—down. "Do you understand me, young lady? Enough!"

Red flashes in front of my eyes and they're there again. The birds, their severed heads and beady eyes, staring, accusing. I wanted them to be free, to show that they could escape their fate. But maybe I'm just like them, destined to die in my childhood home, the ghost of my mother forever disappointed at what I can never become.

I choke back a sob.

My father moves toward me and I turn away, slamming my hip into the side of his desk. I cry out in pain. He grabs my wrist and twists. My elbow smacks the lamp. It crashes to the floor and breaks into pieces of wood and glass. I pull my arm back and take a wild swing at the air. My father tries to block the hit. His hand slips above me and slaps awkwardly against my cheek.

"Lizbeth, stop!"

I raise my fist again, and this time his block is successful. He grabs both of my hands and squeezes hard enough to make me flinch. My skin goes all tingly and numb. Bits of memory flash like strobe lights through my vision, bright, dull, bright, dull—

Swipe.

I grab the letter opener off his desk and raise it over my head. *Swipe.* I jab it into the side of his temple. *Swipe. Swipe.* Blood spurts, spurts, spurts from the hole. He turns toward me, eyes wide, mouth open—

Swipeswipeswipe.

"I think you should leave," my father says, voice eerily calm. I search his face for blood, for some kind of injury, but there's nothing more than the shell of the man he's become since my mother's death. It's worse now that Emma's gone. Maybe we're all just empty shells.

His eyes cloud with sadness and he shakes his head. Slowly he returns to his desk and slides into his chair. I can feel the weight of his frustration, his confusion, but I shrug it off. He sighs. "I wish . . ."

I know what he wants—because they're the same impossible dreams we both share. For Mom to come back. For Emma to be home. To turn back the clock to when things were different, simpler, to a time when Father loved us almost as much as he loved our mother, to when *I* was good enough. All the hateful things he has ever said come flooding back, and my knees buckle under the pressure.

"Lizbeth, you killed the pigeons."

I can feel the color drain from my face.

My father reaches into his desk drawer, grabs a handful of pictures, and tosses them across the surface. They skid to a stop in front of me. The images are grainy, printed off a computer rather than professionally processed. I pull one close, squinting.

My head goes light. The picture is of me, standing in the barn loft, with a hatchet raised in the air. It's probably just the way the camera light catches in my eyes, but I could swear they're glowing red.

"I took that off video footage," he says, his voice cool as steel. A sickness curls in my stomach as I realize he's put security cameras in the barn too. What else has he seen?

"You can look at it if you want," he says. "But it's very graphic."

Hazy polka dots cloud my eyes. I *blink, blink, blink,* but they're still there. Growing bigger and fatter, spreading across my vision like poison, a creeping, ominous gray that eventually . . .

Fades to black.

CHAPTER

30

I peer out the kitchen window, through the dust and grime, searching for the kind of light that only Bridget can bring.

There's no sign of her, and I worry she's slipping through my fingers like fine grains of sand, distancing herself from me, my episodes, the ever-present sense of foreboding that cloaks this house in darkness.

I nudge the blinds closed to avoid distraction and turn on the sink, rinsing my hands under hot water before I grate the lemons lined up neatly on the cutting board. Lemon loaf will lure Bridget back.

Chef Emeril murmurs through the iPad tucked into the cupboard.

From the cabinet on the opposite side I pull down the canister of flour, the baking powder, and salt. My throat hums out a familiar tune, and before I even find the measuring cups, my feet feel lighter. I grab the wooden spoon, twirl in a circle, and freeze.

My distorted reflection shimmers through the microwave. I step closer, peering at myself in the glass. Even in the shadowy image, I can see the outline of a fresh bruise on my cheek. I'm sure that's why Bridget left for the day. Why she needed a break.

I shrug off my negative thoughts—they won't bring Bridget back—and return to making Bridget's lemon loaf.

I've wanted to believe for so long that there is something inside of me so wretched that no one could love—it's so much easier than accepting the truth—but then Bridget's attention, her passionate affection, would be fake.

I refuse to believe that.

The grater scrapes against my knuckles and I pull back, shocked. My skin is torn, raw, flecked with blood. "Damn it," I whisper. As soon as the curse even leaves my mouth, guilt punches me in the gut. It's been weeks since I've gone to church. I've skipped Sunday school, the annual bake sale. I've even started to swear.

I reach for the gold cross at my neck, but the chain is bare. How long has it been since I've worn it?

Unexpected tears spring to my eyes and I shake them away. My strength in our Lord has always guided and soothed me, paved a path that is both devout and true. These past months have been difficult, each a test to strengthen my faith, not destroy it. Doubt is common, even natural, I would advise my students. There have just been so many distractions. . . .

I imagine their eyes staring up at me with expectation. How many would notice the lie?

Our Lord Jesus Christ has sacrificed for us, Father Buck would preach. *What sacrifices are you willing to make?*

Bridget?

No. I am not willing to sacrifice her.

As I sift together the dry ingredients, my mind tiptoes through the coveted crevices of my memory, re-creating every tender moment we've shared. Her hand in mine as we walked the winding path through the Public Garden, her laughter, her tears, every subtle wink behind my stepmother's back, hours spent in my bedroom playing the same games over and over. Twenty Questions, tic-tac-toe, Italian Rummy. A subtle touch as we pass each other in the hallway, a whispered joke in the dining room after Abigail has left the table. Bridget's soft lips pressed against mine.

My heart flutters. No, I am certainly not willing to sacrifice Bridget. She's already shown me so much, taught me so much, already means—

So much.

If not Bridget, then perhaps it is my calling I'm willing to give up? For how can I serve a God who will not tolerate my love for Bridget?

BAM! Emeril shouts at the screen, drawing my attention to another of his specialty meals. It's roast beef, drizzled in dark chocolate and blue cheese, the picture on the screen so vivid I can almost smell the cocoa. Defeat settles on my shoulders. How will I ever be able to cook like this?

I add in two eggs, a quarter cup of canola oil, and measure out the sugar. The scent of lemon tickles my nose, and I wriggle it while I *stir, stir, stir*, blending the ingredients until the mixture is smooth and pale.

The sound of a vehicle outside makes my ears perk up. I creep over to the window and peer through the slats in the blinds. It's too early for Abigail and my father to have returned from the city—another opportunity for Abigail to shop, for my father to complain. He's been doing more of that lately, but last night, as I lay in bed listening to the hushed whispers of another argument, I heard my father mutter, "I should just sell this shit hole."

I hate this place, and I understand how a house can both absorb and exude pain, how memories can step through the floorboards and hang from the rafters as if in wait. But this is all I've ever known. A shudder slithers down my back.

The red truck parked in front of the B and B is not familiar. Perhaps it belongs to the new handyman Father has hired? I crane my neck for a better view, but the doorbell buzzes, making me jump. My pulse skips.

I wipe my hands on my apron and then, realizing it's still

stained with cow's blood from the meat loaf, I untie it, and drape it over the counter, revealing an apron-shaped silhouette on my dress. I am covered in flour.

The bell buzzes again, followed by a sharp rap.

"I'm coming," I call out, though there's no way the person on the other side of the door can hear me. Quickly I walk down the hall, trying desperately to ignore the eyes that follow me from the pictures in the wall. Family I haven't seen in years, some already dead, others just simply . . . gone.

Everyone leaves.

Abigail wants to rip these pictures down, and for once we're in agreement.

Three buzzes come in rapid succession and my patience snaps. I swing open the door.

The man standing on the front step stares at me. Unblinking. At first I don't recognize him—the crew cut, the loose-fitting coat. His stomach is fuller, and his close-cropped mustache is peppered with gray. Whatever resemblance this man shared with my mother no longer exists. "Uncle . . . John?"

"Lizbeth," he says with about as much warmth as a stranger.

A bubble of anxiety bounces around in my gut. "What are . . . what are you doing here?"

His gaze drops to the worn suitcase at his feet. The leather is faded, torn, and stained.

"Oh," I say, still confused.

Upon closer inspection, I note that his slacks are faded too, and the collared shirt that hangs off his shoulders is soiled. There is even mud on his shoes.

Our eyes meet, and in his, I find disdain. There may have been a time when Uncle John looked at me with kindness, but my mother's death extinguished the light in his eyes, along with any affection he had for me. It's been so long since I've seen him that I'm tempted to pinch myself.

"I have business with Andrew," he says.

I am instantly on alert. The long-standing feud between Father and my uncle is a Borden legend. Mom's brother never understood why she'd married a man more attached to his wallet than his family, a man who believed women could never rise to any significant social status—but Uncle John never saw the good times, those authentic moments that bound us together then and make me desperately cling to hope that things will someday return to normal.

That's the trouble with people sometimes: they only hear what they want.

"My father isn't home," I say, voice hardening.

"He's expecting me," Uncle John says with another nod toward his suitcase. I consider calling my father to verify, but something holds me back.

"You'll be staying with us, then?" I lean up against the door frame, steadying myself, my hand pressed so tight against the wood that it's gone translucent. *I am a ghost.*

"Yes."

"Right." I draw in a breath and bend to grab his suitcase, but he beats me to it, as if to remind me that I am not welcome to touch his things, like I'm somehow personally responsible for his misery, my mother's death, the war that rages between our families. He's always been angry at my father, but with the peacemaker gone, that hatred now extends to me.

Much as I hate to admit it, the fact of that stings.

I'd hoped things could be different. That maybe his sudden appearance after all these years was a symbol of positive change, rather than a harbinger of doom that hovers over his head like a storm cloud.

Gathering myself, I stand taller, exuding a confidence I don't feel. "Follow me to your room."

As he does, I sense his eyes on my back, burning through my dress. I imagine him cataloging my appearance, judging and criticizing. Once upon a time he would have complimented me, but it's clear now I'm no different from a casual acquaintance. Regret tugs on my heartstrings. Why did our family fall apart?

I take him to the smallest suite, where the pink duvet is faded like watered-down blood, the wallpaper peels like lemon rinds to reveal the dirty drywall beneath, and the carpet writhes with distant memories.

"I see some things haven't changed," Uncle John says, his

face pinched with disgust. "Your father is still the same old cheap son of a bitch." Every cell in my body begs me to say something, but I've got no credible defense. Uncle John tsks. "When is he expected home?"

"Soon, I hope." I sweep my hand toward the bed. "Until then, please make yourself comfortable. If you're hungry, I made a fresh meat loaf last night. There are leftovers in the kitchen."

Uncle John nods curtly. "I remember you being quite good in the kitchen." Despite myself, a shy smile creeps onto my face. Bridget keeps telling me to get "back in the saddle"— this is the first meat loaf I've made since the food poisoning incident. My blood thrums with nervous energy. "Your mother always enjoyed watching you cook," he says. "She'd be pleased to see you haven't given that up. How would you describe this meat loaf of yours?"

My cheeks burn. "It's killer."

CHAPTER

31

Uncle John's shadow enters the kitchen before he does. It's bigger, more menacing in some ways, than my father's, and a sharp reminder of my mother, who always made a grand entrance. Her smile could light up a room.

My father used to call her Sunshine, back when he used terms of endearment to charm his family instead of his backhand or wallet. *Sunshine.* Before she died, Mom started calling me Moonbeam, her beacon of light in the inky dark of her illness. I doubt somehow that Uncle John would understand.

Unlike my mother, my uncle doesn't come into the room with a smile. His perpetual frown precedes him, and it at once erases thoughts of my mother. I refuse to further taint her memories with the darkness of my here and now.

The scent of freshly baked lemon loaf fills the space, but even it can't evaporate the smell of disdain that lingers so close to my mouth I can taste it, bitter like citrus rind. Uncle John's cologne—so familiar from my youth—is overbearing, and the hair in my nostrils curls in revolt.

"You mentioned there were some leftovers," he says, by way of greeting.

I nod, immediately walking toward the fridge, where I pull out the leftover meat loaf. There's lots, since Abigail refuses to eat it now, which suits me just fine. If I make it into Le Cordon Bleu, *this* will be my signature dish, and by the time I step onto campus, I want it to be perfect.

As I move around the kitchen, Uncle John studies his surroundings.

Does he notice the subtle changes in the atmosphere? The walls are the color of grapefruit, except for one, where I've left the floral wallpaper my mother painstakingly applied herself while six months pregnant with me. It's silly to believe in spirits, but sometimes that wall is the only thing that staves off the loneliness her dying has left behind.

Antique pots and utensils hang from hooks screwed into dark-wood hanging shelves piled with cookbooks, recipe card holders, and Mom's collection of salt and pepper shakers that shimmer under the overhead fluorescents. Bridget dusts them weekly, commenting on each with a humor that leaves my stomach sore from giggling.

Uncle John doesn't smile when he stares at them.

"I gave all those to your mother," he says.

Not all. The bride and groom Mom bought herself at a shop in Maine, where she and Father spent a week honeymooning, back when I think they loved each other. "If you want to take a seat in the dining room, I'll bring it out to you once it's heated," I say, willing my uncle to leave. His presence is unnerving. He's unpredictable. Cagey. The kind of guy who always has an ace—or a trick—up his sleeve.

"I hate that place," he says.

I can't imagine he likes anything about this house, but it makes sense he'd avoid the dining room, the last place he saw my mother alive. I know he blames my father, this house, this town, for Mom's death, but Father never laid a hand on her—ironic, perhaps—and she loved Fall River maybe more than she loved my father. More than she loved anyone, even me.

"I can bring it to your room if you prefer."

"I'd rather eat here," he says. "It's marginally cleaner."

He takes a seat at the small table in the corner of the kitchen, settling into Bridget's spot. I want to tell him to leave, that the seat is reserved, but the last person I want Uncle John to know about is Bridget.

I sneak a glance toward the window, grateful, for once, that she isn't home.

Carefully unwrapping the meat loaf, I put a generous

chunk in the microwave and set the timer for two minutes. As I wait for it to heat up, I busy myself with things that don't allow me to make eye contact. Thinking of my uncle as family fills me with disgust, so I pretend he's a stranger. I pull down a dish from the cupboard—one of Abigail's finest in hopes he breaks it—and fill a glass with cool water. I drop a lemon wedge in the top and set the drink in front of him— the stranger—without actually looking at him. Condensation from the glass coats my fingers. I wipe them on a dishrag, head down.

The buzzer on the stove chimes, a welcome reminder to take out the lemon loaf. It's then that I smile. The top is light brown, and the lemon peels I sprinkled over a bed of light sugar have curled into perfect arcs.

Pride swells in my chest, and for a second I forget how uncomfortable I am in my uncle's presence and remind myself that the kitchen is my sanctuary. I set the meat loaf in front of him.

"I'll have a slice of that loaf, too," he says without looking up.

My heart falls into my stomach. "This is for a special occasion."

He gives me a wolfish grin. "What could be more special than a visit from your uncle?"

I begrudgingly lop off a chunk and set it on a napkin. "You sure waited long enough," I mutter under my breath.

The fact that Uncle John never even tried to make contact after Mom died still stings.

I wait while he takes a bite of his dinner, anticipation simmering beneath my unease. I shouldn't want his approval, his praise . . . and yet . . . In this way, I am perhaps most of all like my mother. Despite his flaws, he was her hero, and I long for that kind of a connection with a father figure.

Uncle John chews without comment. I tuck my hands behind my back and rock on my heels.

"You're just like your mother," he says with a grunt. "Fidgety. That woman never could keep her hands still."

I lean against the kitchen counter. My elbow rubs against a stack of photographs from Bridget's camera—not the pictures from Boston, because something happened to the camera and none of them turned out. My stomach twists with fresh disappointment. Bridget says we'll have more adventures, more memories, but I'll always cherish the first. I skimmed through the selfies last night, searching each image for *something* not quite right. Bridget told me to look closer, deeper, but I don't get what she's trying to say. The only thing I keep seeing is me—an alternate version of me. Relaxed, happy . . . free.

What could possibly be *wrong* about that?

I continue tidying my work space as the silence between me and my uncle stretches on. I take my notebook out from the kitchen drawer—the pages fresh and crisp, a new journal that's hardly been used—and skim the menu I've planned for a week at the B and B. Meat loaf on Monday, of course, because the new guests expect it. Burgers on Tuesday, with as much garlic as I can get away with. On Wednesday, we'll have pasta, a special ode to Bridget and her Italian adventures. But by Thursday, I'm stuck.

"You look like your mother too," Uncle John says. My chest convulses with a pang of sadness. Slowly I turn around, expecting a sneer. But Uncle John looks thoughtful, a little sad, as though being here has dredged up memories, and he's realized not all of them are so bad. "I wondered how much of her I'd see in you."

"You could have come sooner," I say, no longer able to contain how I feel. I was so young when we lost her, and Father . . . he went to a dark place. Emma tries—tried—but we've all had to deal with our grief. *I needed you.*

"I tried." Uncle John sets down his fork and takes a sip of water. His tongue swipes across his top teeth. "Your father wouldn't have it. My letters were returned unopened, my phone calls unanswered."

A cavernous hole opens up inside me, and from it spews a fluttering of emotions. "My father never told me any of that. . . ."

Uncle John snorts. "And risk losing you?"

My eyes go wide. "Losing me?"

He pushes his plate aside and dabs the corner of his mouth with the edge of the linen napkin. His mannerisms are so like my mother's that I get sucked back into her world. I *miss* her. Him. The family we once were.

"A few years back, I came to the B and B, Lizzie. I had every intention of taking you and your sister home with me." His eyes shimmer. "My sister would have wanted that." He looks away. "Your father refused to let you go. Said you needed to stay here . . ."

Trapped.

". . . close to your mother's memories and things." Uncle John sighs. "And at the time, I guess it made sense. I don't know, maybe I should have tried harder. Should have gotten you out of here."

My heart thrums like a hummingbird. "Yes," I say simply. "You should have."

Because now I don't know if I'll ever be able to leave.

32

My father's voice reverberates through the thin wall that separates the dining area from the lobby, where I've been sitting, hands under my butt, for the past hour. It's strategic that my father is hosting the meeting in *that* room, the very room Uncle John abhors. Both will use whatever advantages they can. Which is perhaps why Father didn't bother acknowledging Uncle John last night, prolonging the inevitable blowout that is happening now.

Their insults ping-pong back and forth until I can't tell who's ahead, only that I despise them both the same. I tuck my head between my knees to block the sound, but their voices carry over the constant buzzing.

"You killed her," my uncle shouts, for what may be the tenth time.

There's a loud crash, a shattering of glass. I squeeze my eyes shut. *Swipe.* "I never laid a hand on her," my father yells back.

That much is true. For all my father's faults, his love for my mother was concrete. But Uncle John isn't far off the mark either. Mom had found an experimental treatment, a medical procedure that wouldn't grant her immortality but would prolong her years with us—with me—by a half dozen. Maybe more.

Father refused to pay for it.

Too big a risk.

Too expensive.

Too public.

End of story.

There is another bang from the dining room. A guttural scream that makes me flinch.

"You've always been a cheap son of a bitch," Uncle John says.

"You dare insult me in my own home?"

I picture Father standing over my uncle, hands on his hips, trying to use his considerable height to his advantage. My uncle's no pushover, though—he's shorter, but stocky, with arms that resemble tree trunks.

"My sister's estate should have been divided between us," Uncle John says. "The remainder to her children." He grunts with disgust. "Not wasted on this piece-of-shit business. My suite is filthy. Infested with spiders, for God's sake."

That is a lie. It has to be.

Bridget is terrified of spiders. Those I haven't killed, she's massacred with insect repellant and a strict cleaning regimen that begins with batting at loose cobwebs with a broom that's stretched as far away from her body as possible. That bedroom might not have fresh paint and newly replaced rugs, but it could pass a white glove test. That I know for sure.

"The children will have this B and B when I'm gone," my father bellows. Another lie, given what I know of his plans to sell it. "Do you think it's cheap to run?" He launches into a list of things *he* must care for: maintenance, upgrades, staff wages, paint, gardening supplies, heat, power, *Internet*. All lies. We haven't had Wi-Fi since Emma left for college, and the only thing my father has lifted in the past two years is his hand.

"If your sister had been more frugal . . ."

Another crash; this time I'm sure it's the china cabinet. A noise overhead lets me know someone else heard it too. Abigail? Bridget?

"My sister?" Uncle John gasps, and I can imagine steam rolling off the top of his head, his face red with rage. "You need to rein in that selfish bitch you married. At least then you'd have some money to turn this place into something decent. Something Sarah would be proud of."

My chest tightens at my mother's name. Insulting Abigail won't go well for my uncle. A similar comment from me would have ended in a solid backhand. I don't know if my father loves her, but he won't stand for anyone insulting her either. Not even when it's the truth.

My father explodes with anger. "You ever talk about my wife that way again and—"

Uncle John has clearly had enough. "Don't you threaten me, you arrogant bastard."

"Or what? You'll take me to court?" My father huffs. "Go ahead."

There's a dramatic pause where I know my uncle is calculating his response. It's an argument that continues to swirl in a vicious circle. Nobody knows what my mom wanted— she died before finishing her will. Something else Uncle John blames on Father. And probably another truth.

A thump overhead makes my back go stiff. The dragon lady is crawling out of her dungeon, and for this matchup, I refuse to cower in the corner like some damsel in distress. For once, this isn't my fight.

I creep to the end of the hallway. Peer into the dining room, heart racing. Broken glass litters the carpet. Two of the dining chairs are upended, the leg from one wedged into the wall. My father and uncle face off across the table, light from the chandelier casting shadow on one face, brightening the other. It's the illusion of yin and yang when they're far too much alike.

Abigail swoops into the room, the tail of her silk robe dragging like a wedding train. White fur circles the cuffs, her neck. Uncle John barely acknowledges her entrance.

"You should see yourself to the door, John," she says.

My uncle's stare never leaves Father's face. "I'll leave when I damn well get what's coming to me."

Father's hands clench into fists. He holds his arms at his sides, the veins on his neck tightening into thick cords. He's a volcano set to erupt. I should back away.

I don't.

Abigail moves closer to my father. "Really, John, you need to leave. Andrew is—"

"A pussy," Uncle John spits.

My mouth drops open in shock.

"Get out, or I'll call the police," Abigail says. I'm almost impressed with how calm she remains. Her chest heaves, pushing her boobs up so high I'm sure they'll pop right out of the red nightgown underneath her robe.

"I'm going," Uncle John says, his eyes still on my father. "But this isn't over. You'll pay for this. If it's the last thing I ever do . . ."

The threat trails off at my father's raised voice. He stands taller, thicker, fueled by adrenaline—I know this look well. He points a finger at my uncle's chest. "Go. Now. I'll have Lizbeth gather your things. I never want to see your face again."

"Mark my words," Uncle John says with surprising calm. His breath seethes from between his teeth. "The only way I'll set foot in this house again is to kill you myself."

I gasp.

"Should I take that as a threat?"

Uncle John sneers. "Consider it fair warning." He moves

toward the door, pausing at the threshold, so close I can almost feel the vibrations of his shaking body. I've never seen, *felt*, so much hatred. "If not for my sister's memory, I would have put you out of your misery sooner. Don't tempt me, Andrew. My patience has worn out."

Taking my cue, I scramble back to the lobby, waiting for my father's instructions to gather Uncle John's things. But there is a whirlwind of activity as my uncle stomps from the dining area to the guest suite. A dresser drawer pounds closed. The door shuts with a resounding slam. *Thump, thump, thump* down the stairs.

I am sick with the thought of a confrontation.

Uncle John storms into the lobby, his hand gripped around the suitcase handle tight enough to turn his knuckles white. The expression on his face twists my stomach into knots. I know without a shadow of a doubt that this will be the last time I ever see this man, and I'm overcome with an inexplicable sadness. He's all that's left of my mother's family, my last blood link to her. She wouldn't want this.

"Lizbeth," he says, his voice soft. Almost kind.

I blink away a tear.

His mouth opens. Closes. A heavy sigh erupts from somewhere deep in his chest. He yanks open the front door and pauses, his hand clutching the knob. "You're not safe here," he says without turning. "Your father is a dangerous man. Get out. Leave before he hurts you—or worse."

CHAPTER

33

I stare at the wooden door that leads into my father's study, willing it to open on its own, to save me from knocking, disturbing, losing the courage I've built up in the hours since Uncle John left.

Bridget continues to slip away, lengthening the distance between us, and the only way I can stanch it, to stop her from going forever, is to get us both far away from Fall River, this house, my parents. It's also the only way I can contain the madness that makes me do, say, *feel*, unspeakable things.

Things are different now.

I'm different.

My fingers close tight around the wrinkled envelope in my pocket, and my heart skips a full beat with excitement. I did it—got accepted at Le Cordon Bleu! Father will be angry at first, but he'll come around. He'll see that I'll be better off at school, like Emma. He has to.

With Bridget at my side, I can do this. Control it. Beat it. Find out who *I* am.

My entire body trembles, but it's more than just nerves. I touch my finger to my lips, still swollen from Bridget's kisses. Our mouths are in tandem, but something isn't right with our hearts. A sliver of doubt has put a notch in our passion, and I'm willing to do anything to stitch the wound closed, before it festers with an infection that can't be cured.

Anything.

Even if it means facing my father.

I breathe in, my hand hovering on the handle. Exhale. I decide to knock, out of respect, to maybe start him off in a good mood. He doesn't answer at first, so I knock again, this time a little harder. "Dad?"

He doesn't respond. I open the door wide enough to peer inside his study. The desk light above his rolltop shines over his head, making the gray in his hair silvery and metallic. He seems older every day.

It should make me sad, but this sign of weakness gives me strength.

"Do you think we could talk?"

He looks up from his papers, and there's a beat of confusion, like he doesn't know who I am. Whatever work he's engrossed in has him kind of zoned out. I might be able to use that to my advantage too.

"Dad?"

He blinks, and his annoyance is instant. His brow creases over, and his lip turns down into a scowl. "What is it, Lizbeth? I'm very busy."

I step tentatively into the room. My father's study is the most eccentric room in the house, filled with trinkets and antiques, gifts from clients and his peers. He may not be the most well-liked man in Fall River, but he commands respect. Even if it's by intimidation. As the owner of one of the most prominent banks in the state as well as the local undertaker, he holds the financial fate of thousands of people in his hand.

I can't imagine what it might be like to be that powerful—or feared.

"Can we talk?" My voice is soft, a little reminiscent of my mother's. Whether that's to my advantage or not is a fifty-fifty chance. "There's something I need to tell you. Ask you."

My admittance to Le Cordon Bleu comes with a full scholarship, but I can't go without his blessing. I'll get a job in Boston, and Bridget will help out when she can, I think. If I can just convince my father that I'm able to make it on my own . . .

I chew on my lip.

"If this is about money, don't bother. We're about to be officially broke."

It's not quite an invitation, but I take the seat in front of his desk anyway. Paperwork covers the surface. Bank notes. Legal jargon. I'm too far away to read the fine print, and asking about it is pointless. Father doesn't talk business with me.

On the wall behind him, my father's awards, commendations, and framed certificates form two parallel lines. They're hung exactly two inches apart, centered on the wall with painful precision. The last remnants of my mother's desire for perfection. Abigail has destroyed that in every other room of the house.

My father scratches his signature on a piece of paper and sets it aside. I catch the name of our Realtor on the top. It's not uncommon for my father to deal with mortgages, rentals, and foreclosures, but he doesn't normally work so late into the night.

My pulse thrums.

I shift in my seat, trying for a better view, but the overhead lamp casts all kinds of weird shadows that make the letters impossible to read. My father folds his thick hands on his desk and stares at me. I'm obviously intruding.

"What is it, Lizbeth?"

I gather my courage. "Is everything okay? You seem . . . distracted."

He blows out a huff. "We're being sued, Lizbeth, for a ridiculous amount of money."

I blink. "Sued? By who?"

He gestures toward the stack of paperwork. "About a dozen of these town pricks."

My father hates losing money. He's frugal, calculating, a shrewd businessman at his core. The result is a growing list of enemies. I've heard the whispers at church, the way some of the locals stare at him with contempt.

"Never mind," he says. "You obviously came in here for something." His lips turn into a sneer. "Spit it out, then. I haven't got all day."

Carefully, I withdraw the crumpled envelope from my pocket and set it on his desk. I use my palms to flatten it, tracing my fingertips over the return address, still not convinced I've really, truly been accepted. I haven't even told Bridget yet—I'm going to surprise her with dinner, and if things go well with Father, I'll go to her with a plan.

A way to take us both away from here.

A chance to be totally free.

My lips form a smile, and my chest inflates, filling with pride.

My father takes the envelope and holds it up to the light. "What's this?" He reads the lettering on the envelope. "Culinary school?"

I nod, grinning wildly.

He snorts. "Don't even bother applying," he says. "You'll never get in."

The words set my confidence back a step, but I hold my

chin high. Still smiling, I say, "I've already been accepted. That's the letter, right there. Read it."

He blinks, as though disbelieving, and then unfolds the paper, manhandling it with such force I'm sure he'll tear it in half. I hold my breath and watch his eyes skim back and forth. His expression is unreadable, but the tips of his ears have started to turn red.

I can feel the dread begin to uncoil from my chest.

My father crumples the letter into a ball and tosses it into the garbage at the foot of his desk. I cup my hand against my mouth to trap the scream of protest. My heart is on fire, burning me from the inside out.

"You're not leaving the B and B, Lizbeth," my father says firmly, stiffly. "We need you here. This is your home."

Prison.

"We could hire a new cook," I say hopefully. His eyes darken. "Even for just a little while. I could go to school and work here in the summers. . . ."

My father shakes his head. "This isn't a gourmet restaurant, Lizbeth. The food you prepare is fine."

"I don't want it to be fine." My voice is strained. "I want it to be good. *Great.*" *Brilliant.* "This place, this life, isn't enough for me anymore." I want to *be* someone—the kind of person who follows her dreams and chases new adventures. Someone more like Bridget.

My father's eyes darken. "Some girls would be grateful for what they have."

I swallow hard. "I want more."

He shuffles the paperwork on his desk. "Get used to disappointment. I can't afford the tuition."

"My tuition is paid by the scholarship," I say. "I'll get a job to pay for expenses."

"You have a job, and I can't afford to replace you. Not now."

"But—"

My father slaps his hand on the desk with a resounding *thwack*. "That's enough, Lizbeth," he says, his voice rising to a yell. "You're staying at the B and B and that's final."

My lip quivers. "And if I leave anyway?"

"I wouldn't advise that, Lizbeth." He regards me with cool, hard eyes. "You won't make it out in the world alone, not with your sickness." He blows out a deep, cold breath. "And you'll leave me with no choice but the alternative."

CHAPTER

34

Abigail slams the carton of milk on the countertop. Frothy liquid sloshes out the side and onto the polished granite. What the—? I turn so she can't see me scowl, and head to the sink for a dishrag and run some hot water.

I should be used to this routine.

Abigail's moods have become increasingly darker over the past few days. Maybe it's because I'm not letting her push my buttons. Despite what my father says, I'm not giving up—I'm getting out of this place. With Bridget at my side, I can do anything.

I spin around, a smile plastered on my face, dishrag raised high with enthusiasm. But my expression falters under Abigail's smug grin. Something is up. Something beyond her usual brand of awful, and a shiver of fear trickles down between my shoulder blades.

"What is it, Abigail?"

"You've been lying again, Lizbeth." She is in full show mode now, taunting me. Parading her evil like a runway model. "And this time I have proof."

I snag the milk carton and shove it in the fridge behind a two-liter of cherry Coke. Soda isn't allowed in the B and B—another of Abigail's ridiculous rules—and for an instant, I wonder if that's what she's going on about.

But her face is too smug, her expression too devilish for this to be about whatever contraband she's found hidden in the kitchen, and I worry that she's chosen now to reveal what she knows about me and Bridget. I steel myself for confrontation.

"I know about the poison under the cabinet," she says, tracing her fingernail against the granite countertop, *tap, tap, tapping* it in slow succession. My back goes rigid, but I don't give in. Father knows I bought the cyanide too. What's her angle?

Ripping my apron off the hook behind the door, I put it around my waist and tie it behind my neck. "We had rats."

"In the barn?" Abigail says, her eyes flashing with amusement.

"Yes, the barn," I say, voice clipped.

"Where you slaughtered the pigeons?"

I grip the edge of the sink with both palms while my stomach twists and churns.

Abigail throws her head back and cackles. "I saw the video footage." Her eyes narrow. "You're quite the little demon child, aren't you?"

Cold dread washes over me. I expected Father would tell Abigail about what I have done, but the consequences of those actions are starting to become crystal clear. With this footage, Abigail has exactly what she needs to convince the authorities that I'm not well.

Rage thunders through me, a weak attempt to deflect my fear. "Just say it." Heat flushes across my cheeks. "Get whatever it is off your chest and leave, Abigail. I have a lot of work to do."

"Oh, I'm sure you do," she says.

I hate the sound of her voice, laced with innuendo. My eyes flit to the sink, where a bread knife teeters on the edge of a cutting board, the points of its serrated edge glistening like fangs. I could grab it, run its jagged blade across my stepmother's throat, and stop her from talking right this second. Lord knows I'm tempted.

Bile rises up from my esophagus and I blink away the horrible thought.

What the hell is going on with me?

"I know you were in my bedroom," Abigail says now. Her voice scratches across my temples, creating grooves in my skin that pulse with pain. "You may have convinced your father otherwise, but I know you took the antique watch." She leans across the counter, inching closer to me. Her breath reeks like rotting flesh. "Didn't you?"

A shiver of revulsion traipses down my spine. "You stole my mother's things."

The watch is still stuffed in my cardigan pocket, hanging from a hanger in my closet. Hidden in plain sight, almost taunting Abigail with its presence. I'll give it back if she returns my mother's necklace and crocheted doily, but not one second sooner. No matter how many times my father tries to beat it out of me.

"That watch belonged to my grandfather," she says.

I chew on my lip. I haven't admitted anything, though I haven't denied it either. This is the kind of lie Father Buck might preach about in a sermon. A fib by omission is still a sin. I add it to the mental list of things that I someday may have to confess—if I were ever planning to go back to church.

Catholic guilt hangs over me like a heavy cloud, probably always will. But I just keep thinking of Bridget as my silver lining and it lessens some of the weight. I have to believe she'll be enough.

"You've been a bad girl, Lizbeth."

I wish I could spit in her smug face.

My heart thumps too fast, making my breath catch. Abigail mistakes it for fear, and her laugh grates under my skin. "Get out of my kitchen," I say, mustering as much force as I can manage.

She stands. "I know all your secrets, Lizbeth. Every last one." She creeps closer and lowers her voice. "Even the one you think you've told no one else about. . . ."

My pulse thrums with dread. I don't know for sure what she knows about Bridget, what she's seen or what she's heard. But even a little is too much. Because if—when—she tells my father, it's over. The *actual* end. He'll send her away, lock me in this prison forever—or have me committed.

I am not okay with any of those options.

"What do you think you know, Abigail?"

My hand slides to the knife. Her eyes flick to the sink. She takes a step back, holding her hand up to her chest. "Oh my," she says. "You really are losing it, aren't you?"

I grip the knife in my fist.

"Put it down, Lizbeth," she says. The slight tremor in her voice betrays her fear. For a brief moment, I am empowered. In control. "Put the knife away before your father gets home," she says, holding up a hand.

But there's no time for that, because at that instant, I hear him storm through the front door, and he's mad as hell.

35

"L izbeth!"

My father's voice booms down the hallway and into the kitchen. The force of it is so intense, my knees knock together. Whatever strength I had going into this day is obliterated. Gone.

"Uh-oh," Abigail says, regathering her confidence with my father's impending presence. Her heroic knight, swooping in to save the day. "I guess I'm not the only one who knows you've lied."

"Stop saying that." My voice is panicked, paranoid. I have so much to hide that I'm thinking the worst. Does my father know about Bridget somehow? Or is his anger rooted in something much more ominous? Has he spoken to Father

Buck? Good Lord, does he know that I ran off to Boston with my girlfriend? The lump in my throat swells to the size of a grapefruit.

My father's shadow looms at the threshold of the kitchen. I clutch the dishrag and squeeze. Water drips down my wrist and hits the floor. I want to go with it, to slide *under* the tiles and avoid whatever wrath Father has planned.

"Lizbeth!"

"I'm in here!" I shout, though it's little more than a squeak, because fear has my voice in a stranglehold. "Here," I say again, somehow louder, with more authority. I can do this. Face the consequences of my actions. I have to.

It's the only way Bridget and I can ever be free.

My father fills the doorway, his face menacing, posture rigid with anger.

"I have had enough of your lies," he thunders. "I just spoke with Father Buck."

My stomach bottoms out. I hold my breath, afraid to talk, to move even one single inch.

He doesn't need to continue—I already anticipate what he's about to say. The priest has told him that I did not attend the church retreat as promised. That I was not on that bus, didn't sing "Kumbaya" around a campfire, or practice scripture until my brain hurt. I did not "get over" my unsanctioned feelings, did not resist temptation.

I succumbed to sin.

Forgive me, Father.

In this moment, I'm not sure from which "father" I beg forgiveness. I hold my chin high, anticipating the backhand that always comes when I've disobeyed him.

"Where were you? When you should have been at church—" His mouth twists into an evil smirk. "Where. Were. You?"

I want to tell—to confess all of it to him, to Father Buck, to whoever will listen. But damn it, I'm too much a coward, even now. I wrap my arms around my chest to ward off the chill that creeps into my bones, knowing somehow that this is the end.

There is no going back from this.

"I asked you a question, Lizbeth."

I open my mouth, but the voice that comes out is not my own.

"She was with me . . . ," it says.

Swipe.

Bridget cowers behind my father, her eyes wide with fear. It happens so fast I don't know what to think, feel. I brace myself by holding on to the counter, sure I'm about to have an episode. . . . I struggle to contain it. Stuff it deep inside my stomach, hidden from . . .

Swipe. Swipe.

Vomit rushes into my mouth, bringing with it a rush of anxiety. The madness seeps through my lips, spilling out with heart-pounding speed.

My father doesn't turn to Bridget's voice. He's too angry. Focused. He stares at me with anger and my knees knock together with fear. He's cartoon-character mad—steam spitting from his ears, skin red as an overripe tomato. His forehead is beaded with sweat.

"You lied," he says again, and I can almost see the spittle fly from his mouth when he says it.

Behind him, Bridget lifts her chin, stands taller. I'd be proud if I wasn't scared. Holy shit am I scared, because my father is not a nice man. I'm no match for him in this state, and neither is Bridget.

Save her.

I charge toward my father, who turns to avoid a crash. I fling myself onto his back. My feet dig into his rib cage and I hang on to his neck as he whirls around in an attempt to shake me. My back hits the kitchen cupboard. Dishes rattle. A sharp pain races up my spine.

In my peripheral vision, I catch sight of Abigail, one hand at her throat. The other is dangerously close to a knife by the sink.

I squeeze my father's neck tighter, terrified I might choke him to death, terrified I can't—won't—let go. He jerks to the left and my head knocks against the ceiling fan. A strand of my hair tangles in the whirling blade and is ripped from my scalp. I yelp but keep hanging on, desperate not to let him win. There is shouting around me. Bridget. Abigail. Their voices blur into white noise.

"For God's sake, Lizbeth," my father says through gritted teeth. "You're going to bloody well kill me."

Shocked, my grip loosens. My limbs slacken, if only for a split second.

He takes advantage of the moment to fling me off his back. I land on the floor with a thud, already feeling the bruise that will spread from the bottom of my thigh to the top of my hip. Blood fills my mouth from where my teeth have punctured my lip.

I scramble toward him, crawling on all fours, and dive at his ankle. He sidesteps out of the way, and my fist punches into the table leg. A bolt of electric pain zigzags up my arm. I don't stop. I keep crawling forward, yanking my leg free of Abigail's fingers curled around my ankle. She grunts. I don't look back.

My father wipes his mouth with the back of his hand. Sweat drips from his forehead, where two strands of hair are stuck to his skin. His shirt hangs loosely out of his dress pants, both wrinkled and greased with my blood.

A guttural roar erupts from my chest.

My father delivers a backhand that splits open my lip.

I turn my head in pain, and in my peripheral vision, I see Bridget go into a cupboard. She pulls out a glass vase and raises it high over her head. Tears stream down her cheeks. Her eyes are wide with shock, with anger. In this moment, I have no doubt she will use the vase to smash it over my father's skull.

The blow will be fatal.

Swipe. Swipe. Swipe.

I blink away the image and scream, "Bridget, no!"

Everyone freezes.

My father tilts his head to the side, jaw slack. "Who the hell is Bridget?"

CHAPTER

36

Bridget's palm presses against my cheek, soothing the heat from a bruise that covers half my face. The skin is tender, but it is nothing compared to the sharp pain in my chest. A deep sense of foreboding turns my body numb.

"He almost killed you this time," she says. Her fingertips trail down to my neck and circle the marks imprinted on my flesh.

I can't focus on what she's saying. My father's question hums at the back of my skull. *Who the hell is Bridget?* I stare into Bridget's eyes, needing to see myself reflected in her pupils. How could he not know who she is?

The question brought an abrupt end to our fight, my father storming from the room, shaking his head and muttering about my mental state. I didn't bother to call after him. The way things were going, it's conceivable one of us may have truly ended up dead.

"I was choking him too," I say softly. My throat is swollen and sore, but it's the least of my pains. My head hurts, my ribs hurt, everything hurts. Especially my heart. "I don't understand his question."

Bridget averts her gaze and tends to another wound. She presses gauze up against my skull to clean off the blood.

"Of course he knows who you are," I push, needing to understand. "He pays you a monthly wage, for goodness' sake." My chuckle sounds hollow even to my own ears.

"I keep to myself," Bridget says softly. "It's best to stay out of your father's way."

Sure, but something still doesn't feel right. My father had to be blinded by his rage, not thinking clearly or something. It's the only explanation that makes sense.

Bridget tosses the gauze on the mattress next to the first aid kit. "You should be at a hospital," she says, though we both know why I'm not. She folds her hands on her lap, twisting her thumbs together nervously. "Lizzie, I can't live like this anymore."

The cold chill of rejection seeps under my skin.

"And neither should you."

"We can run away," I say, grasping to hold on to her. The words ping off her like they've hit armor. Her walls are up, and it's already too late to claw my way back in. I should have acted sooner, figured out some way to crawl out from my father's control.

"Can we?" Her eyes search mine. It's too intense, and I look away. My gaze falls on her backpack, puddled at the door of her bedroom, brimming with her personal belongings. I turn back and take in her attire. She wears the same skirt as when she first came to Fall River, and the scarf I love is wrapped around her throat. She's leaving—already half-gone—and there's nothing I can do or say to keep her. "Maybe we can leave this town, your parents, the memories of everything terrible that's happened in the last few months, but . . ."

She gathers her breath and exhales.

I blink, knowing exactly what she's going to say next.

"It's more than just this place," she says. Her hand slides into mine, already lacking in warmth and comfort. It takes all my willpower not to pull away. "It's not even the abuse—though I wish with all my being you'd tell someone about that. It still wouldn't be enough."

I am not enough.

She doesn't say it aloud, but God's voice whispers over my shoulder, reminding me of my broken vows, the sins I have committed for which I have yet to repent. I don't deserve someone like Bridget. I am not worthy.

I am tainted, damaged goods, just like Father has always said.

"I'm not equipped to help you," she adds carefully.

My voice cracks. "Because you think I'm not well?"

She blinks away a tear. "I saw you burn the diary, Lizzie. And the pigeons . . ." She swallows. "The hatchet was in your hand. You stole poison from Mr. Bentz." She's crying now, and I'm not sure whether to touch her or move away. "I'm not safe."

I open my mouth to tell her I'd never hurt her, but even I can't make that kind of promise. It doesn't matter if I'm guilty of the things she's accused me of—Bridget believes it. Right now, that's the only thing that matters.

"I don't think you're safe either," she says. Her lips curve into a sweet, sad smile. "And more than anything, I want that. I *need* that."

"Don't go," I whisper.

Swipe.

"Oh, Lizzie." She presses her lips to my forehead. "I'm already gone."

A single teardrop falls along the bridge of my nose, pooling at the top of my swollen lip. The salt gets into the open wound. It doesn't hurt. Nothing does.

I'm numb to the pain.

Everyone leaves.

As I watch Bridget walk away, the rainbow backpack slung over her shoulder, I wait for her to turn and wave. To say good-bye just one last time. She doesn't.

My heart cracks, splits right in half, swirling the madness

up through my chest, waiting to be unleashed. *Swipe.*

A guttural roar of anguish is pulled from my chest. I bang against the window, trailing my fingernails against the glass like raindrops. She disappears from view, and my stepmother stands in her place, hands on her hips, staring up at me from the garden.

Judging.

Mocking.

Swipe.

This is her fault. And my father's. It's because of them that Bridget left.

Everyone leaves.

A web of pain crackles through my body, spreading like freezing water on a sidewalk. My abdomen cramps. I double over, gasping for breath.

I press my palm against my pelvis and inhale. Breathe out.

A wave of nausea hits me hard, and for a second I'm light-headed before—

—swipe—

Everything goes dark.

CHAPTER

37

I *am dying.*

Pain zigzags across my shoulder blades, along my spine.
My abdomen is stretched out and bloated. Cramped.

I try to lift my head, but it doesn't move. It's like I'm
pinned down by bricks. The scent of blood is overwhelming.
Coppery. Fresh. I'm steeped in it.

Where am I?

A steady pulse hammers against my skull. It's fierce,
unrelenting, the most powerful migraine I've ever felt. My
world is dizziness. I curl my legs farther into myself, cradled
in the fetal position, waiting for the light-headedness to pass.

It doesn't.

Swipe.

I peel open one eye. Sunlight streams in through the curtains, blinding me. I shut and reopen them. White spots form hazy polka dots in my vision. *Get up.* I push upward on my palms but fall back against the carpet. I'm too weak.

My arms are like lead.

Swipe. Swipe.

I turn my cheek away from the window and scan the room for something, anything that I can prop myself up against. I try to call out, but words don't come. My mouth is dry, pasty, thick with a metallic taste.

A shadow in the corner catches my eye.

At first I think it's a pile of discarded laundry, Abigail's dresses back from the dry cleaner. But of course, that doesn't make sense. What are they doing in the guest suite? Why haven't they been hung?

Heat flushes my face. I need to get up.

I prop myself up on my elbows, dizzied by a fresh wave of nausea. I press my lips together to stop from gagging and focus on the discarded clothes to shift my attention. I place my weight on my right elbow and drag myself forward, then to the left. Haul myself closer. My vision blurs around the edges, forms halos and tunnels. I keep dragging my body toward the pile of clothes.

Abigail will be furious. I need to hang them, or get rid of them before she sees. Before she tells Father and I'm punished.

Drag.

Slide.

Draaaag.

Sliiiiide.

My body is slimy and heavy.

Something doesn't look right.

Swipe.

The mound is too small, too formed to be random. I squint and focus on it. Two stockinged legs protrude from the dress. I register the shoes, the designer labels on the underside of the heel, and my skin goes cold.

"Abigail?" I croak.

I slide closer, using my elbows to inch forward. I raise my knees to help with the effort. At first they don't hold my weight. My heartbeat picks up speed. I'm on all fours now, crawling toward the bed. Abigail is slumped facedown on the floor and something is horribly wrong. My skin prickles with unease. Did she have a stroke? A heart attack?

Adrenaline floods my veins and I come to my feet, walking closer when—

I freeze.

A red stain blooms around her like bathwater. It inches closer to the tip of my shoes. I take a step back. The scent of her blood hits me. I sway, almost knocked over. I steady myself on a chair. "No, no . . ." I barely recognize the words coming out of me. It's as though I'm possessed. I creep closer, one hand across my chest, the other at my mouth. I want to close my eyes to block whatever comes next, but it's too late.

Swipe. Swipe. Swipe.

I see the bone fragments first, small pieces that pepper the floor where her head once lay. There's almost nothing left of it now—the back of her skull is almost entirely missing, as though it's been bashed in. Bits of brain and bone blanket the floral wallpaper, and blood splatter covers the walls in elongated, angry slashes, mixed with patches of matted hair. I step forward and something squishes under my foot. I lift my shoe. A clump of . . . brain.

My mouth opens to scream, but vomit spews out. I catch it in the curtain of my dress. It runs like drool down my face. I stop it from running onto the floor. Even its rotted stench can't compete with Abigail's blood. I have never seen so much—

Swipeswipeswipe.

The image of Abigail's corpse doesn't disappear.

I reach for the dresser to steady myself, not trusting my balance to stand. My gut twists into knots. I want to look away, but I'm transfixed by the horror, somehow disbelieving it could be real at all.

My voice drops to a whisper. "Abigail?"

She can't answer. Will never speak again. Somewhere in the back of my mind that fact resonates with the kind of thrill that makes my blood boil with fresh guilt. I drop to my knees and begin to sob. "Abigail . . ." My cries go louder until I'm able to shout. "Abigail!" My voice echoes between the walls.

I drag my eyes from her bloody body and stand. My fingers and toes have gone numb, my heartbeat barely stutters. There are things I must do. Call the police. Tell my father . . .

Dear Lord, my father. What will he do?

Anguish overcomes me, and it's enough to force me to turn away. I stumble to the hallway, images of Abigail's battered skull pulsing in my vision. My fingers wrap around the banister as I take tentative steps down the stairs. My legs are weak, my body limp.

Who is responsible for this?

There's no murder weapon in sight. My mind flits through the inventory of the room. Is it possible I missed something? I shake my head. The police will find it. They will sort this out.

My ankle rolls a little, and I lose balance, almost fall. My hand clings to the banister and I breathe deep. *In. Out. In.* I tamp back the nausea threatening to cause a blackout.

I wet my lips, cool to the touch. *You can do this.* I work through the steps. Turn at the landing. Walk down the hall to the sitting room. Pick up the phone. Everything moves in slow motion, each step, each thought. I'm a dead woman walking.

No, that isn't right.

I'm alive.

Abigail is dead.

Murdered.

The back of her skull literally bashed in.

Swipe.

A sob of anguish erupts from somewhere deep inside my chest. I shuffle to the sitting room and almost fall through the door. I hang on to the frame to steady my balance. I lift my chin and he's there. Father.

Sleeping on the couch.

He looks so peaceful I don't know how to wake him, how to tell him this news. But as I walk toward him, I'm hit by another wave of the same metallic scent. Blood, seeping through the vents, filling the house. Vomit rushes up my esophagus, but this time I push it back down. I must be strong for Father.

He'll need me now.

"Daddy?"

I move closer, steady and slow.

His head is tilted to the side, shadowed by the shade of the curtains. In the back of my mind it registers that he shouldn't be home yet—it's not even noon—but I keep moving forward, drawing courage for what I must do.

The smell of blood is overwhelming. I can't get the image of Abigail's skull out of my mind. *Swipe. Swipe. Swipe.*

I blink and her corpse disappears, but it's replaced by a new horror. My heart is like a pump, pounding a scream from my chest. My father, the left side of his head gone. Chopped right in half. I slump to my knees and lift my head to stare at what's left of his face. Fresh blood still drips from the wound and pools on the expensive Persian rug beneath the sofa.

Drip. Drip.

Drip.

I reach out to touch his skin, still warm.

My gaze drops to the floor and a scream so animalistic I don't recognize it erupts from my chest. Amid the blood—so much blood—bone fragments, hair, and pieces of brain, is my father's eyeball, practically sliced in half.

In death, he stares at me with accusation.

CHAPTER

38

eporters and bystanders surge to the crumbling stoop of
the courthouse like blood cells coagulating at the site of
a wound. I stand between my lawyers, shielding my face
from their judgmental stares. Across the street, a group of kids
play jump rope, their melodic chant seeping under my skin.

"*Lizzie Borden took an ax,*" they sing, "*and gave her mother
forty whacks. When she saw what she had done, she gave her
father forty-one.*"

Their song echoes long after we enter the courtroom and
I am seated before a jury of twelve men, and a judge whose
nameplate reads DEWEY. He peers at me through glasses,
expression stern and disgusted, as though guilt radiates from
my soul.

My eyes are drawn to the side of the court, where pictures of my stepmother and father dangle from an evidence board. Their inanimate eyes follow me, just as they have in my dreams, and in the waking hours since their death. Below the board is a small table, where their skulls sit on display, as though at a museum.

The left eye socket on my father's is missing. Light shines through the gaping hole in the back of Abigail's—jagged bone fragments casting shadows on the wooden surface of the table.

My head goes light and I cup my mouth with trembling fingers.

Swipe.

I stand over my stepmother, hands raised, the hatchet heavy in my grip. *Swipe.* My arms swing downward. *Swipe.* *Swipe.* Blood sprays across my face, my skin—

Swipeswipeswipe.

An electric current of unease rockets through me.

I did not kill them.

How could I have done something so horrible?

I stand firm in my denial, and still their corpses are all over me, their decay and sadness in the grooves of my thumbprints and gummed up in my mouth. They reek of evil and of loss, creeping out of memory and back into life. Over and over and over—

Judge Dewey clears his throat, raps his gavel on the lectern. The room silences, but the children's voices float through the window, the words of their rhyme adding fertilizer to the seed of doubt pitted at the bottom of my stomach.

"Counselor," the judge says, addressing my lawyer. "Does your client wish to enter a plea at this time?"

He nods toward me, and I fumble with the hem of my dress, and then stand.

"Miss Borden, you have been charged with murder of your father, Andrew Borden, and your mother, Abigail Borden. Do you have anything to say?"

My fingers tremble. "Abigail is not my mother."

Judge Dewey clears his throat again. "Miss Borden, do you have anything to say about the brutal murders of your father, Andrew, and your stepmother, Abigail?"

The voice that speaks is hardly my own. "I am innocent," I say, and a murmur ripples through the crowd. "I leave it to my counsel to speak for me."

Mr. Jennings squeezes my hand as I sit, but it's as though antifreeze bleeds into my veins. I'm as cold as snow. Numb with shock and sadness.

My lawyer stands. "A young woman who led an honorable life has been accused of a shocking crime," he says. "You do not have to decide how this brutal deed was done or who did it at all. All you must decide is whether it can be proven beyond a reasonable doubt that Lizbeth Andrew Borden is guilty. If you cannot do that, you cannot take her life."

I turn in my seat and scan the crowd. The room is packed,

filled with unfamiliar faces, and of those I've known my whole life, too. Mr. Bentz is there, along with Father Buck. Neither of them will look at me.

Mr. Jennings begins to refute the evidence mounted against me.

I am too small, too frail, to wield a hatchet. I lack the strength to slice into my stepmother's head with nineteen whacks—not forty as the schoolchildren sing—and then drag my lithe form down the hall to deliver another eleven—not forty-one—blows to my father's skull. The blood from that would cover me, and I was not covered in blood, Mr. Jennings says.

This is the basis for the defense the best legal team in the state will use to acquit me of a crime so heinous, so vile, my stomach twists into knots at the thought. *Blood.* So much. I feel it, like a sheen of sweat on my lips, and watch it *drip, drip, drip* through my dreams. A shiver judders along my spine.

Swipe. Flames lick the mint-green porcelain of the bathtub, engulfing my dress in fire. *Swipe. Swipe.* The material curls and shrivels, turns to ash—

I blink clear the vision. Not my dress, my journal. I burned my diary.

My lawyer's gravelly voice *tap, tap, taps* at the back of my consciousness. "Lizbeth Borden was an abused young woman," he tells the court. The room is silent. Listening. Waiting. I refuse to look over my shoulder, to see the doubt—shock—on their faces at this revelation.

Mr. Jennings paces the front of the room. "Throughout her entire childhood, she lived in fear for her very life." He pauses for dramatic effect. "Some of you may think that gives her motive for murder."

There is a murmur from the crowd.

His words etch their way into my bones, giving me a chill. He's right, I had reason to murder them both. I wrap my arms around my waist to ward off the cold, but it doesn't stop another shiver from traversing down my spine. It's so intense my entire body shakes, as though I'm going into a seizure.

In any other trial, this evidence would be enough to convict me, but somehow my small frame and history of abuse may be enough to cause reasonable doubt. My pulse spikes. Sweat glistens on my forehead.

I can feel the stares from the back of the courtroom on the back of my neck. My attention drifts to the collective faces of the jury. None of them will look at me for longer than a second. Their eyes skim over me as though I am a monster.

Am I?

Tears gather in my eyes and I *blink, blink, blink* them back. I am afraid that the madness will leak from my tears and spill into the courtroom, drowning the judge, the jury, the people of Fall River in my guilt.

Not guilty.

One of the jurors risks a glance. His eyes flit from me to the skulls, and to me again, as though trying to process the evidence of a crime too horrible to understand. My mind is like the flapping wings of a dozen monarch butterflies racing through my intestines. My esophagus vibrates with the need to scream: *I didn't do it.*

I crane my neck and search the crowd for familiar, kind faces. But even Father Buck still won't look at me. In him, I search for truth, for belief, for an ally in all this. But it's clear from his body language—the way he shifts ever so slightly to avoid making eye contact, the way his brow is creased, the subtle way he fingers his rosary, as though praying for the Lord to have mercy on my tainted soul—that he believes that God has forsaken me.

Anger thrums through me. Well, fuck God.

My throat closes in around the vulgar curse. I want to stand now and shout it at the top of my lungs, proclaim my innocence: *I did not kill my fucking father and stepmother! I did not bludgeon them with a hatchet.*

But there is no one to refute the evidence.

I lean over to my lawyer and whisper, "Has anyone found Bridget?" Her name is a whisper of hope on my breath. "She will testify for me."

His eyebrows peak. "Bridget?"

"Sullivan," I say, swirling my tongue over my teeth. "She was my . . ." I can't stomach saying the words that acknowledge the end of our relationship. "The maid."

Mr. Jennings looks down at his file. "Isla was the maid," he says, pointing to her name on a long list of my father's employees. "No one has been hired for that position in"—he skims more paperwork—"almost a year."

"No, that's not right. . . ."

I mentally flip through the past few months, remembering all the time spent with Bridget, searching for tangible evidence, something to prove to the court—to myself—that Bridget was real. But I'm drawing blanks.

My heart presses against my rib cage, swelling with such pain it's like it has split in half. There's obviously been a mistake.

I search for Bridget here, scanning the faces of the curious, the disappointed, and the smug. But there is no wild siren call of her red hair in this crowd. Instead I find a dozen or more potential killers—the handyman my father refused to pay, the former gardener whose affair with Abigail was cut short, the men and women who have lost their homes in the wake of cruel business practices. Any of these people had a motive to kill my father.

But Bridget is not among them.

I lean over to my lawyer and say, "There is security footage. A camera at the front door." The hollowness in my chest widens as I remember the exact moment Bridget and I first met—her perfect smile through the peephole, a brilliant ray of sunshine on a dismal and gray Christmas Eve. I can recall every detail of that moment, but my memory is not enough. "The footage will prove Bridget was there."

Mr. Jennings smiles thinly. "I believe you, Lizbeth, and we will certainly take a look at the footage if it becomes necessary," he says, voice low and reassuring. "Let's see how this plays out."

The tips of my fingers start to tingle as the prosecution continues to mount evidence—my dress, soaked in blood, burned after the arrest but before DNA could be collected; the fact that the house was locked—it's always locked—before, during, and for some time after the murders; that I was alone in the house with my stepmother and father. The fighting. Screaming. Threats and abuse.

My head is like cotton as I try to sift through memories to assess what is real, even as the horror of the crime continues to roll out on public display.

Good Lord, how my father would be mortified.

I can't help but wonder how many people in this room knew that things were not how they seemed in the Borden household. *Bridget knew.*

Where is she?

My chest is heavy, not only at the loss of my parents—God grant them peace in death—but also because of the niggle of doubt that further conflicts my emotions. I did not—could not—kill my father and Abigail, but in the wake of their death, my long-sought-after freedom is within reach. There is no one to stop me from chasing my dreams. I can go to cooking school, be with Bridget, be . . .

Me.

Unless . . .

Is it possible that none of it—even Bridget—was real?

My heart squeezes with pain so intense I gasp aloud.

Mr. Jennings covers my hand with his. "Are you feeling okay, Lizbeth?"

My mind drifts to the crime scene. *Swipe.* "I felt good enough to eat a pear." *Swipe. Swipe.* The police officer looked at me, eyebrows raised. "A pear, Miss Borden?" My grin is small and ominous. *Swipe. Swipe.*

"I'm having trouble," I say softly, "knowing what's real anymore."

He opens his mouth, perhaps to offer words of wisdom, but is cut off as the prosecution enters into debate. They cross-examine, exchange theories and conspiracies—I acted alone, with an accomplice or maybe an entire team—but nothing they say makes sense. I am numb to them, to all this, to everything.

The door opens at the back of the courtroom. My heart leaps with hope. But Bridget doesn't walk through that door. It's just Uncle John, standing among the gawkers and disbelievers, his expression unreadable. I think back to the two days he spent at the B and B—surely he must have noticed the presence of a maid? But even now, at the height of my desperation, I remember how he spoke of the inn. The spiders, the dust, the musky scent, as though Bridget had not cleaned that room.

Had never been there at all. Impossible.

I flatten my fingers against my lips to stop from throwing up.

All of this is a result of this sick witch hunt, the opportunity to blame a troubled young woman for a hideous crime. Shock has filled me with self-doubt, caused me to question what's real, what's not.

I close my eyes and take a long, steadying breath.

No matter what happens in this courtroom, I need to find a way to reconcile my memories with tangible facts. The dismal truth is, I *don't* remember those final moments leading up to my parents' death. I can't account for my whereabouts, can't recall anything that happened after Bridget broke up with me.

A sharp pain jabs at my chest.

Losing Bridget was the most pain I've ever felt. It still hurts, as if someone has reached into my soul and clawed it from my body. That kind of heartache can't be faked.

Can it?

As the prosecution continues to count down the hours prior to the murders, fragments of memory flash through my mind like a black-and-white film reel stuttering through a slide show: Uncle John's red truck at the end of the street, the hatchet, heavy in my hand, Bridget's blurred reflection in the dirty windows.

Except none of *that* was real. Uncle John's wife says he was at home with her during the murders. Bridget had left—I can still see her silhouette disappearing around the bend. And the hatchet . . .

Yes, of course.

The lack of a credible murder weapon is troublesome for the prosecution. I burned—*swipe*—the pictures of me killing the pigeons in the barn, but what of the video footage Father spoke of? If I find it, will I also find evidence of Bridget?

My attention turns to my lawyer, who stands, hands clasped, before the jury. "Lizbeth Borden had motive to kill her father, that much is true," he says. His tone is solemn. Controlled. "But there are other factors to consider."

I am instructed to look at each of them now, to demonstrate remorse, sorrow, but never guilt. A picture of innocence, the image of an abused child, now without parents, accused of a horrible crime. We have practiced this until the movements are mechanical. But if I am innocent, shouldn't this come naturally?

My lawyer continues his defense. "She was drugged, taking medications for symptoms that didn't correlate with her true mental state."

My memories flip back and forth to the fragments of time when I was off the pills, and then forced back on them. I glance over my shoulder at Mr. Bentz. Will he tell them about the poison? Will he lie about the citrus peeler he claims I stole?

A shiver runs along my shoulders. What if my father is

right? What if the kitchen gadget wasn't a birthday gift from Bridget at all?

"Lizzie Borden was not depressed, as her diagnosis suggests," my lawyer continues. "And this misdiagnosis led to medications that worsened her condition, rather than provided the respite she so desperately required."

He lifts his finger. "But even so, she did not swing that ax."

Hatchet.

I picture it now in the cellar. In the barn. Soiled with pigeon blood.

Abigail's blood?

Even the judge keeps mixing them up, but there *is* a difference. Hatchets are smaller, so if you find yourself in a cramped space, you can execute a backswing. The bedroom where Abigail was murdered was open. My father's head was propped up against the couch, a wide, uncramped shot. Technically, you could use a hatchet to chop down a tree—or chop into a skull, *skulls?*—but it would require more strength, my lawyer argues.

The kind of arm and core muscle I don't have.

I stare down at my biceps, thinned from lack of sleep, food, movement. I have lived in a perpetual state of numbness and depression, alternating between incarceration and the psychiatric ward. Poked and prodded. Questioned and accused.

And not once has Bridget been to see me.

Why not? If our love was true, if Bridget was *real*, wouldn't she have at least visited? Checked to see that I was okay? Or didn't I mean enough?

My gaze returns to Uncle John, who lowers his chin in a slight bow. Is he sending me a message? What is he trying to say? When all this is over, will he stand at my side or forever walk away?

Everyone leaves.

I swipe at a tear. Is my mother watching over this trial from somewhere above? She would not have approved of this—

She loved my father.

This town.

Me.

She would be horrified by what I have done . . . *not guilty* . . . by what I have been accused of doing. *Forgive me, Father, for I have sinned.*

Guilt slithers down my throat. Lord, I don't even know what I'm confessing to anymore. The halo that once hovered over my head is tarnished, but not bloody. It can't be.

But what if it is? I'm no longer able to trust myself to separate reality from fantasy. I've already begun to forget what it feels like to be loved and touched and kissed by Bridget. Is it possible that she was all in my head?

No. I won't—can't—believe that.

I shake my head back and forth, squeezing my eyes shut. Images of Bridget flit through my vision, but they're so faint I can hardly make out the details. How is it possible that I've already begun to forget what she looks like? Unless . . .

Unless she never existed at all.

The judge taps his gavel on the lectern, drawing silence from the crowd. Distracted, I don't notice that someone else has entered the back of the courtroom, and the murmurs of the audience continue to grow animated even as the judge commands order. I follow the direction of the crowd's collective gaze and my heart stutters. Almost comes to a full stop.

Emma.

Our eyes meet, and in hers I find unconditional love and support. I work to contain my emotions. My fingers curl into the chair, grasping hold of this reality. After everything, and nothing, Emma is here. She is real and I know that her presence will calm and soothe me, help me get through this trial.

My lawyer places his hand on the bench in front of me and stares at the jury. I know these men—former Sunday school students, the clerk at the candy store, the man who runs the camera shop. They know me, too.

How can any of them believe I would do this?

"Members of the jury," my lawyer says, forcing me to focus. "I ask that you consider the evidence carefully. That you take into account the years of Lizbeth Borden's abuse—physically at the hands of her father, emotionally at the will of Abigail. And the years of medication for a *mis*diagnosis."

"Objection. The victims are not on trial here," the prosecution says.

My lawyer dips his head in acknowledgment, but the seed has been planted. "In any case, I must insist that there is not enough evidence to convict this young woman. Please. Do not send her to her death for crimes she did not commit."

Not guilty.

The room is so silent, a pin drop would echo like a shotgun blast.

My chest heaves in anticipation as both sides debate their closing arguments. The evidence is reiterated, Uncle John is talked about, the words between lawyers go back and forth, back and forth, until I am almost dizzy with confusion.

I search once more for Bridget, but I know she won't be here.

Was maybe never here at all.

And if Bridget wasn't real, if I made her up, is it possible that I could have also committed this heinous crime?

The idea leaves me breathless.

The judge dismisses the jury for deliberation, and as they exit stage left, I watch the way they walk. Study their subtle glances at the crowd, at the lawyers, at me. I keep an eye on their expressions—try to assess on which side of the vote they stand.

But it's impossible to tell.

My lawyer rests his hand on my shoulder. "I've done what I can," he says. I look up to see the defeat in his eyes, and fear spikes in my heart. His voice is solemn. "The jury will weigh the evidence—we'll know the verdict soon enough."

NOT GUILTY

The idea of going into Bridget's room fills me with cold, electric fear, a deep dread that feels as though it's sewing my heart shut stitch by stich. White spots form on the yellow walls, making my eyes blurry. I *blink, blink, blink*. The spots don't change, don't disappear.

Instead they become camouflaged in the halo of dust that circles in air that carries the musky scent of neglect. The suite feels not only *empty* but somehow hollow. A cavernous black hole.

A sharp pain is pulled from my belly button with an intensity that brings me to my knees. *Swipe.* I crawl on all fours toward the wall and scrape at the paint, carving my fingernails into the rough and gritty texture of the grime-covered drywall.

Scratch. Scratchy, scratch.

Scraaape.

The underside of my nailbed is yellow, tinged with dirt.

I draw a line of white, the paint peeling as though skinned from a ripe pear, and watch as flecks fall to the stained carpet. I rub at them, grinding them farther into the carpet, anything to make them fade. Go away. Disappear.

Swipe.

I roll onto my back and stare at the closet. Empty hangers dangle from thin wooden rods. I close my eyes, imagining myself buried in Bridget's clothes, my nose pressed against the material to smell her cotton-candy scent. But there is nothing but the stale stench of emptiness.

There is no essence of Bridget. Not even a drop.

My grandmother's quilt is folded on the top shelf of the closet, the plastic packaging still crisply taped shut.

Dirt is everywhere—not just here, but throughout the entire B and B. In the wall crevices and the corners of the baseboards. Spiderwebs dangle from ceiling tiles, the bookshelves are layered in dust. It's as though no one has cleaned this place in more than a year.

I curl into the fetal position and stare at the shelf on the bedside end table. The gold leaf lettering of Father Buck's travel scrapbook glints under the overhead light. I crawl to it, breath held, and flip to the first page. The Duomo cathedral glares at me, ominous in its perfection. I imagine the angle

Bridget would need to stand at to take this shot—but it's Father Buck's writing on the description.

The words go blurry, fading into the dialogue Bridget and I shared about this very image—the number of steps, the people she met, the view from the top. *Swipe.* Father Buck turns the page, carefully noting the details of another cathedral, this one in Milan. *Swipe. Swipe.*

And last, a picture of Bridget's "parents"—though the inscription beneath the image marks them as Father Buck's niece and her boyfriend. I stare at their picture, searching for some kind of likeness to Bridget, but even her explanation about them no longer rings true. How can I blame Bridget for lying when it's clear I've been lying to myself?

I slam the scrapbook shut and toss it at the wall. It bounces back and knocks over the end table. A series of photographs scatter across the carpet. I flip through them, heart beating, looking for images of Bridget—there's me in the field, me with a daisy in my hair, me with a smile on my face, me, me, *ME!* A dozen or more selfies, taken at just the right angle to hide my imperfections and flaws.

I'm in Boston, alone on the swan boat. At the diner, eating a burger. My stomach roils with denial. There's a picture of Le Cordon Bleu, the hotel room, even the café where I met Emma.

Where are the pictures of Bridget? Of me and Bridget?

Where are the memories *she* captured on film?

My throat feels raw.

I stand and go to the window to peer out at the barn. The rotting slats of the wood look more decrepit now, as though they've metamorphosed over the summer, turned into something haunting and eerie and surreal.

The echo of pigeons chirping *tap*, *tap*, *taps* against my skull. They peck at my eye sockets, through my flesh until they hit bone. A guttural sob erupts from within me and shakes the windowpane.

I slap my palm against the glass. Once. Twice. Flattening my hand against my distorted reflection. Pain trails along my wrist, but I hit the window a third time. No matter how hard I hit, it won't break.

I am already broken.

Tears stream down my face. "Bridget!"

She can't hear me.

She's not here.

Not anywhere.

Swipe.

I spin on my heel, surveying the empty room where we once lay, looking through photographs, dreaming of travel, counting stars through the open blinds. *Someone should have told me not to fall for a girl with stars in her eyes—they blinded me, like a deer caught in headlights.*

Could I truly have been so blind that I'm unable to see the truth?

Vomit spills out my mouth and onto the floor. I dip my finger into it, a hot, sticky mess, and drag it into the carpet, swirling the watery mixture into letters and symbols. Bridget. Hearts. Broken hearts. I stand and grind my toes into the rug. It mixes with blood, feces, wine wedging under my toenails.

Swipe. Swipe. Swipe.

My heart explodes into tiny shards of glass. I pick at them. Stab my arm with tiny pinholes that draw blood. *My* blood.

I lick my wrists, coating my tongue in the copper-scented liquid, until my mouth is full and I can hardly swallow. I drag my arms across the bedspread, imagining Bridget's body there, but even her imprint on the bedspread is gone. The sheets smell stale, a hint of Isla's lavender perfume lingering under my nose.

Scratch. Scratchy, scratch.

Swipe.

I spin around, listening for the source of the grating sound. It grows louder, more insistent. I can't find the source. I open and close the closet door, searching for the insect or rodent *scratch, scratch, scratching.* Isla's uniform hangs at the back of the closet, her name tag crooked on the pinafore. I yank it off the hanger and scrunch it into a ball.

The *scratch* comes again.

I slither on my stomach, Isla's shirt still gathered in my

hand, and peer under the bed for the monster that won't

Shut

Up.

Shut up, shut up, shut up.

There is nothing but darkness.

Emptiness.

Scratch. Scratchy, scratch.

I cover my ears, but it doesn't block the sound. It pulses against my temples. *Scratch.* STOP! *Scratch.* "STOP! Please, God, stop!" But my words mean nothing to a God that no longer believes in me.

A God I no longer believe in myself.

Scratch. Scratchy, scratch.

Swipe.

I pull open the dresser drawers, pawing at the emptiness inside. I slam the top drawer shut. Open the second. Nothing but a handful of loose change, a gray *Star Wars* sweatshirt, and two pairs of black underwear rolled into a ball. The name written on the inside waistband is ISLA.

Fresh grief hits me like a cold wave. There is no Bridget. She was nothing more than a twisted manifestation of my madness, a hallucination, a mirage.

Scratch.

Scratchy, scratch.

What is that fucking noise?

Goose bumps rise like the hair on the back of my neck.

A tingle runs through to my bones. *Clackety, clack, clack.* Desperate, I yank open the bottom drawer and suck in a sharp gasp at what I find. My heart leaps into my throat. It isn't possible, and yet—

I *blink, blink, blink.* It's still there.

Swipe.

I pinch my arm, digging my fingernails into my flesh, hard enough to draw blood.

Swipe.

A monarch butterfly begins to flutter in my chest, and I drop to my knees. Tears cloud my vision, but through the mist, I still see it.

The sun, the moon and stars, the whole constellation— Bridget's scarf—carefully coiled into the shape of a heart.

Author's Note

"Lizzie Borden took an ax
and gave her mother forty whacks.
When she saw what she had done,
she gave her father forty-one."

Shortly before noon on August 4, 1892, the body of Andrew Borden, a prominent businessman, was found in the parlor of his Fall River, Massachusetts, home. Hours later, police discovered the body of his wife, Abigail Borden, in an upstairs bedroom. A week later Andrew's youngest daughter, Lizzie, was arrested for the double murder.

In an era where women were considered the weaker sex, and female murderers were far less common, the trial—and Lizzie's quick acquittal—sparked a media frenzy and a stream of theories and speculations that continue to fester even today, more than 125 years after the horrific crimes were committed.

As is the case with many historic mysteries, there are more theories than truths, and Lizzie Borden's story has been the source of much creative inspiration, tracing back to the origins of that haunting nursery rhyme so many of us seem to know by heart.

The author of the rhyme took some creative liberties, of course—forensic evidence shows that Andrew Borden was killed with ten or eleven blows, not forty-one, and Abigail nineteen, versus the forty sung by schoolchildren skipping rope. The murder weapon was actually a hatchet, but obviously "ax" sounded better in the rhyme.

I've taken some creative liberties with my story as well. So how much of what you read is real? Quite a bit, though I admit, researching this story led me down some interesting and conflicting rabbit holes.

Do I think Lizzie Borden killed her parents? I can't answer that, even now.

But what I have been able to discern is that neither Abigail nor Andrew were well liked in Fall River. Andrew, a successful undertaker and banker, was worth about ten million dollars in today's money, but he was frugal—perhaps to a fault. The house they lived in didn't even have proper plumbing, though it did have—for its time—a state-of-the-art security system. Andrew was reportedly a very paranoid man.

It's also known that Lizzie did not like her stepmother

and in later years took to calling her "Mrs. Borden," or "ma'am." Both labels infuriated Abigail.

The Borden family was quite religious and attended church often. Lizzie served as a Sunday school teacher and was active in many religious organizations. She is described as being shy, kind, and family-oriented.

It's true that Lizzie had a medical condition that affected her menstrual cycle, and her mental health was often questioned. But of course, I've exaggerated these facts for the purpose of fiction. It's also been hinted at, though not proven, that her father was physically abusive, and that she was attracted to women. Lizzie never married, but after her acquittal, she was rumored to have been in a relationship with an actress.

Obviously that was not Bridget.

Lizzie had a fondness for animals, and it's true that she harbored pigeons in the barn behind the house. The pigeons were found dead in the barn, though no one ever took credit for the crime—killed because they ate the pears, which upset Lizzie's stepmother because she loved pear pies.

Several days before the murders, Lizzie tried to buy prussic acid from a local store owner—Eli Bentz—but he refused to sell it to her. That same poison was responsible for a bout of food poisoning Abigail and Andrew suffered after eating Lizzie's infamous meat loaf, but Mr. Bentz's testimony was not admissible in court. It's probably a good thing for Lizzie that he couldn't testify, since she repeatedly stole from him, a fact her father covered by simply paying off her debt each month.

Lizzie also loved to cook. Her meat-loaf recipe is on display in Fall River at 92 Second Street, her former house, which has been turned into the Lizzie Borden Bed & Breakfast and Museum. Guests can tour the property, watch an actual dramatization of the events, stay overnight in the bedrooms originally occupied by Lizzie, Emma, and their parents, and even enjoy the same breakfast the family shared on the morning of August 4, 1892.

And then there's Bridget.

Bridget Sullivan was hired to be the Borden maid at the time of the murders, and while I have completely fabricated much of her backstory in *Lizzie*, it's well-accepted that Lizzie and her sister shared a fondness for her, even nicknaming her Maggie.

The remaining details are less clear. As I wrote this book, the story seemed to drive its own narrative, and the lines between fact and fiction became far less clear. It's possible—probable, even—that I've blurred these lines for you, but I hope that regardless, you've enjoyed my interpretation of one of America's oldest unsolved mysteries.

If there's anything I didn't include here that you're curious about, fact or fiction, please feel free to ask. You can find me at dawnius.com or via Twitter @dawnmius.

Thank you so much for reading.

Acknowledgments

Even before I'd finished writing *Anne & Henry*, my good friend and brilliant illustrator, James Grasdal, sat across from me at Starbucks and while innocently doodling, asked, "So, which kick-ass female from history will you write about next?"

He suggested Lizzie Borden. And only seconds after agreeing, I got a lump in my throat—*how the hell was I supposed to do that?*

As always, James, you challenge and inspire me. Thank you for your unwavering support not only on this book, but in all things—and especially for planting the seed that became *Lizzie*.

Obviously, that seed has required some nurturing.

Massive, gargantuan thanks to Agent Awesome, Mandy Hubbard—who knows damn well I am crying as I write this—for championing not only *this* idea, but *me*, the writer, the person, the dreamer. I can't imagine this journey without you in my corner and I am grateful every day for all that you have taught, and continue to teach me. I love you.

To my amazing editor, Jennifer Ung. Thank you for "getting" my vision for this book, and for not firing me when I turned in a shaky first, second, and maybe third draft. You forced me to dig deep for this, to work harder than I knew I was capable of, and because of you, *Lizzie* is the book I *wanted* to write. Your patience, diligence, and belief is appreciated beyond measure. So much love.

Thank you also to Sarah Creech, who designed a more creepy and beautiful cover than I could have imagined, and to my production editor, Chelsea Morgan, and my copyeditor, Valerie Shea, whose unbelievable diligence saved me much embarrassment and from a lot (a lot!) of ridiculous throat- and chest-tightening moments. As a young girl, my dream was to be an author for Simon & Schuster (yes, that specifically)—thank you to the entire Pulse team for making that dream come true, for the third time!

I could not have written this book without my amazing sister, Dr. Jessica Driscoll, whose expertise helped to inform the difficult scenes in which Lizzie struggles with her mental health, and whose steadfast love and support are a beacon of light in even the murkiest waters. You are the best sister and friend anyone could ask for, and I'm so glad you're mine.

A huge debt of thanks to my critique partner and friend, Kitty Keswick, who powered through many revisions of this, despite having no "Nick" to crush on. I don't deserve you.

Much love and thanks also to Nancy Traynor, Lee Bross, Rocky Hatley, Megan Lally, Jennifer Park, Kyle Kerr, and Kimberley Gabriel for reading this in various stages of completion. I cherish your feedback and friendship.

To Jamie Provencal for venting, coffee, and pep talks—you'll always be my IR whether you like it or not. Huge hugs to Sue Worobetz for your steadfast support, and for helping me celebrate the milestones. To Matt and Bernadette Tracy for your amazing friendship—and for always displaying my books face out on your shelf. Kate Cosgrove, your love and support grounds me. Thank you for all you do and continue to do. Simone Demers-Collins, your belief in me is astounding. I look forward to many coffee dates going forward.

A special thank-you to Karen Dyck, who practiced extraordinary patience as I wrote this book—*Lizzie* is for you, my dear. (Hope it's creepy enough. Nah, who am I kidding? Nothing is . . . but I'm trying!)

As always, I thank my mentors Gary Braver, Steve Berry, James Rollins, and Jacqueline Mitchard for believing in me when I didn't, and who taught me to write often, write tight, and write well. I am forever in your debt.

Of course, I could not do this without my extraordinary family (the one I was born with and the one I was lucky enough to be married into)—thank you. I know I can be scatterbrained, anxious, busy, and forgetful, but I love you all very much and appreciate your support.

Thank you, Mom, for reminding me always that "imagination is more important than knowledge." Dad, I'm quite certain you will hate this book, but I know you'll still be proud, and that's awesome enough.

To my sweet Nona, whose light on earth burnt out this year. I love you, and I hope you're up there making sure Nono isn't still cheating at cards. Give him and Grandma Ruth a huge hug for me, please.

And of course, to my two beautiful stepdaughters, Aydra and Hailey, who make me laugh (and cry), and inspire me to work hard and be someone they can be proud of.

Last, but never least, to my husband. I have no fancy metaphors this time, no clever ways of saying how much I love and appreciate you, Jeff. Quite simply, you are my soul mate, my lifeline . . . my everything. I love you. Always.

ABOUT THE AUTHOR

Dawn Ius is the author of *Anne & Henry* and *Overdrive*. When she's not slaying fictional monsters, she can be found geeking out over things like true love and other fairy tales, Jack Bauer, sports cars, Halloween, and all things that go bump in the night. She lives in Alberta, Canada, with her husband, Jeff; their giant English mastiff, Roarke; and their Saint Bernard pup, Charley.